Liberation

a novel

Joanna Scott

BACK BAY BOOKS
LITTLE, BROWN AND COMPANY
New York • Boston • London

Back Bay Books / Little, Brown and Company
Hachette Book Group USA
237 Park Avenue, New York, NY 10017
Visit our Web site at www.HachetteBookGroupUSA.com

Originally published in hardcover by Little, Brown and Company,
November 2005
First Back Bay paperback edition, February 2008

The characters and events in this book are fictitious. Any similarity to
real persons, living or dead, is coincidental and not intended by the
author.

Portions of this novel have been published in *Black Clock* and
Conjunctions. Special thanks to editors, and to the Lannan
Foundation and Yaddo for their support.

Library of Congress Cataloging-in-Publication Data
Scott, Joanna.
    Liberation : a novel / Joanna Scott. — 1st ed.
        p. cm.
    ISBN 978-0-316-01053-5 (hc) / 978-0-316-01889-0 (pb)
    1. Italian American women — Fiction.   2. World War, 1939–1945 —
Atrocities — Fiction.   3. World War, 1939–1945 — Italy — Fiction.
4. Portoferraio (Italy) — Fiction.   5. Senegalese — Italy — Fiction.
6. Middle-aged women — Fiction.   7. Women immigrants — Fiction.
8. Friendship —Fiction.   9. Soldiers — Fiction.   I. Title.

PS3569.C636L53   2005
813'.54 — dc22   2005000147

10 9 8 7 6 5 4 3 2 1

Q-MART

Book designed by Brooke Koven

Printed in the United States of America

*For my mother and
for my daughters*

The stage was set. The weather was fine.

—W. G. F. JACKSON, *The Battle for Italy*

Liberation

Inside

SHE REMEMBERS HEARING SHOES SHUFFLING, HICCUP OF her mother's stifled sneeze, water trickling down a pipe, soft breathing, whispers like pages of a newspaper blowing across a deserted piazza, the neighbor's dog barking in the field, grunt of a curse, click of her teeth on her thumbnail, rattling of rain or water boiling or bicycle wheels turning, creak of a chair as whoever had been leaning back replanted its front legs on the floor, crackling of gunfire across the harbor or maybe someone had thrown a fistful of pebbles in the air, "ssss" in place of *stai zitta*, "ssss" in place of *silenzio*, strike of a match, her uncle clearing his throat, three quick coughs, suck of a cigarette, murmur of prayer.

What time is it now, now, and right now? Huddled in the cabinet beside the kitchen sink, she cared about nothing else but the time. If only she'd known the exact time, she could more easily have endured the night. She pressed her fingers between the hinges of the cabinet door and stared into the darkness. Even without any trace of light, she persuaded herself that she could see the outline of the door. The more intensely she stared, the more transparent the darkness became. A soft glow began to pulse through the crack between the hinges — she imagined that this was the motion of time. She'd made herself forget that the lamp on the kitchen table had been put out. And then she realized her mistake.

Understanding everything and nothing. She didn't even know what questions to ask. She didn't know why the Germans had come without warning and bombed Portoferraio in September or why a week later a submarine had torpedoed a ferry full of islanders on their way home from the mainland or why the bombs had fallen again one day in March. And now again.

How easy it would have been to knock on the cabinet door and ask for the time. And how stupid. They had already spent half the night up in the orchard — or had it been less than an hour they'd sat wrapped in blankets while planes strafed the ancient port across the bay and gunboats poured fire onto the coast east and west of La Chiatta? At one point there had been a great thud of an explosion that lit up the southern sky, then a grayish, bitter-smelling haze spread inland across the island, shrouding the moon. The steady pounding and crackling of artillery had continued in the distance, but eventually the aerial assault had ceased and the planes disappeared back out to sea. Once the sky overhead was quiet, Adriana, with her mother and their cook, Luisa, had returned inside. Amazingly, she had managed to fall into a deep sleep. How long had she slept before her uncle had arrived from Portoferraio, and her mother yanked Adriana from her warm bed and dragged her into the kitchen and stuffed her into the cabinet?

Her uncle had made it clear that any noise would be the end of them all, so Adriana only pretended to hum, holding a finger against her lips to feel them move in the darkness while she imagined treating her ears to a trace of a melody, her voice too quiet for anyone else to hear. They could go on assuming that she was a good girl doing just as she'd been told. You mustn't make any noise, Adriana. You must stay inside the cabinet until it is safe to come out. When would it be safe? Only when her mother said it was safe. Sooner or later it would be safe. Unless the Germans made her mother and uncle and Luisa disappear, just as they'd made General Gilardi disappear last September, and Adriana would be left to rot inside the cabinet. This was a possibility that her mother hadn't considered. Weeks would pass, months, until one day Lorenzo's Angela would at last come to clean the kitchen and unlatch the cabinet doors in search of rags, and out would fall Adriana Nardi's dusty bones.

Didn't it occur to anyone to ask her how she was faring? She was thirsty and hot and had done nothing to deserve such misery. She wanted to remind her mother that she would be eleven years old in two weeks. Eleven years — undici anni. Undici, undici. It was a number that deserved a melody. Music was always a good way to pass the time. She imagined singing all the songs she'd been taught in school. Caress the music with your voices, ragazze. Not too heavy down below, not too reedy on top. Do not sweep between two notes. Balance the tone. Now sing. Color the sound with memory. Every note signaling the passing of another second. She imagined humming the songs she couldn't sing aloud. She hummed silently to keep herself from asking what her life would be worth if she were to be killed before dawn. The dives she'd been perfecting off the rocks at Viticcio. How could her life end before she'd become a champion diver?

Her grave a cabinet beside the kitchen sink. Her mother and Luisa and her uncle Mario keeping watch in the kitchen of La Chiatta. Each world inside another world. The music she was hearing in her head matched the music she would make if she'd been humming aloud. It was as real as the fact of her growing. Luisa had predicted, judging from the size of Adriana's grandissimi feet, that she wouldn't stop growing until she had reached two full meters. She was growing continuously, irreversibly. As she grew bigger, the cabinet grew smaller, and her knees poked against her chin. She was like a hen packed in a hatbox. She couldn't stand it. Either she had to stop growing or she would suffocate. Hiding from the fighting wouldn't do her any good at all if her confinement made it impossible to breathe.

What, she wondered, could be worse than death? She was old enough to be able to imagine a multitude of brutal endings. The worst, she'd been taught, was Christ's suffering on the cross. A crucifix was a reminder that dying wasn't easy. She didn't want to die. There was nothing she wanted less to do than to die. What could surpass the misery of dying?

Whatever it was, it seemed to be something that could only happen to children — to girls, in particular, of a certain age. Only she'd been hidden in a cabinet. The adults were sitting comfortably in chairs around the kitchen table as though they'd just finished a meal and were waiting for visitors.

Deep inside her growing body, inside the cabinet, inside the kitchen, inside the walls of La Chiatta, she let herself consider what could happen. She could guess that it had to do with the advantages of strength over the stupidity of innocence. Adriana Nardi wasn't stupid. She'd always considered herself exceptionally knowledgeable and didn't find it difficult to surmise at least a part of the truth from which she was being protected. It had to do with young girls and soldiers and how, if a girl's growing body was too little for their pleasure, they had to make it bigger. Even as she was wishing to fit more comfortably into the cramped space of the cabinet, she imagined expanding like a balloon. She thought about how the soldiers would make this happen.

She was a girl, worthy enough to be hidden in a cabinet. Yet no matter what might be done to her, she couldn't imagine choosing death. Having long been assured by her mother that there was no such place as hell, she could believe that even the worst suffering wouldn't last forever. When the suffering ended, she wanted to be alive. She was as deserving as any child and had a right to live past tomorrow. She'd rather have faced a hundred Barbarossas than end up dying in an effort to hide from them. Was it really necessary for her to stay where she was? Did her mother think that death was preferable to defilement? Did she realize that her daughter was desperately uncomfortable?

"Mamma," she whispered through the crack in the door. Actually, she didn't even whisper. She made the sound of blowing out a candle flame, and her mother couldn't have heard her. And she made the sound of *ʒ*, for her zio Mario, and the murmur of Luisa's name. Didn't they understand that Adriana wanted to be with them?

There was a muffled, rhythmic knocking, maybe of someone nervously tapping a shoe beneath the kitchen table. The smell of cigarette smoke seeping into the cabinet had the coarse sweetness of automobile exhaust. The adults, unable to come up with anything better to do, must have passed a pack of cigarettes among themselves.

Tired of her troubled thoughts and the necessity of hiding, Adriana let herself feel angry at all of them for treating her as though she were some sacred vestment being hidden from the Turks. Let me out! She tried to think the demand forcefully enough for them to understand. But still no one bothered to check on her or offered her as much as a sip of water.

And then, abruptly, all activity seemed to stop, or at least the sounds of activity ceased. Adriana prepared to emerge into the open space of the kitchen. But for some reason she was not released. The darkness remained absolute, and the adults didn't move from their chairs. She wasn't sure whether it was after dawn or still the middle of the night. She listened for some evidence that the danger had passed, if only temporarily, but all she heard was the silence of inertia. The adults, having abdicated all responsibility, could do nothing else but sit and wait for someone to tell them what to do. Adriana would tell them what to do if they'd just let her out.

She was preparing to bang on the cabinet door, but right then she heard the far-off sound of the piano, notes of a fifth played separately, a tinny A and E, then E and B, then the slam of a chord.

For God's sake, why had the piano tuner come now, in the middle of the fighting? Adriana wasn't insane. She was the only sane one left in the world. The island was burning, soldiers were prowling for young girls, and the adults were sitting around the kitchen table while Rodolfo tuned the piano.

It didn't occur to her that she was asleep. As far as she knew, her eyes were open, and she was a good girl doing just as she'd been told to do while everyone else went mad. Pazzo Rodolfo, go home. Someone let her out. Mamma, what is going on?

The hammer hitting the string, again, beat of two notes, and then another note, and another. Trill down, trill up. The strange sounds of human ingenuity. With this that our ancestors have made for us. Pianos. Bicycles. Books and microscopes and air-planes. Bombs and vaccines and grammar and ink and radios. The challenge is figuring out what makes sense in the long run. Never knowing whether the most fundamental expectation will prove reliable. Unable to estimate what is happening simultaneously. She being a young girl wanting merely to assure herself that she would survive the war and be blessed with a good long life but knowing all the while that she couldn't even guess what would happen or what was happening elsewhere, no more than she could see through the door of the cabinet. Thinking of something while something entirely different occurred. Listening to the imaginary sounds of the piano while the Allied troops spread out across the island, following the road beside the Fosso Galeo toward Procchio, from Procchio to Portoferraio. Not seeing into the future or even into the recent past. Not seeing anything but the dim form of herself and the drainpipe. Not knowing that the soldiers had taken turns with the fourteen-year-old daughter of Sergio Canuti, whom they'd dragged from her home on the outskirts of Marina di Campo, and then they'd finished the job with bayonets, so by the time other troops had reached the Ambrogi estate next to La Chiatta and shot one of Lorenzo's pigs, Sofia Canuti was al-ready dead.

She could only be wrong if she tried to wager a guess. But at least she could vaguely sense the confounding scope of what she couldn't know, and even as she dreamed about Rodolfo tuning the piano, she had a dim notion that beyond the confines of her perception almost anything was possible.

In the mysterious night surrounding La Chiatta, the war raged on, and in her sleep clever Adriana Nardi knew not to be surprised by what she didn't understand. It was a lesson she'd begun learning when the Germans had bombed Portoferraio back in September. After that first attack, Adriana had found a woman's slipper when she was sweeping behind the men clearing the rubble from her school. She didn't understand what the slipper was doing there, since the bombs had fallen when the school was empty. And there was more: her friend Claudia had found the crushed carcass of a cat, and two boys claimed to have found a finger, though they dropped it and lost it when they were running to the office of the carabinieri. They reported that the finger still had the indentation of a ring encircling it, although the ring was gone. Adriana believed them.

She believed many things. She believed that there were diamonds on Volterraio. She believed in God. She didn't believe in hell, but she believed in the devil, and she blamed the devil for the fact that the sea was full of the souls of the dead. When she was swimming in the sea and her hand brushed up against something that felt like a spiderweb, and when afterward she found that the back of her hand was streaked with red, that meant she was almost caught by the souls of the drowned. If they ever got a firm grip on her, they would pull her under. And then she would have to do the same to others.

She remembers wanting to stop believing everything she was told. But how did she know what to believe as long as anything was possible? It was possible that the war would never end. It was possible that she would never see the light of day again. It was possible that the entire island would be blown to pieces during the glorious liberation.

When she was a young girl hiding in the cabinet, she didn't yet know that it would be called the liberation, nor would she have understood what was being liberated. She'd come to think of the Germans who had occupied the island for nine months as tourists — untrustworthy, to be sure, known in particular to have such a fondness for silk shirts that they would steal them right off the clothesline. Adriana had only seen the German soldiers from afar, though she often dined on their rations, since her mother sent Ulisse into Portoferraio to trade with them: eggs, dried figs, and cured olives in exchange for canned beans and salt. And occasionally Uncle Mario would arrive with a huge beefsteak — a gift from a German officer he'd befriended — which Luisa would cook in a stew to make it last for a week. Life may have been more dangerous because of the Germans, and it was even more dangerous if you were a partisan or a Jew. But there weren't many partisans left on Elba, as far as Adriana knew, and there definitely were no Jews. Anyway, visitors never came to the island to stay. They left when they grew bored, usually when the autumn rains started.

The first night of the Allied liberation of Elba would turn out to be only the beginning. The night she spent hiding in a cabinet beside the kitchen sink. Let me out! Cracks of light graying the darkness. Hating to be where she was but grateful not to be somewhere else. Where?

Shrieks of a dying pig. Intake of breath. Thudding rush of blood in the ears, reminding her of the few times she'd cut her finger and sucked the wound: she imagined that lemon mixed with the pulp of a rancid tomato would taste like blood. How disgusting! Ragazze, attenzione! Ah-eh-ee-oh-oo. Please, Mamma, when would Rodolfo finish his work and go home? The sound was giving her a headache. Try to sleep, Adriana. She couldn't sleep. She was asleep. She didn't hear Sofia Canuti screaming. Of course she didn't.

She imagined hearing the gurgle of milk spilling from a bottle tipped over by a cat. She imagined hearing the snapping sounds of someone gathering kindling. And Rodolfo playing scales. She thought about all the sounds that a violin could make in a half step. Once upon a time she'd wanted to learn to play the violin. But her mother had insisted on the piano.

She thought about the sweet smell of bonfires. She thought about a flip book she'd bought at the market last week showing a man blown from a cannon to the top of the Tower of Pisa, his weight bringing the leaning tower crashing down. What about all the good jokes she'd retold? Or climbing up to the rocky summit of Monte Capanne? Or the restless tapping of a pen on blank paper?

She remembers imagining that all the fighting going on across the island was just a ruse and the explosions as harmless as fireworks. She remembers feeling irritated by the inconvenience of it and angry at her mother — why had Giulia Nardi chosen to live in a place where war would come? Why hadn't she had better foresight? What, exactly, was happening? When would it be over?

The Germans would have left on their own eventually — that's what the Elbans thought. Instead, the French Colonials, with a backup of British Royal Marine Commandos, had to force them out, and by the end of the first night, everyone who wasn't alive was dead. Only hours into the invasion, Sofia Canuti was dead, the Signori Volbiani were dead, six Senegalese boys were dead, fifteen Germans were dead, nine British commandos were dead, and seven troops of the Bataillon de Choc had decided that the long drive between the road and the villa of La Chiatta was too long, so instead they went to La Lampara and killed a pig while Adriana, not knowing much of anything about anything, past, present, or future, dreamed about crazy Rodolfo the piano tuner, who had to make the piano sound better than perfect and always stayed for hours.

Forgetting in her sleep to hope that eventually the sun would rise, the door to the cabinet would open, and she would tumble out into her mother's arms, more confused than she'd ever felt in her life, joints aching, mouth parched. Only after she'd been revived with a cup of water would she consider it her right to demand from her mother proper recognition for her hardship. But Luisa would scold Adriana for this. She would tell her to give thanks to God for protecting her during a night when so much had been lost.

Not guessing what would be involved in the many stories she'd have to hear before she really understood what had gone on that night and through the following days around the island while the savage fighting continued up in the mountains. It would be three days before the Germans surrendered — and longer before the interim government secured a reliable peace and demobilized its troops, ending officially what the French would call Operation Brassard, the Italians would call La Liberazione, and the British Royal Marine Commandos would call a bloody little sideshow.

SIXTY YEARS LATER, the woman known to others as Mrs. Rundel is riding on a train through New Jersey. Mrs. Robert Rundel — with her cap of hair a blend of gray and white and streaks of satin black; her face fitting neatly inside the frame of her curls; dark pools of flesh completing the circles of her wide dark eyes; her right eyebrow raised at a sharp angle, pushed upward by a chronically swollen lachrymal gland; her overlapping front teeth hidden behind the beak of her mouth — this is who she has become, a woman who is convinced that she will always, everywhere, be perceived as a foreigner.

The truth of her own future would have shocked her when she was a young girl if a Gypsy had told her what was in store, though after decades of the same routine there should be no surprises. She is on the train heading into New York. Today is no different from any other weekday. She is staring indifferently out at the factories and warehouses, the parking lots, the FABCO sign, Shakey's Garage, the ninety-nine-cent value promised at Shoppers World, the power station, the graffiti on the concrete wall below the flyover: "Leo DaMan," "JJ Excavator," and "I Luv Pedro." Her mind drifts to her husband and children, their faces and voices, and their gathering the previous evening in celebration of her seventieth birthday. She thinks about how this need to mark the passing years seemed strange to her as she raised her glass in a toast. So she is officially seventy. Seventy! She's not the only one who finds it hard to believe.

She'd like to indulge her pride — how often she is complimented on her vigor! — but she is distracted by the slow sharpening of a new awareness. She felt fine just a moment ago, but in the time it takes to clear her throat, she feels less than fine. She wonders if the feeling has something to do with the memory of last night's dinner and the conversation with her family, the stories she told and retold at their urging. Could it be that despite all she said, she didn't say enough? There's always plenty left out of any account. Still, she might have missed an opportunity. There wasn't enough time. There is never enough time. Why didn't she understand this before it was too late? Too late for what?

Forget about it. She has to concentrate on breathing. Her body longs for a saturating inhalation, yet for some reason she can only take quick, shallow breaths. Panting like her daughter's little terrier on a hot day. In her flustered state she imagines that she is on the verge of drawing attention to herself. Really, the inconvenience of it is appalling.

The sensation of mild heartburn seems to spread backward, gripping the thoracic vertebrae, causing her to stiffen in her seat. She presses her right hand against the plastic armrest, though at the same time she is seized by the desire to lift her arm and curl the fingers into a tight fist. But the plastic has turned to glue, binding her hand in place.

She reminds herself that she has felt worse on other occasions. In her seventy years she has survived whooping cough, pneumonia, and malaria — all this after surviving the war. It occurs to her that she talked about the war with her family last night. What part of the story did she forget to tell? What is she trying to remember? All the reasons not to panic. She is admirably fit for her age, according to her doctor. Surely this disorientation will pass in a few seconds. The dizziness could be attributed to . . . She doesn't bother to finish the thought. It's enough to have confidence that her condition could be attributed at all.

Outside, beyond a band of junipers, brown smoke hangs motionless between the chimneys of a foundry and the sky. If she'd noticed, the scene would have added to her mistaken sense that the world had momentarily paused to accommodate her, like traffic waiting for an old woman to cross against the light. Then be quick about it, Mrs. Rundel. Avanti, svelta! Had she been on her feet, the momentum would have caused her to stumble. She can't stumble, not here. She must get to the other side and can't risk even a quick look back. All her concentration must be focused on getting the air she needs into her lungs, from her lungs into her blood. The brain is hungry — breathe, Adriana! Memory needs oxygen. Breathe. She will not panic. Breathe.

The confusion at the Newark Station — passengers spilling out of the train, passengers trying to get on — keeps others from noticing that the elderly woman in a window seat is having difficulty breathing. Even the man who occupies the seat beside her doesn't notice. He's got his ear pressed against his cell phone and the newspaper folded open to the front page of the Business section. Across the aisle from him a woman is absorbed in a thick report on freshwater resources: water stocks and flows, desalination, international watersheds. Beside her by the window another woman is refreshing her lipstick.

"It had something to do with the anchor on the service door," the man in the seat directly behind Mrs. Rundel is saying to his companion. "No one would explain what was wrong, but we sat there on the runway for three hours. . . ."

A college student in the seat in front, exploring the brown-bag lunch his mother has prepared for him, groans, "Liverwurst again!"

Two seats ahead, a man whispers into his phone, "It doesn't have to be this way."

Hubbub of lives lived by strangers. . . . *It was like, like, it was so incredible the way you said there on the runway what is called I said it doesn't have to be this way if you she they . . .*

Mrs. Rundel doesn't notice them, and they don't notice her. That's good. She wouldn't want to give anyone a reason to stare. In another state of mind, she would have recollected past occasions when she inadvertently drew attention to herself, such as when she lost an earring while waiting for the crosstown shuttle to take her from Times Square to Grand Central or screamed curses in Italian at a newscaster on the television screen above a bar. Really, Ma, her daughter has said, can't you be a little less impetuous?

If like the time, you know, if you'd listen to me when I it would if he she having been advised concerning arsenic poisoning of Bangladesh groundwater if only.

ALTHOUGH THE FIGHTING continued elsewhere, the sounds around La Chiatta were ordinary again — leaves rustling, roosters crowing, gentle waves sloshing against the rocks outside the back gate. But because Adriana had a faint notion that something terrible had happened the night before, the ordinary sounds were newly ominous. What had happened, exactly? Paolo would explain. While Luisa was brushing Adriana's hair, Paolo, Luisa's nephew, skidded on his bicycle into the courtyard. He was fourteen years old and small for his age, with handsome features but skin so marred by blemishes that it seemed tinged with a perpetual blush. Adriana laughed whenever she saw him, even in the middle of a war, even now, as he bumped through the doorway into the kitchen. She laughed into her cupped hand, and Luisa tapped her lightly on the ear in admonishment.

Paolo had ridden his bicycle across the island to bring the news that Marina di Campo had already fallen to the Allies and the German antiaircraft batteries had been bombed into oblivion. Luisa's sister and her family were safe, he said, but the daughter of Sergio Canuti, a girl who never did what she was told, had opened the door when the African soldiers came knocking, and they'd dragged her away and killed her. Luisa collapsed into a chair, her exclamation of "Madonna!" escaping like air from a bellows. Sergio Canuti — who was that? Mario asked what Adriana was wondering. Sergio Canuti, Paolo explained importantly, was a grocer, and his daughter, Sofia, who everyone always said would come to a bad end, was dead. How exactly had she died? Adriana wanted to know. Paolo didn't bother to reply. He said that the forest on Monte Bacile was burning and that the French flag had been raised over San Martino. He said that he'd seen an unexploded shell half buried on the beach at La Foce. He said that he'd passed Lorenzo's Angela on the Santa Clara road, and from her he had learned that the Ambrogi family and all the servants at La Lampara were unharmed — they'd spent the night up in the hills and saved themselves from an encounter with roving soldiers. But Belbo the pig had been killed and left to rot in the yard.

When Luisa heard about the pig, she stopped genuflecting, wiped her eyes, and said they must send for the carabinieri. "Ma che," Mario said. Think about it: What good were the carabinieri in a war? he asked. Or priests, for that matter? Adriana wanted to add. Either you were spared or you weren't. Either you were Adriana Nardi and the soldiers didn't bother to walk down the long drive to La Chiatta to torment you or you were Sofia Canuti from Marina di Campo and you were dead.

How did she die? No one would explain it to Adriana. She shouldn't even ask the question, her uncle said. But she understood enough to know that what she'd imagined had been confirmed. First one soldier taking advantage, then another and another. There were African soldiers involved, apparently — Moroccans and Senegalese. After spending most of the night inside the cabinet, she was not afraid to imagine it: soldiers taking turns while the girl just lay there with her skirt up to her neck.

She watched the bump in Paolo's throat slide up and down beneath his thin skin as he gulped a cup of water. It occurred to her that in general skin was an inadequate surface. For that matter, the whole human body was needlessly vulnerable. All a soldier had to do was plunge a bayonet into that bump in the throat. It was far too easy. Maybe those who were still alive were simply lucky. Lucky for Paolo that he had survived. He'd ridden his bicycle all the way from Marina di Campo. Would Adriana have had the courage to do that?

Mario lit another cigarette while Paolo stood with his hand on the shoulder of his aunt, who was bent in her chair whispering a prayer. Giulia, sitting beside Luisa, looked helplessly at the table, as though recalling that once she would have been able to find an answer there. The question they couldn't ask themselves was what to do next. It was clear to Adriana that beyond what information Paolo had brought, none of the adults knew anything worthwhile.

She left them, wandered out of the room, and quietly unlatched the door to the courtyard. The inland breeze slipping past her already carried the warmth of the midmorning sun along with the perfume of jasmine and an unfamiliar tangy residue. Somewhere someone was chopping wood—the distant clacking of the ax was reassuringly steady. And the buzzing of a lone plane passing overhead was as serene as the chortling of the doves. Adriana heard the birds but did not see them, though she knew they liked to tuck themselves beneath the roof or hide in the palms.

There were many places to hide around La Chiatta — in the walled garden, in the bushes at the edge of the fields, or between the rows of vines. How could she be sure that soldiers weren't hiding in the vineyard now, crouching behind the thick tangle of wires and leaves, waiting for an opportunity to jump out and seize her and carry her off and do to her what the Africans had done to Sofia Canuti? The glint of a metal pail at the end of a row made her think of a soldier's helmet. How many soldiers were hiding in the vineyard? Merely to contemplate it gave credence to the fear, and fear gave irresistible power to her curiosity. What would happen if she were as brave as Paolo and ventured out alone? she wondered. How does God reward courage?

She set her bare foot tentatively on the stone step, as though testing its strength. She was so prepared for the sound of a voice calling her back that for a moment she actually thought she heard the sharp command to return — Adriana, vieni qua! But no one called, and she broke forward, skipping lightly, surprising herself with her convincing performance of ordinary cheerfulness. An ordinary girl on an island lit with the creamy sunshine of a perfect June morning, the fields still damp with dew, the sky a tranquil blue, everything in place and everything that was dangerous either elsewhere or nearby and invisible.

Although she knew she was supposed to stay inside, where, if necessary, she could be stuffed back inside the cabinet within a moment's notice, she craved the freedom to prove to herself that there was nothing to fear. Either there were soldiers hiding in the vineyard rows or there weren't. Either they would try to catch her or they wouldn't. The only way to confirm the truth was to go see for herself.

Maybe the bleating horn of a ship in the harbor was signaling that the world was safe again, or maybe not. Maybe the Germans had already surrendered, or maybe not. What would happen if she padded in bare feet across the courtyard, where the cobblestones were furred with moss, the cracks yellowed with tile dust, and if she crept along the first grassy row of vines, keeping close to the wires, using her hands as though to propel herself through water? How much would she risk in order to know the truth? She should probably figure out the real value of truth before heading off in pursuit of it. But already she was moving with the ease of a snake slipping through grass. No one would suspect that she was there. Where? Here in the second row. Here in the third row, where she just missed stepping on a pair of rusty shears — a useful weapon, a gift of coincidence or divine grace. Which was which? How did anyone ever tell the difference? And would the difference matter if she were compelled to make use of the shears, plunging them through the paper-thin skin of an enemy soldier?

One element of the truth was that Adriana Nardi couldn't distinguish enemy from ally. Last year the Germans were said to be friends. Last month they moved among the Elbans like guards among prisoners. Last night the French Colonial troops killed everyone they found. Who could be trusted?

Adriana was better off stuffed inside a cabinet — then she wouldn't have to find answers to unanswerable questions. Short of that refuge, she could crawl through the vineyard, and now and then she could squat on her haunches and sniff the air for the scent of a predator.

The pale green grapes were tiny and hard — she slit one open with her thumbnail and dropped the shreds in the dirt. As she peered through the vines she let the velvety underside of a leaf brush against her face. That felt good, along with the sunshine warming the back of her head and the crumbled earth beneath her feet. The freshness of the morning was a comfort not quite sufficient to distract her from her search. She was looking for the soldiers who had killed Sofia Canuti, in order to prove that they couldn't do the same to her. She was armed with rusty shears. She was stealthy and agile and would vanish into the thicket of vines as soon as she inflicted the necessary fatal wounds. Wasn't vengeance as fair as consequence was inevitable, after all? Maybe, or maybe not.

"Madonna!" That was Luisa's common exclamation of surprise, and Adriana borrowed it only sparingly. She used it now, or at least part of it, dropping the shears as Luisa's nephew, Paolo, came up from behind and caught her by the wrist.

"Paolo, tu sei un'idiota!" Sneaking up on Adriana like that and startling the breath from her . . . But Adriana was a troublemaker of the first order. A young girl shouldn't wander off at any time, and especially not during a war. Now come inside, Adriana. And keep your head down in case there are snipers nearby looking for a target.

So far, the war hadn't bothered to come to La Chiatta. The war had passed them by. Adriana couldn't admit that she was secretly disappointed not to see more evidence of the invasion in the vineyard or the olive groves — a trampled path, for instance, or empty shells. Or a corpse. With all that she'd witnessed in the ten years of her life, she still had never seen a corpse.

Had Paolo seen the dead body of Sofia Canuti? Adriana asked, but he didn't answer. He just trudged ahead, his back to her, his shoulders hunched in a pretense of impatience, as though he had to let her know that he had better things to do than to go chasing a silly little girl through the vineyard.

"Guarda, Paolo" — look at that. But he didn't look. He ignored Adriana and didn't see what she saw: the group of planes in the sky, each the size of a hummingbird, so high up that she could barely hear the sound of their engines. They were heading inland toward Marina di Campo, flying in an even V. Maybe they were carrying bombs or maybe not. Maybe more people would be dead in a few minutes or maybe not.

Adriana squeezed her eyes shut and rubbed the sunblind from them. She blinked and purposefully stared at her grimy toes to regain her vision, then raised her eyes to scan the hectare of vines extending toward the seawall, looking just in time, as though in expectation, to see what at first she took to be the peak of a powerful wave. No, it was a man — he had clambered up the opposite side of the wall and was heaving himself over the top. A shirtless man, shrunken by the distance, his dark back glistening like the quartz-speckled granite in the mountains, plummeting toward the ground, disappearing into the weeds.

She stared at the place where he had been, expecting to see him pick himself up and run. Vaulting the wall, he had given the impression that he was running for his life. Amazingly, he'd gotten as far as the Nardi vineyard, yet surely this wasn't far enough. Get up! Run! Without considering the sentiment, Adriana wanted to cheer for him. He'd been trying to escape. She wanted him to escape. But the scene remained absolutely still, devoid of even a ruffling breeze. The solidity of the wall and the pristine line of its top edge made action seem an impossible concept. Nothing moved or would move again.

Adriana would have been the first to concede that images were easily mistaken at such a distance. She thought she'd seen a man running for his life. She could as easily have seen a bird, a heron, perhaps, or a cormorant, more likely, plunging from the top of the wall to carry food to nesting chicks. Or else she'd seen the shadow of a plane.

She turned to Paolo for confirmation — he would tell her what she'd seen. But Paolo wasn't there. So eager was he to return to his duties as messenger that he hadn't even noticed Adriana was no longer following him, and he had gone on ahead. There'd be a great clamor as soon as the adults greeted him in the kitchen and he realized that he'd left the girl behind. The door would swing open, Giulia would rush out to fetch her wayward daughter, Mario would stand glaring in the doorway with Paolo behind him and Luisa behind Paolo. Until then, Adriana would watch and wait, but the vineyard would refuse to give up its secret, leaving her with no choice but to conclude that she'd seen nothing.

WHERE HAD HE ARRIVED, and where was here in relation to there? Here wasn't clay baked underfoot and coated with dust. There wasn't terraced with vineyards and olive groves. Here piles of kelp rotted on the rocks between the water and the beach. There he had to check his boots for centipedes. Here he was told to check his boots for snakes. There the rising sun melted like wax over the metal roofs. Here the sun rose like a plump orange from the sea. There he would stand outside the lycée and listen to the teacher playing piano and think that if only he were given the chance, he, too, could play the piano. There he had talent for everything. Here if they caught him they would kill him slowly. He'd been warned: whatever happened, he mustn't get caught. He knew of soldiers who carried poison in their pockets. But he wouldn't swallow poison in self-defense. He'd rather defend himself by running away. He was not afraid of being called a coward. Whatever story was told about him, he could tell a better one.

In this current story he, Amdu Diop, wasn't fleeing from pursuers. He was running toward the next chapter of his life. He was good at slipping away unnoticed because he didn't begin like other boys his age with a noisy burst of speed. He scuttled like a centipede out of a boot, across a rocky slope, behind a house, and onto the path paved with pieces of broken pottery.

He imagined an angry wife smashing all this pottery, casting one plate after another onto the ground after her husband announced that he had spent what was left of her dowry. He'd learned from listening to conversations about the people of this country that the women preferred to save money and the men liked to waste it. Also, they sat for three hours at their midday meal. Also, they wept over every holy transubstantiation as though from one Mass to the next they'd forgotten about the truth of miracles. Also, they didn't know how to hide during a night of war. Please, madame and monsieur, do not stay in your houses with the shutters closed. Try instead a cave in the mountains. Or better yet, leave the island altogether and go to some uncontested place, like, say, the Fouta Djallon highlands, and live in peace.

In all operations, Amdu was assigned to the rear. But when the rear was a beach and the only retreat possible was into the sea, he had no choice but to go forward up the hill toward the dark village, where the residents were hiding inside their houses like birds in the tall grass, like little mangemil birds after they have mauled the peanuts. These people were as guilty as the mangemil. They were guilty because they'd tolerated the German occupiers instead of joining the Resistance. But they weren't the enemy and they didn't deserve to be destroyed.

While the air assault on Portoferraio was under way, the British admiral T. H. Troubridge directed naval operations from an infantry landing craft in the Golfo di Campo. He had begun by ordering a unit of commandos to capture a German gunboat, and he had watched helplessly from the bridge when a stray German shell hit the gunboat and touched off its ammunition. With the cold ferocity of a man who knew he couldn't make up for his losses after that, he had sent off the Colonials in their rubber boats across the sandbars, wave after wave of them pushing forward through the storm of fiery shrapnel. Jumping from their boats into the water, the troops had made what the admiral would later describe as "a curious humming" that could be heard even amid the thunder of exploding shells.

Ahead of the main body of the Ninth French Colonial Division, the Bataillon de Choc crept single file up the slopes, but they couldn't locate the German gun positions in time, and soldiers of the Thirteenth Regiment of the Tirailleurs Sénégalais climbing directly behind them were forced to scatter when the top of the slopes began to flash with interdicting artillery fire. That's when Amdu found himself alone.

He was known for being useless — he'd killed no one in the battles on Corsica and had managed to lose his regiment more than once, returning only after the fighting was over. Each time he'd been forgiven, not only because he was by far the youngest soldier in the Ninth French Colonial Division, the unofficial mascot who was thought to bring good luck, but because he was the grandson of the great General Jean-Baptiste Diop and was forgiven for anything.

His belt snapped as he ran, spilling the attachments. He grabbed his canteen but left the sheath knife and extra magazines where they lay. Call him crazy, but he had no intention of reloading. Beyond the town he made his way into a dense pine grove, where he stayed until he could count to one hundred between the bursts of gunfire. One hundred and one, and he walked through a meadow in the direction of the sea. One hundred and two, he was flat on his belly, eye to eye with an immobile gray toad the size of an apple, while a plane passed low overhead. One hundred and three, he was on his feet again, scrambling along a muddy gully in search of better shelter.

In this story, he wanted to find a waterfall like the Felu, where he had once traveled with his family. He wanted to fall asleep to the roar of cascading water and then wake and find a monkey squatting next to him, picking burrs from his hair. And then the monkey would surprise him by talking in French and telling him his future.

In the future of this story, he would play lovely music on a piano, and a boy whose name he didn't know would listen through an open window of the lycée. Many years later the boy would remember Amdu's music at a moment of indecision. The memory would cause him to choose the path leading to happiness instead of sorrow.

This pleasant story occupied Amdu's thoughts while he made his way to the end of the field. The moon, bright behind the haze of smoke, silvered the bristles of high grass. He heard the distant sound of an engine, though he couldn't tell whether it was a motorboat or a motorbike. His father had promised him a motorbike when he returned from the war — this would be his reward for staying alive. Of course he'd stay alive. He didn't like to speak of it to others, but he knew God had planned an important life for him and through these difficult times would offer absolute protection.

He headed down a road that turned to dirt and led to a row of concrete bungalows perched on the edge of a steep, rocky slope above the sea. Amdu guessed the inhabitants were huddling inside their homes, trying to keep their dogs from barking and their children from crying. The silence was the sound of their fear. They had every right to be fearful, given what the general had told the captains to tell their men at the outset of Operation Brassard: *tout est permis.* Anyone found by troops of the Ninth French Colonial

Division was at risk of being humiliated — or worse. But they didn't have to fear Amdu, who had been in the war for almost a year and still hadn't fired his rifle at anything alive. He made no secret of the fact that he would never kill a living creature. He considered himself as close to a saint as he could come without actually communicating with God. At the very least, he was a good man — a seventeen-year-old man with noble aspirations and swift legs. Despite his reputation as a coward, he was liked by everybody who knew him. Even the people hiding in their houses would have liked him if they'd known him. He had come to their island to help them and make friends. But he had no way of declaring his good intentions.

A toad — slightly larger than the one he'd seen in the field, its gray skin blotched with charcoal patches — hunched lazily on the step of a lopsided well. The toad blinked at Amdu. Amdu blinked at the toad. He wondered what the toad knew of the war. He wondered what had happened to his comrades. He hoped that the German battery had already surrendered and his friends in the Thirteenth Regiment were having a good long smoke now that the invasion was over.

Feeling a sudden urge to participate in victory, he fired his rifle at the moon. He liked to fire his rifle at the moon. It was an irresistible action, though he would always regret it once he remembered that he couldn't predict where the bullet would come down. But he enjoyed the kick of the grip and the sound of the shot melting into the night air and returning with the loud snap of an echo. It was fun to shoot a rifle without the intention to kill. Yet a soldier should always have a reasonable target — a coffee can across the yard instead of the moon. See what could happen? The falling bullet could hit you in the eye. Fortunately, it didn't hit Amdu in the eye. It grazed him on the shoulder, stinging like a thorn stings with a quick sharp pain followed by an aching. His own bullet. Except it wasn't his own bullet. It was the glancing bullet from the rifle of a sniper on the roof of one of the bungalows, though Amdu didn't realize this until the man fired a second shot, which sent up a spray of gravel as it embedded in the ground beside his boot.

Run, Amdu! Of course he would run. But first he'd slip off the sling of his rifle and grab it by the barrel and send it plunging down the well. Why for heaven's sake did he do that? Because it wasn't fair to shoot an unarmed man. But why throw the rifle down the well? Because the well was there. There was not here. Here was where he had to run from, the place where God had failed to protect him.

Amdu, God fails in nothing. Of course — he knew this as surely as he knew his own name. But how do you explain . . . ?

War is war is war. To be alive during a war is to be guilty. Amdu was as guilty as the residents of this island. Amdu was as guilty as his fellow soldiers. For every boot of the tramping warrior in battle tumult and every garment rolled in blood will be burned as fuel for the fire. Be broken, you peoples, and be dismayed. Be wounded in the shoulder. Be bloody and afraid.

Amdu was afraid and would make no secret of this fact to anyone watching, but at the same time he was grateful for his many abilities, especially his ability to run so quickly that he was out of the line of fire and was heading down the steps leading to the beach before whoever wanted to kill him could locate him again in the rifle sight.

Under the hazy moon, the pebbles on this island were as smooth and round as duck eggs and were covered in a yellow film that seemed to radiate a dusty phosphorescence. Amdu was grateful for the moonlight, since it enabled him to see his way. To his right was a small wooden pavilion and to his left was a jetty extending into the sea. He headed in the direction of the rocks, clambering up and over and splashing along the edge of the water.

He was grateful to be able to move among the concealing forms of the huge boulders. He was grateful to find himself alone and far away from the fighting. He was grateful that the pain in his shoulder was no worse than a toothache, and once he'd taken off his shirt, he saw that the blood was hardly oozing at all. The bleeding would soon stop altogether beneath the cloth he'd ripped from his undershirt and twisted around his upper arm. He was grateful to be alive and had faith that whatever happened would be necessary and just. And he was grateful to find a reward for his faith in the form of a rowboat wedged against a grassy point bar. A boat! He could take the boat and row himself back to the ship that had delivered him to this island, the same ship, anchored offshore, that would take him home. He wanted to go home now, please, and take up the important work of ministering to his people. He'd seen enough of war to prefer to avoid it.

Everything was supposed to make sense, even in the absence of understanding. So when Amdu saw the giant toad perched on the bench in the boat, a gray wrinkled mass just sitting there as if it owned the world — by far the largest toad he'd ever seen, bigger than a full moon in the night sky — he took it as a sign of prohibition. If the toad could have spoken, it would have said, Do not take the boat, Amdu! All right, he wouldn't take the boat. He would keep walking in the direction he'd started, away from all that he wanted to leave behind and toward wherever, scrambling over the rocks and through the shallow water of the estuaries, and when a single plane swooped low between the bordering peninsulas and dropped some sort of cargo into the water — a bomb, Amdu assumed as it was swallowed by the sea, no, an extra fuel tank — he would know for certain that he had been right not to take the rowboat, for if he had taken it he might very well have been floating in the middle of the inlet directly beneath the jetti-soned tank. He might very well be dead by now.

He couldn't know how to interpret in any reliable fashion the mysterious evidence of fate, but so far he hadn't made any obvi-ous mistakes. The best anyone could do was pray for wisdom and trust lessons learned from past experience. Just as a good farmer will plant millet one year, peanuts the next, and then let the field lie fallow, Amdu, depending upon the situation, would enjoy the company of his family, listen to the stories of his friends, or run from danger. Family, friends, danger. Millet, peanuts, fallow. Yes, everything made sense if you had faith.

He was alive because he had faith. Yet he was being tested. Which way was the direction of happiness? He could keep fol-lowing the coastline, but this would take him farther away from his regiment. He could retrace his steps and try to make his way back to the well, but this would return him to the bungalows. The only other option was to cut inland and try to find a road leading to the marina where he and his fellows had landed. In all likeli-hood there would be troops stationed in the central piazza, and they would tell him how to make himself useful.

Between the line of the sluggish surf and the fields were boul-ders stacked steeply, with jagged footholds. Even without the full use of his left arm, Amdu could climb slowly to the top lip and from there look out over the empty expanse of the inlet. Other than the circle of foam still floating over the spot where the fuel tank had disappeared, there was no sign of life — no sailboats moored offshore, no planes overhead. He knew that the marina was hidden behind the far peninsula and figured that he could reach it by traveling a wide arc up and around the bungalows and past the meadow. As long as he moved furtively, he would be safe.

Family, friends, danger. Millet, peanuts, fallow. Folly is a joy to him who has no sense, but a man of understanding walks aright. Amdu walked aright through the low grass and onto a dirt lane that led directly uphill between halves of an old orchard. The grass in the field was waist high, and vines webbed the neglected fruit trees. Puddles of rotten peaches filled the night air with a sweet, foul fragrance, giving Amdu the impression that the yield of this land was excessive. The soil was too fertile, the sea too calm, the people lazy.

He thought about his own land — there instead of here. The warmth of fine, silky sand beneath his bare feet. The smell of fresh rain on the streets of Dakar. Riding the train between Dourbel and Kaolack — looking across the compartment at his father, who was reading a book. Wasn't his father always reading a book? His face hidden behind the pages, his thoughts as far off and unfathomable as the action of Operation Brassard. What was going on, and where? Amdu could only make his way slowly toward the place where the action had commenced. The beginning of a plan following the sequence of thought, one idea leading to another, logic supported by belief in logic, belief in logic supported by faith in God, faith in God reaffirmed in an unfamiliar setting.

He was somewhere on an island, somewhere in the night. And at the same time there was something calling or crying, a shrieking sound — he couldn't tell whether it came from an animal or a person, but the plea conveyed by the sound was easily perceived. If help was needed, danger was present. And what do you do in the presence of danger, Amdu? Run!

He ran. But in order to escape danger he first needed to identify the scope of it, so instead of running away from the awful shrieking sound of pleading, he ran toward it. He ran toward chickens being slaughtered, cats being swung by their tails, beached whales, and warthogs being devoured by hyenas. He ran toward monkeys gabbling in French. He tore through bramble wheels, damp from the previous night's rain, stumbled over the broken cylinder of an old wasp nest, kept running through the orchard toward a shed, where whatever had been calling for help, calling directly to God's servant Amdu Diop, offering him the chance to do a good deed, had already fallen silent.

Amdu gazed through the broken window of the shed, through the pane on the lower right. A flashlight propped across the rim of a wheelbarrow lit up the aftermath of the show. Amdu's fellow soldiers crowded inside — four or five of them from another regiment in the Ninth French Colonial Division. He recognized at least one, a captain he'd seen conferring with General De Lattre de Tassigny en route from Corsica. Now he was talking to his own men, muttering something in his own language, and they were muttering back, arguing about who and what while at their feet, with her bare legs spread at the thighs but crisscrossed at the ankles, lay a young girl, naked and ribboned with fresh blood.

Don't look, Amdu! Too late. He was a dark face at the broken window, looking and seeing. Too late. He couldn't unsee what he couldn't deny was beyond the general's liberal directive of *tout est permis*. Surely this act wasn't covered by *tout est permis*. Anything goes . . . except this. This was not war. This was something else, unworthy of a witness. Amdu wished he'd remained with his own regiment. Too late. And what would have shored him up under other circumstances — the Lord delivers and rescues, he works signs and wonders — only reminded him of his mistake, which was to have lived long enough to have seen too much and then to stand there stupidly until he was seen, drawing one by one the attention of the men, their gazes locking, the captain the last to notice Amdu but the first to react, slowly shaking his head, mouthing what Amdu interpreted as a description of what would happen to him if he ever dared to speak of what he'd seen.

The obvious truth being that Amdu would have been better off dead. The bullet that had grazed his shoulder should have killed him. Or the fuel tank that had fallen from the sky should have crushed him. At each turn he'd made a mistake and so had ended up at this wrong place. From here there was no turning back and no going forward into the remarkable story of his life. He could only run away.

Two soldiers had rushed from the shed and were coming after him. Run, Amdu, before they cut out your tongue! And don't bother clinging to any tired notion of punishable sin. A fair god would have cracked open the heavens and rained fire. Instead, the liberation of this rotting island continued, crimes would remain unpunished, and there was nothing he could do about it.

At least Amdu could outrun anyone he challenged to a race. As the voices of his pursuers faded in the distance, he ran this way and that, along dirt paths, through pine groves and fields, up rocky slopes, down rocky slopes, along paved roads and gravel drives and back to a narrow strip of beach. When he wasn't running he was staggering — away from a barking dog or the sputter of a jeep. Or he was leaping into the air like a startled gazelle. He stayed alive, thanks to no one but himself. He hated himself for wanting to survive. He had no right to survive. He and everyone else deserved to be dead. Life designed for the destruction of life made no sense. The liberation made no sense. The rising sun made no sense.

Warm, sweet, foul air of morning. Pebbles beneath his soaked boots gave way to a sandy belt lapped by the sea, where splinters of quartz, iron, amber, mica, glistened in the sunlight. Stupid sea. Stupid sky. Stupid wall separating Amdu from the private lives of the islanders. He and they, whoever they were, everyone everywhere sharing the capacity for enacting the unimaginable. Monsieur, tell Amdu who started this fooking war anyway. And tell him where those fooking planes flying overhead were going to dump their fooking bombs. Here? He'd rather be not-here. There. Somewhere. The other side of the wall would be preferable.

NORMALLY, the two layers of the pleura slide over each other, allowing the lungs to inflate and deflate smoothly, passing inhaled air via the trachea into the branching bronchioles and through the thin alveolar walls into a network of tiny blood vessels. Normally, the heart rate for a healthy sedentary adult averages seventy beats per minute. The diaphragm flattens as the intercostal muscles contract, the heart pumps blood through the arteries and arterioles, the ten thousand million nerve cells in the brain receive their fuel, and the mind keeps producing complex thought.

On the train between Rahway and Penn Station, on the stretch through the Kearny Marshes, Mrs. Rundel is busy thinking, her mind focused on the task of identifying the source and significance of her discomfort. Breathing in is difficult. Breathing out feels better, she discovers, and she is able to control her panting by extending the exhalation. Should she be worried? Is it, in fact, an extreme situation that would require her to seek immediate help?

Is she experiencing a disorienting introduction to an unusually potent influenza? Or could it be that the premonition of illness has produced symptoms that have no actual physical cause? At this point of calm, her cerebrum observes the misfirings of brain stem activity with skepticism. She is having difficulty breathing. But she knows she could do herself real harm by translating the possibility of an illness into a psychosomatic reaction.

Whatever the actual basis of her condition, she doesn't want to involve anyone around her. She has ridden this train for twenty years and rarely has she exchanged even the mildest greeting with other passengers. Non parlare a stranieri — don't talk to strangers. It was a lesson her children grew tired of hearing from her, and it is counsel her mind summons to consciousness now that she might be in need of aid.

It's not that she's uninterested in the lives of others. Just the opposite — she is full of curiosity. But any stranger — the man in the seat beside her, the people in front and back — might be a swindler. Hai capito? Un'imbroglione. She can't explain why she suspects this, since she's never been a direct victim. Maybe she gleaned the danger from the novels she read when she was trying to improve her English. Or maybe the need for caution came to her through intuition. Whatever its source, the possibility that she'd lose something of value to a fast-talking American has haunted her since she arrived in this country. Without a proper introduction, she will work hard to stay aloof.

She's determined at this moment to keep others from involving themselves in her predicament, though if she were home she would stumble from her chair and make her way to Robert's study and throw herself into his arms. He would take care of her. It is reassuring to remind herself of this. Just as she would take care of him if need be, he would take care of her. His concern would be hidden behind a tranquil mask — the sweet crescents his eyes make when he smiles, the thick skin buckling into wrinkles, the gray bristles muffling his chin. Dear Robert, who came into her life nearly fifty years ago in a café on the Île de St.-Louis in Paris, bumping her table as he was trying to pass and then lingering to apologize. He stretched his apology into courtship, courtship into marriage, and she's been Mrs. Rundel ever since.

But she doesn't have the leisure to remember their beginning right now. On a train bound for Penn Station on a morning that started out like any other weekday morning, she's not thinking of their past together. She's not thinking about that time he startled her, catching her by the arm while they were crossing the Place des Vosges. She's not thinking about how he brushed his lips against hers and then pulled back with an expression of surprise on his face, the intimacy confounding him for a hundred different reasons, so she slipped her hand around the back of his neck and eased him toward her. Both of them runaways. The luck of finding each other in the crowded world. Good luck marking these two individuals with an identical and permanent impression, a shared relief that would even have a gradual physical effect, so that over the years those who knew them would note an actual resemblance, as if they were siblings or cousins. And who can say for sure that they are not related by blood? He was born the youngest son in a large family and has so many relatives he never bothered to learn all their names. She was a foundling — an English word she came to love for its fairy-tale conjurings and abhor for its meaning: a baby deserted by unknown parents . . . and found, and claimed, when no one else would have her, by Signora Giulia Nardi of La Chiatta.

But she's not thinking about any of this on the train to Penn Station. She's not even thinking about what she'd been trying to remember a moment earlier. She's not considering the influence of memory upon consciousness and doesn't contemplate how her past experiences will affect any decision she might make in regard to seeking the help of strangers, nor does she have any idea that because of her years of smoking, her platelets are sticky, making her vulnerable to hypercoagulability and deep vein thrombosis. She's not thinking about how it has started to rain. She is not wondering how the brokenhearted man talking on his phone will end his sentence — "what I'm trying to say is what goddamnit I'm trying to say if you'll just listen to me so I can say what I'm trying to say is that" — or what happened to the man sitting behind her, who is still complaining about the delay of his flight to his friend, a software designer heading into the city to look for a new job. She is not interested in the issue of water as a human right — the subject of the chapter being read by the woman across the aisle. She is not concerned about the college student's disappointment over his liverwurst sandwich. And she is certainly not wasting her time wondering what she's not thinking about.

All she knows during this clarifying action of an extended exhalation is that she needs her husband and would call him at home if she could find her own cell phone, but as usual it is hidden in the mess in her purse. Here are her cigarettes and lipstick, her checkbook, her wallet, a pack of tissues, a pack of gum, old receipts, her address book, paper clips and Post-it pad and mints and nail file and pens and aspirin. But she can't find her cell phone. The rain, invisible in the air, splinters on the window, and she can't find her cell phone. Her husband is at home, and she can't find her cell phone.

She can't see what she can't find. She can hold her cell phone in her hand and stare at it and still not see it, and then toss it back into her purse and continue searching, oblivious to the fact that she just found what she'd been looking for because the effort has already struck her as futile. Useless desire. What is happening is happening, the embolus is stuck in an artery, and if she can't find her cell phone, she can't find her cell phone. It all makes irritating sense. There is nothing to be done, no way to translate effort into success and find what she assumes is lost. Her husband could be seated beside her right now instead of a stranger, and Mrs. Rundel wouldn't see him.

AFTER THE FIRST NIGHT of the liberation, during the quiet stretch following a pranzo that consisted only of cheese and bread because they had no meat left and Mario advised them not to light the stove to heat stock for soup, Adriana was at the piano rocking her hand between the opposite notes of chords in an attempt to mimic the sounds Rodolfo had made in her dream. Now that the bombardment had stopped, the war seemed very far away, though the fighting was said to be continuing as close as the alleys of Portoferraio as well as across the island in Porto Azzurro and the forests around Marciana Alta. The adults were still unsure who would emerge as victor.

With her face hidden in the crook of her left arm and her right hand tapping sound from single notes, Adriana thought about what she knew. She knew that she could trust her mother to protect her and to find her enough to eat, even during a time of scarcity. She knew that her uncle would continue to tell her what to do. And she could assume with good reason that when the war finally had gone elsewhere, shutters would still be painted green, stucco would be chipped, stone steps marked with smooth grooves, pistachio berries would be red, the caps of acorns brown, and the Scoglietto light-house would still be standing.

C, G, she played. C, G; D, A. How easy it was to predict, abstractly, the sound of the note she was about to press. And yet she couldn't really hear music before she played it, just as she couldn't experience morning in the midst of the night or smell a rose in her imagination. What had she been hearing during the night? What had happened? Uncertainty was like an itch she couldn't satisfy by scratching — this was a good comparison and it deserved to be shared with her mother, along with other things, including how, though she knew a little about a little, every passing minute seemed to erase a piece of memory.

Giulia Nardi sat across the room, chain-stitching a scroll on a linen napkin. Luisa was snoring downstairs in the kitchen, having fallen asleep in her chair. Mario had gone to La Lampara with Paolo to find out what Lorenzo knew about the situation. And Adriana was at the piano, trying to re-create the sounds of last night's dream.

Quiet, lazy pausa. The air felt both buoyant and restrictive, the world muffled by inertia. Today was . . . what was today? The eighteenth day of June in the year 1944. Just another afternoon in a villa surrounded by olive groves and vineyards, midway between Magazzini and San Giovanni. Just another war in the history of an island.

A, E; C, G. That Adriana had noticed the fuzz on her legs darkening in the same week in September that the war had come to the island seemed more of an insult than a coincidence. Her body's changes would have been hard enough to accept — but coinciding with the German occupation, they became unbearable. Everything that was happening was happening without the consent of those most deeply affected. Everywhere was occupied territory. Was resistance absurd? Was she really supposed to accept the fact that everything familiar would gradually be modified? Or worse, she could paint her nails and lips and smile at soldiers of any nationality. She could use the war to her advantage and do what she'd heard adults talking about when they thought she wasn't listening.

But these were ridiculous thoughts. Infantile, girlish thoughts. War was one thing, and growing up something else entirely. That the fighting on the island would continue for days or weeks or months had nothing to do with the fact that she would grow up. And if she couldn't meet the challenges of life with courage, she might as well take back the porcelain doll she'd given away to Paolo's little sister. Of course she wouldn't do that. She was through with dolls, and someday she'd be through with cartwheels, handsprings, and her amazing dives off the rocks at Viticcio. She would grow up willingly and would be as beautiful and superior as her mother — a woman who knew how to stay in control of her life.

Other mothers were shrill in their worry, with voices that rang morning to night with admonishments. Not Giulia Nardi, with her dignified demeanor that was just short of severe. Other mothers were subordinate to their husbands and had little interest in the world outside their homes. Not Giulia Nardi, who had traveled widely, spoke French and English fluently, and never bothered to marry. Giulia Nardi was the woman Adriana expected to become — unmarried but never alone, clever with numbers, regal, stoic even during wartime, setting the example for others.

But it was true that she hadn't remained entirely stoic during this current invasion. The clatter of bicycle wheels on the drive made her gasp. Her daughter's absence made her frenetic. Do not go outside without your mamma's permission, Adriana!

As the afternoon wore on, there was nothing to do but roam the shuttered rooms of the villa and stay out of Luisa's way as she swept the stone floors or rubbed copper pots with wood ash and lemon juice. There wasn't even the interesting sound of gunfire in the distance to remind her that she was living in history. Occasionally she could hear the buzz of a plane passing overhead, but it seemed to be a leisurely sound, like the sound of a bee drifting from flower to flower.

Her mother encouraged her to read a book. But there was no book that could hold her attention. Then she might draw a picture. She didn't want to draw. Then she should practice the bagatelle she'd been learning, fill La Chiatta with music, and ignore what she couldn't affect.

The hours passed slowly. Finally, Mario and Paolo returned with Lorenzo Ambrogi, who sank into the chair across from Giulia and announced that the Germans had retreated from the central regions of the island into the forest on Monte Capanne. This was good, they all agreed, except Mario, who was not convinced that an Allied victory would be preferable. "Senz'altro" — without a doubt, Giulia insisted. Without a doubt it would be preferable. "Senz'altro," Mario echoed coldly. What did Giulia mean by preferable? he wanted to know. Was what the African soldiers had done to the daughter of Sergio Canuti preferable? And what about the Signori Volbiani, who were caught hiding in their barn in the hills outside of Procchio? This was news Lorenzo had already shared with Mario and now was obliged to repeat for Giulia and Luisa. The Signori Volbiani of Procchio had been killed, slaughtered like animals, like goats, their throats slit when they were found hiding in their barn. Sofia Canuti had been killed. Corpses of soldiers were scattered in the woods. And Belbo the pig was dead — shot in the snout.

If it was already this bad, then it should be worse, Adriana wanted to say, though she knew that the adults would consider her foolish, so she kept her mouth shut. But she went on thinking it. If people were killed brutally for no reason, then the killing should happen elsewhere. If there was no place left on an island that would serve as a refuge, then there should be no refuge left on earth.

Foolish child. War made all children foolish. And at the same time that it left people dead, it made dogs bark. Lorenzo's dog, Pippa, having followed her master through the fields, was barking in the courtyard. Luisa told Paolo to go see why Pippa was barking. Adriana asked to go with him. "No, assolutamente no!" Luisa said over her shoulder as she left the room. The other adults continued arguing. When Adriana followed Paolo to the ground floor and out into the courtyard, no one noticed, not even Paolo, who quieted the dog and then went back inside to hear more of the important talk.

What was so important about talk? Talk, talk, talk. Adults talking during a war were like dogs barking. Sss, Pippa, silenzio, and come with Adriana! "Vieni, sss." There was something Adriana wanted to check, and she would feel safer with Pippa along. Quick, veloce! Back along the grass corridor between the two halves of the vineyard, hurry, hurry, to the wall extending from the gate along the edge of the field, to the stretch of stone netted in ivy, through the briars, to the patch of weeds flattened by a falling nothing.

Veramente, nothing had fallen over the wall. Nothing had scrambled through the briars and run away. Nothing could interrupt the serenity in this far corner of La Chiatta's vineyards. There were no footprints or bits of torn clothing to be seen, nothing more than a few twigs broken either by some animal or by the most recent rain. All Adriana had seen earlier that day was a dark nothing spot of sunblind.

Having confirmed what she'd believed, Adriana knew she should hurry back inside and station herself at the piano bench before anyone noticed that she'd left. She couldn't afford to cause more trouble. But she was distracted by the interesting show put on by the natural world. She watched a pair of kestrels plunge one after the other into the grass, probably in pursuit of a snake. The swallows overhead curled in a design as intricate as the scroll in her mother's linen. Above the swallows, a single gull glided in a wide arc. Unseen beyond the wall, the sea splashed against the rocks. What else wasn't she seeing, she wondered? She looked around, trying to take in everything. Pippa sat smiling, panting, her tongue lolling. She gave a little whine of impatience. Yes, Pippa, it was time to go. But a quick motion in the grass caught Adriana's eye — a nice, plump cricket had hopped onto a broken twig. She cupped her hand in anticipation, since it wasn't possible to see a cricket without trying to catch it. She even had a cage waiting for it in her room — a house of wire and painted wood made by Ulisse, La Chiatta's gardener. He had given the cage to Adriana when she was six and had shown her how to sneak up on a cricket and catch it in her hands. He had instructed her on how to feed it lettuce leaves. If before the end of three days it sang for her, he said, the Nardi family would have good luck. If it didn't sing, life at La Chiatta would go on as before. Either way, the cricket must be given its liberty at the end of three days. But if the cricket died in captivity, Adriana would have to find a witch to undo the curse.

None of her crickets had ever died, though not all of them had sung for her. But this one looked as if it could be coaxed to sing. La Chiatta needed good luck right then. The insect seemed to

know that it was under inspection and might even have been en-
joying a moment of vanity as Adriana drew closer to it and prepared to catch it. She was quick, but the cricket was quicker —
with a triple set of hops it was off the twig, out of reach, and hidden in the grass.

This was a disappointment — good, cleansing disappointment,
like a bucketful of cold water thrown over a floor and then swept
away with a broom! It felt fine to be disappointed by a cricket and
to forget, momentarily, about Sofia Canuti and the Signori Volbiani and the corpses of soldiers in the woods. If a cricket's escape
was the worst that could happen, then war was really just a confusing idea to be debated by adults over cigarettes and coffee.
There was only the here and now and the feeling of being in the
world. And as though to reaffirm the value of immediate experience, the cricket, hidden in the grass, gave a long, pleasant chirp.

Sunshine. Cricket songs. The faded petals of a primrose. The
unreal reality of war. Adriana would have liked to wander the little labyrinth of box hedges in the garden right then. Or she would
have liked to slip through the gate and wade in the shallow water
along the beach. But there was a war going on, and she was supposed to be sitting quietly with the grown-ups. Vieni, Pippa! Pippa
was a good dog — usually. She had wandered off to sniff around
the gate and the boathouse, and when Adriana called to her, she
gave a yelp and ran in the opposite direction. Pippa! The dog ran
up the aisle between the rows of vines, not in pursuit, as Adriana
would have expected, but rather in flight, chased by a small calico
cat whose loping gait made it seem as though the pursuit was just
a game to her.

Cricket songs and yelping dogs and predatory cats. Yes, this
was the patch of the world that Adriana was pleased to call home.
But this bright thought provoked its grim opposite. What if the

fires spread or the bombardment resumed during the night? What if La Chiatta was destroyed? The possibility aroused a childish anger. Who turned the idea of war into reality? Who invited the soldiers to the island anyway? First the Fascists, then the Germans, then the Africans. The war had been going on longer than forever, with one army arriving on the island with its bombs and guns, forcing the occupying army to retreat. As they passed across the land they left behind corpses and ruins. They burned the olive groves and let their fat horses graze in the wheat. In memory she heard Luisa's exclamation: Madonna! And her mother's voice: Adriana! She really should go back inside. Luisa would be serving supper, and the adults would be deciding what was safest for Adriana: her bedroom or the kitchen cabinet.

She watched the cat turn proudly back toward the boathouse, its tail standing high in victory. Adriana approached it, chucking softly, stretching out her fingers, but the animal growled, and its fur rose in a spiny ridge. In response to the growl came a soft mew from behind an old dinghy propped against the boathouse — the mew of a kitten, a puffball that Adriana caught and held in her cupped hands, a prize even better than a cricket! As small as a peach and the color of sponge cake soaked in wine, it was the best treasure Adriana had found in weeks, worth the risk of hiding in her bedroom, she thought for a moment, but decided against this when the mother cat began pushing against her ankle, bumping her head and haunches. Certo, Mamma Gatta, the little one belongs to you. And if there was one kitten, there must have been others. After a brief look around the outside of the boathouse, Adriana pushed the door, already open a crack, and, with the kitten still in her hands and the mother following at her heels, she stepped inside.

Somewhere amid the buoys and rakes and ropes, the oars and the tiers of terra-cotta pots was a cat's den full of kittens. She listened for their mewing. She looked for a flash of tawny fur. A slice of fading sunlight fell across the center of the boathouse, but the rest was hidden in deep shadow. Everything was in place, and yet as she stood poised on the threshold, she sensed the solitude give way to a strange feeling that she recognized from her dreams. It was the feeling of standing on stage in a dark theater she'd thought was empty and slowly realizing that the audience was in the seats, waiting for her to speak her next line. It was the feeling of running down an alley and hearing footsteps behind her. It was the feeling of being watched.

No sound. No movement. Who's there? No one. Nothing. Spot of sunblind. Blackness surrounded by light. Adriana, come along now — any minute your mother will notice that you've gone missing again. Chi c'è? Tiny thorns of kitten claws on her wrist. The mother cat was stationed behind her, waiting. Waiting for what? Cat's pupils expanding to absorb the light within the darkness. What if Adriana died now, right here, on the threshold of the boathouse, age ten? Paura: the only suitable expression for this feeling of being afraid, the breathy stumble of the letters mimicking its meaning. La paura. Ha paura. The dream of seeing footprints in white powder on the floor. There were no footprints in the boathouse. The dream of finding herself alone and not alone at the same time. What did she really know for sure about anything? Help: aiuta — another good word. But to speak it aloud would be to invite danger into the open. The dream always ends before you die — until the last dream, which would be just like this: standing on a threshold, unable to go forward or back, locked in place by the eyes of someone hidden in the darkness.

And then she would wake up. The kitten would fall from her hands with a squeak and bounce against her ankle and land unhurt on the floor and scramble ahead of its furious mother beneath a tarp thrown over barrels. A kitten. A cat. A boathouse. A dream, no, a sudden recollection of watching sixteen oxen pull a wagon loaded with a block of marble across a piazza in the mainland village of Avenza. Why did she remember Avenza now? Would this be her last memory?

No, not if she could help it. She would give herself the chance to remember running up the grassy aisle between the vines toward the courtyard and La Chiatta — a foolish girl running from nothing, which was even more absurd than a big dog running from a little cat. A ten-year-old girl — almost eleven — who understood the war either as an abstract idea that made adults angry or as a monstrous something hiding in the boathouse. True, she hadn't seen it, she hadn't heard it, but she knew it was there in the darkness because she'd smelled it — a smell she recognized only in afterthought as the sweat of oxen.

Blame
the
Devil

IT WAS THE EIGHTEENTH OF JUNE, AND THOUGH THE FIGHTING
between the French Colonials and the Germans was continuing
and fires were burning in the mountains, life inside La Chiatta was
hardly less than ordinary, though with more coming-and-going
than usual. Shortly after Adriana slipped back into the kitchen,
her absence unnoticed by the adults, Lorenzo Ambrogi ground
his cigarette stub against the heel of his boot and announced that
he was heading back to La Lampara. He conferred quietly with
Mario in the hall. Some minutes later, Adriana heard him in the
courtyard calling for his dog. After Lorenzo's departure, Paolo
headed to the guest room to sleep, having been forbidden by Luisa

to return home on his bicycle. Luisa sent word to his family that her nephew was safe, the message conveyed by Ulisse, the gardener, to a bold fisherman who had spent the day traveling in his boat along the northern coast of the island, gathering fish from the surface — grouper and bass and whole schools of anchovies killed by the bombs that had fallen into the sea.

Ulisse had arrived at La Chiatta earlier in the day, bringing with him his entire family: his wife, his three sons, and his eighty-three-year-old mother, the Signora Fausta, all of whom were comfortably lodged on the upstairs floor of the cantina, from where the sounds of voices raised in argument could be heard at regular intervals — first the chatter of children, then their father demanding quiet, then the children again, ignoring him, then Ulisse's wife scolding, then the boys, each of the two older ones insisting on their innocence while the baby wailed — as if nothing at all had changed in their world.

The lamp in the kitchen remained unlit, but the shutters had been propped aslant to let in air, and there was enough daylight to illuminate the details of features — the cracked lipstick on Giulia Nardi's lips, the prominent mole on Luisa's temple, the tips of gray on Mario's mustache. The harbor of Portoferraio was carpeted with corpses, Adriana overheard her uncle say. Not just fish, he insisted. The harbor was full of human corpses! Giulia rebuked him. Don't speak that way in front of the child! But Adriana was already imagining a carpet of dead bodies so thick that a light-footed cat could have walked across it. Bodies of soldiers, of old men and women, of girls, bobbing like so many corks in a row — a vision she could entertain only because she imagined that all of the dead had never really been alive. And even if the war was nearby, it wouldn't come inside the safe haven of La Chiatta. That's why the others had come here for refuge. Surrounded again by the comforts of the kitchen, where the air was filled with the sweet smell of the stove's cold ashes, Adriana felt newly confident that she was safe, they were all safe here under the roof of La Chiatta, and her confidence made her annoyed at her mother, who continued to talk with Mario about a possible refuge. Where could they go to escape the fighting? This was the topic absorbing the adults now that night was returning. With thousands of soldiers scouring the island and the defiant Germans holed up in their concrete redoubts, the forests were no longer safe, the ports would be vulnerable again, and snipers were posted in the villages.

Hundreds of Elbans had fled into the hills, where they were hiding in caves and old mining tunnels. Some of them had been there for weeks, and a few peasant families had taken their herds of sheep and goats into the mountains when the war began and lived there ever since. But it was too late to join them, since now the fighting was heaviest in the hills. Mario suggested taking refuge in the church of Santo Stefano, but Giulia insisted that its open position in the meadow made it vulnerable. Luisa broke into mournful reminiscence: in the time of her povero papà, war stayed away from the island. In those days people feared lightning and famine, not soldiers and bombs. God did not make man in his image to be blown apart by soldiers and bombs.

Ignoring her, Mario suggested the boathouse as a hiding place.

"The boathouse," Giulia echoed quietly, considering the prospect.

Not the boathouse! Adriana imagined blurting it aloud. Not the boathouse! What did Adriana know about the boathouse? her uncle would demand. What was wrong with the boathouse? Would she rather spend the night in the cabinet again? Sì, sì, certo, put her in the cabinet and nail the doors closed! At least the cabinet didn't have extra space where the war could hide, biding its time. Yes, the cabinet was preferable to the boathouse. What did she know about the boathouse? the adults would demand. She didn't know anything for sure and would only have condemned herself to punishment if she'd admitted that she left the villa while the adults were absorbed in their conversation. And even if she did confess that for a second time she'd ignored the prohibition against going outside, what could she say about the boathouse? She couldn't say that she was afraid. Afraid of what?

The clamor of voices drifted from the cantina again — the voices of Ulisse and his family. Hadn't Ulisse begun tying the vines just yesterday? No — it was the day before yesterday. The ashes in the stove had been cold for two days.

"What will happen to Ulisse?" Adriana offered this question as a distraction. Ulisse and the children of Ulisse, the wife of Ulisse, and old Signora Fausta? If La Chiatta wasn't safe, then neither was the adjacent cantina. "What about Ulisse and his family?"

"Ulisse should take his family and go back to Magazzini," Mario growled.

"Ulisse has come to us for refuge," Giulia countered.

Mario said he didn't think there was a law obliging a woman to provide shelter for her servants during a time of war — a remark that drew a huff from proud Luisa and sent her stomping from the room. Giulia rose to go after her and then thought better of it. Sinking back into her chair, she said that she didn't think there was a law obliging her to provide shelter for her brother-in-law. Mario was appalled at the insinuation. He'd come to La Chiatta to offer aid and advice, not to beg for protection. Truthfully, he would have preferred to join his neighbors in the hills while Portoferraio was under attack. If his help was no longer appreciated, he would leave.

The gray edge of his mustache looked as if it were coated with the residue of foamy milk, and the web of wrinkles on his forehead made him appear perpetually displeased, even when he smiled. He hardly ever smiled. His severity might have been enough to cause Adriana to dislike him, but instead it increased the effect of the few flashes of amusement. In the years since her aunt had died, Adriana had learned to relate to her uncle with charm designed to distract him from his gruffness. And her success had made her fonder of him. Smile, Uncle! Laugh! Listen to the stories Adriana has to tell. . . . On another day he might have enjoyed listening to her, but not now. Now he had other things on his mind.

He swung his arm into the sleeve of the jacket he'd left hanging on the back of the chair. He was leaving. But first he would remind Giulia of all that he had done for her and Adriana over the years. What he had done for them? Did he have no sense of gratitude? Had he forgotten the money she had loaned him? How dare she speak of debt! Mario retorted. What insult! As if he'd used the money for himself. As if — this part he left unsaid — he hadn't done everything possible to care for his wife, Teresa, Giulia's sister, during the terrible final weeks of her illness.

"Come se," Giulia echoed. As if. "Come se niente," she said bitterly. As if nothing.

"Com'è vero Dio!"

The ugly argument was growing uglier, so Adriana decided to follow Luisa's example and go elsewhere. She hesitated at the threshold of the dining room, half inclined to announce her exit, but then decided to slip out without a word. She wandered through the expansive rooms and settled again on the piano bench. With her right hand she began playing the opening of a little folk song she had memorized when she was eight and now remembered in bits, each phrase leading her into the next, the childish music reassuring in its simplicity, reminding her of the simple promise of time. There was yesterday and there would be tomorrow. Tomorrow, or the day after tomorrow, Luisa would stir together melted chocolate and eggs for budino di cioccolato, Giulia Nardi would propose a shopping trip to Livorno, and Adriana would make her uncle smile.

The thought of ordinary life brought to mind the celebration that would come at the end of the war. Crowds would gather in Piazza Repubblicà in Portoferraio; all the girls who had been hidden in cabinets during the fighting would be out dancing in wooden shoes while soldiers tossed spools of paper ribbons into the air. The tune Adriana played on the piano might soon be played in victory. Or this one for a quadrille. How did it go? She paused before trying to sound it out. Something like — no, that wasn't right. Then try this.

Before she'd found the note to begin, she was interrupted by an abrupt sound coming from the terrace below the loggia. It was the sound of a hammer hitting a tree stump or a bucket falling from a tree. It was the sound of metal against stone or wood against metal. It was the sound that the representative of the war would make if he had wandered from the boathouse up to the terrace and accidentally knocked over a rake that had been propped against the wall.

Who was out there? It wasn't difficult to imagine an answer. Blame the devil. The devil could make a daydreaming girl think terrible things.

She could imagine that a soldier stood in the garden outside the library's shuttered door. Un marocchino, black as the black sand at Topinetti, with the blood of the Canuti girl caked beneath his fingernails. Thanks to the devil, Adriana could guess what she couldn't have known otherwise — that the same man who had jumped over the wall and hidden in the boathouse was now crouching outside on the terrace. He was four meters tall, wearing only drawstring trousers, his hands were as big as rabbits, and he was waiting for an opportunity to attack a defenseless girl.

In her imagination, she could follow this possibility to its ugly end. And then, because she would not let herself be as easily tempted toward horror as all that, because she liked to hear people say about her, Che coraggio!, she could return in memory to the instant that the black man had tumbled over the wall into the grass, the nothing that she'd seen, a nothing that was nowhere near four meters tall, and she could remind herself that her first impulse had been to cheer for him, whoever he was, whatever he'd done.

From one perspective, the meaning she gave to the brief noise she'd heard outside the library had a magical prescience. Without adequate evidence, somehow she knew that she was right — a soldier was in the garden, drawn by the sound of the piano, and he wanted to communicate with her. But from a more pragmatic point of view, her understanding of the situation was entirely reasonable and in fact would have been reached earlier if she'd been willing to acknowledge the reality of what she'd seen. The explanation was quite simple: a solitary soldier had fled the fighting and made his way onto the Nardi estate, and now he was finding comfort in the songs Adriana played.

She played for him again — first a beginner's version of Tosti's "Non M'Ama Più," and then a rendition of "La Serenata." She played for her invisible audience of one, and because she imagined her listener had never heard anyone play the piano before and couldn't judge the merits of her playing, she imagined that he would think her brilliant. She imagined his admiration and pleasure. She played with a confidence that previously she'd felt only when she was diving and her girlfriends who didn't even know how to swim were watching in awe. Ma che coraggio! And when, at last, she had played all the songs she'd memorized, she swiveled on the bench to face the loggia, intending to wait as long as it took for him to open the shuttered doors from the outside, forgetting in that period of calm that the violence could resume without warning. Just when she had no interest in anything beyond her immediate experience, there was a rude banging on the door facing the courtyard, a clamor of voices in the front hall, commands in a foreign language, Luisa screaming in protest, Mario trying to reason, Giulia ominously silent, the crash of a plate swept off a table onto the marble floor, more screams, more shouts, words she didn't understand followed by the sound of a single gunshot.

HE KNEW what he knew not because his knowledge had been clearly verified but because what he knew about himself and his relation to God had the logic of a sound mathematical equation. Faith founded on the deduction of truth was irresistible. Perceiving himself as blessed, he would go to great lengths to protect his good intentions, even, or especially, during a war.

He wasn't entirely naive. He'd seen the devastation after the battles were over. He had helped to bury the dead. He'd even seen the jerking, pleading motion of life's last efforts when, across a field on Corsica, a comrade took a sniper's bullet in his eye. But he'd always thought that what he couldn't bear to witness was a death that he himself had caused, since to kill someone would have disproved the truth, as he understood it, relating the sanctity of his life to its potential.

Before he learned the value of reticence, he had candidly expressed his desire to become the first Senegalese saint. For this he was considered endearingly childish or even, as the nuns at the mission school had said of him, out of his mind. But the nuns were wrong and he was right. Amdu Diop was not suffering from madness. He knew that what he knew was as trustworthy as $n(C)=2$, which, though lacking in factual content, paradoxically was eminently applicable to reality.

But reality was not supposed to be expansive enough to contain what he'd recently seen through the broken window of a shed, which had been enough to cause him to distrust his faith in the value of his life. He was no longer sure how to measure his value or how to plan the miracles for which he wanted to be remembered. He didn't know what he was worth in a world where he couldn't do any good.

His gloom had been powerful while it lasted. Between then and now, however, his hunger and thirst had taken precedence. He hadn't eaten since yesterday's breakfast and had finished the water in his canteen during the night. He'd missed two midday meals. He hadn't yet tasted the sweet wine the general had promised his men once the island was liberated. Forget about all the blessed who would be chosen for everlasting happiness. He would have traded his own place in heaven for a big cup of clear water, an orange, and a bowl of mutton stew. He would have stolen bread from a child. Maybe he would even have killed the child. To what length would he go to fill his empty stomach? While he was arranging the sails and tarp in the boathouse to make a concealing place to rest, he entertained himself with this idle question. To what length would he go? And then the door to the boathouse opened, sending a pillar of light across the floor, sunlight blotted by an imposing shadow, making the question suddenly relevant. Hiding behind the folds of the musty tarp, Amdu wondered whether he would kill simply in order not to be killed.

He would have insisted that this was the first time he had contemplated the hypothetical necessity of killing. Pressed on the issue, however, he would have had to admit that in his lazier moments as a soldier he'd allowed himself to wonder how easily he, Saint Amdu, could have been corrupted.

Nothing, he'd discovered, corrupted an innocent soul as easily as hunger and thirst. The longest he'd ever fasted was from sunrise to sunset, having been invited to participate in Ramadan by a Muslim cousin. A whole day without nourishment had been tolerable, even if it hadn't changed Amdu's mind about the faith he'd concocted for himself. But now he was discovering how after thirty hours every thought of some particular fulfillment felt like a pin pricking the soft tissue of his brain. Mon Dieu, what he would have done to be free of desire. What would he have done? He could only wonder in retrospect, for already the light was stripped of its bulky shadow and the intruder was gone.

He was alone again, and solitude gives a corrupted man the chance to consider missed opportunities. What would he have done, if he'd had the chance? He would have pointed his gun at the nose of the stranger and demanded, in French because he didn't know how to say it in Italian, a loaf of bread and a jug of water. Except that his gun was at the bottom of a well, remember. Stupid Amdu. Once upon a time he'd planned to be a saint. Now he couldn't even bully a stranger into giving him food and drink. But what did he know about bullying? For most of his youth he'd been too small and frail to bully others. Then he'd grown tall and become a soldier. And then he'd thrown his rifle in a well. Now here he was, alone in some stranger's boathouse, hungry, thirsty, willing but unable to commit a mortal sin to replace desire with fulfillment.

He heard the rustling of the kittens, which he mistook for mice. Once upon a time he'd gone so far as to imagine that someday, with God's blessing, he'd be able to talk to mice. And to birds, following the example of Saint Francis, and to fish, like Saint Anthony. The language of fish was a silent language, a language of motion and glance. He thought of this now. If the people here spoke no French, he could say what he needed to say by pointing to his mouth. Kiss me here. No, he didn't mean that! I am thirsty. I am hungry. I am going to kill you unless you bring me a loaf of bread and a jug of water.

He was a disgusting wretch, but so what? His temper would improve if some kind soul would only offer him assistance. Whoever had nearly discovered him in the boathouse might have been able to help. And if that same whoever had been willing, maybe the willingness would extend to another place at a later time. He had nothing to lose. He could step from the confines of his hiding place, he could go to the door, and he could follow the girl whose shadow he'd seen on the floor of the boathouse. First he could follow her with his eyes, and after she'd disappeared into the stone palace that must have been her home, he could follow her on foot. And when finally he found her again, he could convey to her his simple needs: a loaf of bread and a jug of water, if you please. And then he would go on his way again, from nowhere to nowhere.

Spikes of sedge poked from beneath the stone steps leading up to a door. Oleander bushes at opposite corners of the wall were heavy with creamy blossoms. Doves made a steady purring sound. The sound of a baby's laughing gurgle drew Amdu toward the adjacent cantina. Keeping low to the ground, he moved close to the open window, trying to summon the will to make his presence known, but a burst of angry voices from the upstairs floor sent him fleeing in a panic along the dirt path leading around the front of the villa and into the nearest hiding place — a meager shelter made by an old door propped against the wall, camouflaged by thick junipers. He sat there with his heart pounding, legs folded, knees tucked beneath his chin.

He waited for a good idea to come to him. He waited to be discovered. When would he be discovered? Sooner rather than later, he hoped. He wanted to be found, dragged into the open, scolded, and eventually set on his feet and appraised. Once he was judged harmless, he hoped that he'd be invited inside for food and drink. The feast would continue late into the night, and his kind hosts, whoever they were, would explain to him in French, if they spoke French, the meaning of this war.

Yet he didn't really need an explanation. The war was what the war had done, and because of it he'd been reduced to a huddled, starving, disgusting wretch, nostrils coated with dust, ears filled not with the gentle sound of rain but with the buzzing of flies. He'd fallen as low as the old Dahomy men, the sons and grandsons of slaves, who built their cardboard homes alongside the railway tracks leading out of Dakar. If no one helped him soon, he would have to do what they did and scavenge through piles of garbage for his meals. He'd live like a dog, in the company of dogs, starting with this gray-muzzled dog sticking her snout into Amdu's shelter, sniffing carefully, cocking her head in thoughtful interpretation of the evidence.

Amdu offered the dog his open palm. She licked his hand, tasted his salty sweat, licked greedily, licked his fingers, his wrist, his arm up to the dirty cloth that was glued fast to the scab on his shoulder. Amdu was delicious, briny and ripe, and unlike most people he didn't mind a dog's slobbering affection.

The animal eventually settled beside him, resting her head on his boot. Amdu thought about Saint Jerome and the lion. He thought about the silhouette of a baobab tree against a white sky. He thought about monkeys speaking French. He thought about food and drink. He thought about the bushland, and it was this thought that drew him into a dream that he was loping on his hands and knees beside a magnificent cheetah, who turned to him as they ran and smiled as though to suggest that she had in mind a secret plan.

"Pippa!"

Amdu woke abruptly to the sound of a man's voice. "Pippa!" The dog raised her head, pricked her ears forward, barked once, then yawned and let her tongue droop lazily over the side of her jaw. "Pippa, vieni!" But Pippa liked it here beneath the door. She liked it when Amdu rubbed the fur smooth along the ridge between her ears. "Pippa!" Amdu heard a man's boots crunch along the path in slow approach. He watched a pebble, kicked inadvertently, roll into the grass. The dog's easy panting and her half-lidded eyes gave her an aura of impermeable lassitude, as though she were used to doing as she pleased. And what pleased her now was to stay with Amdu for a while, her head in the coolness of this shelter, her haunches extending out into the warm sunshine.

But her master had a different idea. Amdu cringed when he saw the man's boot raised, and he pressed his face into his knees so he wouldn't have to look up when the door was knocked aside and the blows started to fall, falling harder than ever because the master would discover two dogs in place of one. But the blows never came. The man, oblivious to Amdu, merely nudged the dog's rump with the toe of his boot, rolling her to force her upright and out of her hiding place, rewarding her when she obliged with gentle pats, which caused the dog to forget her new friend entirely and trot happily in advance of her master back along the path, leaving Amdu to go on rotting and starving, alone on an island where he didn't even know the word for help.

It was hot and cold under this wooden door, dusty and damp, bright at the edges, dark in the center. Amdu stayed there a long while, feeling sorry for himself. He thought of his mother and father. He thought of the Soeur Maria at the mission school. He thought of the wrestler at the stadium in Dakar who was draped in beaded gris-gris. Before the match began, the wrestler had boasted of his strength while drummers drummed and a trio of women sang in praise of him. Amdu remembered the man vividly: the clacking, shimmering talismans hanging from his neck, the stark muscles in his arms, his pride and confidence. It was odd, then, that Amdu couldn't remember whether the women sang in Wolof or in French. Or who had won the wrestling match. Or the name of the officer he'd seen last night in the shed, the captain who would cut out Amdu's tongue if he ever caught him.

Last night was so long ago. Hours were no proper measurement of time. Time could only be measured with food and drink. How do you say food and drink in the language of fish? That's what he wanted to know. And why do dogs deserve to live during a war when soldiers and girls deserve to die? And when would he go home? And who was playing the piano?

The musician, whoever it was, had some technical knowledge but little talent — that was Amdu's conclusion based on the first melody played. The second song, however, was more promising. Perhaps the pianist had talent but no skill. Perhaps there hadn't been enough time to practice. But why, then, wasn't the pianist practicing now? Whatever Amdu heard, it didn't include exercises. The pianist, then, was lazy. Or else the pianist was a spoiled child, a young girl left to her own devices while her parents worried about the war, the same girl, he concluded, whom he'd followed from the boathouse.

What finally drew Amdu out of his shelter and back toward the garden terrace was not the overwhelming desire for food and drink. All he could think to want right then was to tell the girl that she could improve her playing if she only set her mind to it and practiced. Beautiful music doesn't come easily, he would tell her. Just from the way she played, he knew la petite princesse at the piano was a spoiled child. She didn't know what it meant to work toward beauty. Why work when you have more than enough of the things that other people covet?

The world would have been a better place without spoiled princesses who played the piano — badly — during a war. Amdu's parents, blessed as they were with material wealth in a poor country, would never have spoiled their only son. Their plan for him was fixed: mission school to the lycée to the military to Al Azar University in Cairo to study medicine so he could return to Dakar at the age of twenty-three as Doctor Diop. That's Saint Doctor Diop, if you please. Or Amdu Dogboy, if no one saved him from his current plight.

Hear that noise? That was Amdu accidentally knocking over the iron rake leaning against the back of the trellis at the bottom of the steps. And this was the silence of a young girl's apprehension. La petite princesse had stopped playing in order to listen; she was waiting for Amdu to make another sound. But Amdu wasn't going to oblige. She played too poorly to be so easily satisfied. And as though to prove this point, she began playing again, worse than before, because now she played grandly, clearly wanting to impress him.

He climbed the steps, unable to resist the lure of the imperfect song. Listen to me, the music said. Applaud this accomplishment. The song was in an easy tempo, though flexible enough to be elaborated in the treble notes, key against jack, hammer against strings. Amdu knew exactly how the pieces came together and thus had a sense of the instrument's potential and the musician's inadequacy. Eighty-eight notes and that was the best she could do?

Adriana would have gone on playing and Amdu would have gone on listening through to nightfall if there had been no interruption. But when the soldiers entered the villa from the courtyard and began shouting in French, the princess stopped playing. And then there were other noises — the sound of something shattering followed by the unmistakable sound of a gunshot. Amdu didn't consider what he should do next — he just did it. Having already convinced himself that he could only keep running away, he ran toward the opposite side of the loggia, colliding with the shuttered door as it was flung open from the inside.

The force of the impact caused him to stumble, but he managed to stay on his feet. His fingers went automatically to his face. Before he even opened his eyes he became aware of the stickiness of blood oozing from his nose. Groping for a handhold to steady himself, he tried to put his thoughts back into proper order: he was here, newly bloodied. He opened his eyes and discovered that he was no longer alone. He was standing opposite the startled princess, the little dark-haired spoiled child who played the piano badly, the one he'd wanted to ask for food and drink. What were the words for food and drink in Italian? He felt that he used to know these words and that he'd forgotten them. Now the only Italian word he could recall was *pace*.

"Pace!" Stupidly, he said it aloud. Yet as stupid as he sounded to himself, apparently he'd said the right thing. For a moment the girl's eyes seemed to flicker with understanding and relief. This was a beginning. Pace. He started to say it again but couldn't get past the opening popping sound of the *p* because another popping sound, a rifle's second report, came from inside the villa, and the girl slid forward into his arms with such force that Amdu thought she'd been shot in the back. But when she started clawing at him, hissing some combination of a curse and a plea, when she started wriggling to be free of him, he could tell that she was unharmed, and this dance she was doing in Amdu's arms was her crazy attempt to stay unharmed.

He was confused, but he could see that the girl was even more confused. She didn't even realize that she was begging him to help her. What was the word for help? He didn't need to know it. There were soldiers in the villa, guns were being fired, and the girl had fled from her piano bench and ended up in the arms of Amdu Diop.

He would take care of her. Pace, Princess. Amdu had no way of conveying his sense of decency, and the girl resisted him. But he was stronger and could drag her down the steps and across the terrace, yanking her forward by the wrists, dragging her along on her knees when she fell, dragging her through the opening in the box hedge separating the terrace from the olive grove, pulling her away from the place where bullets were flying, soldiers were yelling, women were screaming.

Now the little princess was screaming — a dangerous mistake, for the soldiers would be drawn to the sound of a young girl's desperation. Yet it was understandable that she was terrified. How could she know that Amdu was trying to help her? How could he communicate with her? All he could think to do was slap his hand over her mouth to trap the sound. But she fought hard against him, and with his palm slippery with sweat and his arm still sore, he couldn't keep a tight hold of her wrists. She pulled one arm free and managed to scratch his neck. He was startled, and when the vise of his fingers weakened, she slipped loose and stumbled away, half running, half crawling, back toward the terrace garden in the direction of the villa.

No! She would be killed if she returned! How could he explain this to her? There wasn't time to explain. There was time only to jump on her from behind before she reached the hedge, to feel her collapse beneath the weight of him, to cover her mouth again so she couldn't scream. *Pace, spoiled child.* She wasn't lovely enough to be so spoiled. But she wasn't unlovely. Amdu would have had to admit that it felt good to blanket the girl, to lie there supporting himself with his knees to lighten his weight, confining her without suffocating her, and to smell the sharp lime smell of crushed grass mixed with the dry brown spines from the hedge and to feel the body beneath him accept its defeat. Was this what his comrades had felt with the girl in the orchard shed? The good feeling of being powerful enough to choose whether a child lives or dies.

It was easy for a man to do whatever he pleased with a girl. In some ways, it would be easier to have his way than not, and for this reason most men in Amdu's position would have continued with the expected action. But Amdu wasn't like most men. Though it was difficult to adjust the claim to protect the profound humility he expected of himself, he would have argued that he was better than most men. At least, he was born with the potential to be better. If he saved the girl from slaughter, he would be worthy again. Somehow he must make her understand. She must live — this was the miracle Amdu could perform in order to regain his faith.

If saints could earn the trust of birds and fish and lions, then Amdu could earn the trust of this island girl. He reminded her again that he had come in peace. He spoke in French now, explaining that he wanted to help her, not hurt her. But she must stay very quiet and still — as still as an egg in a nest, he whispered. He felt her lips move against his palm. He lifted his hand. "Whisper," he told her, though it would have been better not to speak at all. She seemed to understand. When she did finally speak, her voice was barely audible. At first Amdu thought she was moaning. But the word she was saying was "mamma" — an easy word to recognize. "Whisper," he said again in French. "You understand?" With the side of her head still resting against the ground, she nodded. "Oui," she said. Oui — signifying the fact of a shared language.

"You do understand!"

"Oui."

"You understand that I am here to help you?"

"Oui."

"And if I let you go, you won't run into the open and make a target of yourself?"

Oui. Non. She meant . . . Amdu assured her that she didn't need to explain. He understood that she understood. He released her, raised himself up and off her as though dismounting from a bicycle. An old bicycle — that was his immediate association. He'd never made love to a girl, but he did have an old bicycle back in Dakar. He remembered that his father had promised him a motorbike when he returned from the war. He wanted to tell the little princess this, but she was rubbing tears from her eyes with the ball of her hand, smearing dirt across her cheek.

"You have a dirty face," he whispered.

"You have a . . . a nose," she whispered back, forgetting the French word for bloody.

The exchange prompted timid smiles, but only for a moment. A cold fury replaced the girl's smile, and Amdu's features bunched in puzzlement. Why was she angry with him if she knew he was trying to help her? He reminded her of this: he wanted to help her.

"But why . . ." she began, choking on the words.

"No sound," he reminded her. "Sound will bring the soldiers."

They waited, sitting separately now, tucked close against the hedge. Amdu kept his head tilted until his nose stopped bleeding. He thought it strange to see a carefree gull gliding overhead. And from the distance rumbled the innocent sound of a motorcar. How could life just go on while nations were battling for control of this insignificant island? And where was the captain who wanted to cut out his tongue? And who was winning the war?

Out of respect for the girl, Amdu avoided looking at her and didn't notice that she was crying, heaving with silent sobs, until she moaned again, "Mamma."

Amdu whispered, "You mustn't worry" — a stupid thing to say, he knew. Of course she should worry. Her mother was probably dead, along with her father and any brothers and sisters she might have had. It would be a miracle if this girl survived. Amdu's miracle. He would make it happen.

They continued to wait, and eventually the girl stopped crying. She wanted to go back to her home. Amdu tried to persuade her to wait. He didn't like waiting any more than she did, especially when he was so hungry and thirsty. "But we must wait," he insisted again when the girl started to rise to her feet.

"What are we waiting for?" she wanted to know. Amdu didn't have an answer, so he made one up. He said they must wait for reinforcements. The girl pondered this. Would the reinforcements save her mamma? Oui. She could wait, then, at least for a little while longer.

The sunlight had softened into late-afternoon haze by the time they heard the woman calling from the back of the villa, calling a name that was like a little song, Adriana, an appropriate name for the girl, this player of little songs.

"Mamma!" she shouted back, springing to her feet.

"Wait," Amdu urged. But Adriana was done with waiting.

"You come with me," she commanded, beckoning him to follow, a positive sign, Amdu thought, a sign that he had earned her trust. But as much as he wanted to, he couldn't come with her. Instead, he withdrew in the opposite direction, scrambling half-upright and loping away, keeping close to the ground, stumbling over loose clods of earth, falling forward onto his hands, pushing himself up, and running between the olive trees toward the wall at the eastern edge of the Nardi land, not noticing that the girl he'd saved was standing with her hands on her hips, watching him.

ON THE TRAIN crossing the marshland of New Jersey, Mrs. Rundel remembers none of this. She remembers only that when she woke up this morning, she felt better than she does now. She remembers this as an abstract idea without being able to recover the sensation. Conscious of mild chest pain, she wonders if she is having a heart attack. Her forehead is damp from the effort of her breathing. There's a heaviness in her limbs, as though she's recovering from anesthesia. Despite her discomfort, fatigue is a growing temptation.

She glances at the man next to her, the one who is moving his lips to form silent numbers as he listens to a recording on his cell phone. He is close enough to bump elbows with her, yet he seems perched at a distance, like a squirrel in a tree. He is not someone she would ever want to seek out for assistance. But then, she doesn't intend to be in the position where she'd need to ask any stranger for help.

They are only ten minutes or so from Penn Station. She tells herself that once she's out of the train she'll feel better. And then she'll go on to work or she'll call her husband from a pay phone and he'll come to get her and bring her home. Either way, this episode will be behind her.

But whatever future she has left feels very far away right now. Even what is real and present seems to be shrinking, receding in the distance. Or if not receding, then losing volume, becoming transparent. The seat in front of her seems made of cellophane, the man beside her of crepe paper and air. Voices are coming through long cardboard tubes. She remembers how her children liked to tape paper-towel tubes end to end and make a pipe reaching up the stairs. Where are her children now? She has to remind herself that they are all grown up. But she often has to remind herself of this. Sometimes she lets her grown daughter remind her.

Ma, I'm not a little girl anymore!

Wasn't there something she'd wanted to tell her children? All that's left of the impulse is the feeling of having forgotten something, and even this has become too vague to matter much. What matters is her effort to orient herself so she can figure out what is wrong. But it's like trying to will a Ferris wheel to stop.

Strange, that she can be so aware of her distorted perception and unable to control it. She knows what the voices should sound like. She knows that the seats on a train are separated only by a single narrow armrest. She knows as well that this temptation of sleepiness is dangerous and she should try to resist it. Didn't her husband have a great-uncle who went climbing in the Alps and fell asleep in the snow? It's said that the mind starts to wander when hypothermia sets in, making it harder for the body to rouse itself against oblivion. She is letting herself surrender, like Robert's great-uncle. Or was he Robert's great-grandfather? Anyway, it's not an unpleasant sensation. Just the opposite, infatti. Like drifting off to sleep after making love. There are some things she'll never forget. The rippling inside her, the smell of Robert's shampoo as he rested his head on her chest, the coolness of the sheets on her skin. And then the jingling of la sveglia, and . . . how do you say it? Up and Adam? The lie of purpose that Americans tell themselves.

She is looking at the world through the wrong end of a telescope while her children are chattering in the kitchen. Who said, *Appearances are deceiving?* The objects around her are not as small as they appear. The shrinking world makes the body tired. She is very tired, but still she knows it's not polite to fall asleep in public, either on a train or during a meeting. Think of all the unnecessary words communicated during an average meeting. All the wrong directions a topic can lead. That meeting last week regarding a mascara ad, for instance, and the time wasted arguing about mirrors. The Germans invented mirrors, someone announced. No, the Venetians invented mirrors. No, the Turks invented mirrors. It depends on what you mean by mirrors.

Isaac Newton solved the problem of refraction by making a telescope that worked with mirrors rather than lenses. Una scoperta dietro l'altra. Cosa? Who pointed out that if Isaac Newton had recorded his discoveries in verse, he would have been left alone? But wait . . . wasn't that said about Galileo?

And then, all of a sudden, the whoosh of the tunnel's darkness, a change so startling, despite Mrs. Rundel's twenty years' experience on this commuter train, that it stops her labored breathing altogether, and the thought that pushes away all other thoughts is of her mistake: she should have asked for help while she could still speak.

She does need help — she'd readily admit this. Now she has only the vaguest sense, hardly articulable, that if she wants to stay alive and remember what she'd been trying to remember earlier, she'll have to depend upon the action of strangers, whoever they are: the woman closing her lipstick tube; the financial adviser, who is hearing that the price has just risen to eleven and fifty cents per share; the husband, who is trying to talk his way back into an affair, pleading, "If you, if you, listen, if you would just listen to me"; the lawyer, who repeats, "Three hours!" to his companion, the unemployed software designer; the student, who is still thinking about liverwurst and how there's something a little bit spiteful about it, given that every night for the past week he has asked his mother for tuna; the woman who is reading in *The Biennial Report on Freshwater Resources* about the water needed to produce an average diet in sub-Saharan Africa.

These are the people in Mrs. Rundel's immediate vicinity. Only the student, who works as a lifeguard in summers, has first-aid training. The woman who refreshed her lipstick is a secretary in a malpractice insurance firm. The woman reading about water speaks English, French, Russian, and Polish fluently. She is from Kraków and has recently come to work in New York after spending three years in the Sudan. The financial adviser has a new baby daughter, and last week he and his wife made an offer on a house in Westfield. The lawyer worries constantly that he's a bore, but he can't shut up. The husband involved in the affair, desperate for reconciliation with his lover, is fifty-nine years old and on his third marriage. No one in the vicinity has any reason to suspect that he is talking to an answering machine.

GIULIA NARDI didn't tell the Moroccan soldiers that the painted plate they smashed, the one where she set outgoing letters, had been a gift to her ancestor from Napoleon Bonaparte's sister Pauline. She didn't say that the scene on the plate had shown a happy satyr chasing a nymph, whose golden hair encircled the full length of her body. The gold tint had been particularly striking, and to reinforce the effect Giulia had placed beside the plate a small basket wrapped in brocade. Such details were her signature. She liked symmetry and echo, subtlety, and unobtrusive symbolism. She was always searching for ways to enhance beauty — but only to the observant eye. The writing desk in the library, for instance, had on its surface carved cupids set against a painted landscape. A visitor would have to look closely to see that the landscape was of the fields of La Chiatta, with Volterraio rising in the background.

The soldiers under the command of General De Lattre de Tassigny did not look closely at Signora Nardi's furniture. They were looking for members of the occupying force — to smash them or to shoot them. Bang! they said, using the English word.

Bang! Despite the warmth, they wore dark capes over their white robes. Their faces were mottled with patches of dried mud. They were obviously weary from the night of battle. They were impatient. They were looking for enemy soldiers. And they were looking for something to quench their thirst. They'd seen the lemon trees in their terra-cotta pots in the Nardi garden. Surely, then, the estate must have a stock of the sweet lemon liqueur — what was it called? — that the men had tasted early this morning in a bar in Portoferraio. No? Mais pourquoi pas, madame et monsieur? Why not? Or are you hiding something, madame et monsieur? You speak French, oui? Bien, nous parlons en français. Vous n'avez pas un peu de liqueur? Que n'avez vous pas, madame et monsieur? Rien? Rien! This is what happens to people who have nothing to offer eager soldiers. One of them fired into the wall. Bang! In the head next time, madame et monsieur. These men have had a long day. They have not been treated to the hospitality that they, the liberating force, had expected from the Elbans. So far they've had to take what they wanted. Bang! Another soldier fired high into the cornice. And what they wanted was Germans who were said to be hiding in the cellars of Fascists. Are you Fascists, madame et monsieur? Oui? Non? If you don't have Germans, then can you provide something to placate the soldiers of General De Lattre de Tassigny? Non? Oui? Remember — bang bang in the head, madame et monsieur.

There was a desperate quality to the threats of these young men, which suggested to Giulia Nardi that they were trying to hide their youth behind bravado, just as they hid their unbearded chins behind their red scarves. She was terribly afraid of what they could do — afraid to the point of feeling a coppery taste in her mouth that made her nauseous, as though she were already tasting their bullets. But she wasn't afraid of their brutality. She was afraid of their ignorance. They would let one thing lead to another simply because they didn't know any better.

Foolish men with guns. She'd been expecting them to arrive after nightfall, if they were going to arrive at all. Instead, they'd come to La Chiatta when the late-afternoon light in the courtyard and gardens had a golden sheen, like the gold on the smashed plate. That plate had been one hundred and thirty years old — and good riddance to it. Giulia Nardi would sacrifice an old plate and the rest of her possessions in order to save what really mattered.

All she could hope to do was keep the soldiers from wandering around the villa and finding Adriana. Giulia would have to keep them distracted. Come with me, then, gentlemen. Gentlemen indeed! They laughed at her invitation and followed her down the stairs to the kitchen. Their bluster softened as she motioned to Mario, who grabbed a bottle by the neck as though it were a goose and began shaking it. Così — Mario will pour grappa for everyone.

"Grappa, grappa, capito?"

"Grappa, oui" — everyone knows what grappa is. Salut, then. Cin-cin.

Adriana would hear afterward about how Mario drank with the marocchini while her mother and Luisa looked on. Her mother would tell her how the grappa improved the mood, and the soldiers became more respectful after a couple of glasses. She wouldn't speak of her worst fear: that Adriana would wander into the kitchen while the soldiers were still there. Later, she would insist that there had never been any real danger. The soldiers didn't look more than eighteen years old, and they clearly shared with every other sane human being a desire to put an end to the war and go home. And when two officers appeared at the door in search of these men, when they reprimanded their troops for entering a private residence, when the officers apologized in French to their kind hosts for the intrusion, the soldiers' bravado melted away entirely, replaced by mute obedience. Once they were inside the room, one of the officers saluted, touching his fingers to the tight-fitting kepi on his head, and promised recompense for any damage. The other Frenchman, apparently the superior officer, expressed gratitude and said that without the help of the Elbans, the Allied divisions could not expect to be victorious in their offensive. "Viva l'Italia!" the officer proclaimed ridiculously. "Viva l'Italia!" Mario echoed, raising his glass. "Viva l'Italia!"

The officers of the French Colonial Division drank with Mario and the soldiers. They ate the bread and pecorino that Luisa laid out on the table. Giulia watched as the soldiers rubbed their fingers to loosen crumbs, their awkwardness suggesting that bread was a novelty to them. She stood patiently while the officers questioned Mario about the depths of the Magazzini inlet. In their interview, they disclosed more strategic information than Giulia would have thought acceptable: there was a special boat squadron waiting to approach the island under the cover of darkness and bring additional troops, they said. But they were uncertain where to land. Mario advised that farther east would be better, since the shallow water near La Chiatta was treacherously rocky — a judicious lie, Giulia sensed, and with silence she signaled agreement. Land the boats on the sandy beach at Bagnaia. That would be better. And the soldiers could follow the road there either toward Portoferraio or across the island to Rio Marina.

How long would it take on foot from Bagnaia to Portoferraio? the officers wanted to know. Or at least they pretended they wanted to know. In fact, they pretended poorly, offering questions to hide their lack of purpose. But Mario played along and asked for a map of the island, and the request gave Giulia the excuse to leave the kitchen.

She climbed the stairs and headed through the salotto to the library. Brown petals from a japonica on the loggia had blown across the floor through the open door, and the perfume of jasmine saturated the air. It was strange to find the world so serene, the sky so empty, and Volterraio as stark and unyielding as ever in the distance. Giulia felt as if she had walked into the painted panel of the writing desk, into a false landscape designed to trick perception, where space was only an illusion and the colors had been ingeniously chosen to hide the reality of war.

In a real war, soldiers hunted for the enemy, and mothers hunted for their daughters. Adriana must have run and hid herself when she heard the gunfire. Che coraggio! Or else . . . forget about or else. She would keep herself safe, wherever she was. Despite her waywardness, she was a resourceful girl. She would do what she had to in order to survive.

Giulia found a map in the writing desk, but instead of returning promptly to the kitchen, she continued to search for her daughter. She went outside to the loggia, surveyed the fields, and headed down the stone staircase leading to the front of the villa, where she discovered only one plausible hiding place, a little den behind the cantina's old back door, which Ulisse had left propped against the wall until he found time to chop it up for firewood.

The space was empty — indicating either that Adriana had fled in another direction or that she'd been taken away. Where had she gone? Only many months later would Giulia reveal to Adriana that in a fit of despair at her uselessness she'd pushed the heavy slab of wood away, sending it toppling into the junipers, and then she'd stood there gazing at the emptiness where her daughter should have been, half-believing that Adriana would appear if she just waited long enough. But she couldn't stand there forever — even if the soldiers hadn't heard the noise of breaking branches, they'd be concerned by her absence and they'd come in search of her.

She returned to the kitchen, delivering the map to the officers and moving aside while Mario traced with his plump, well-manicured forefinger the unmarked roads around the island. The officers looked on, suggesting with their excessive show of interest that they didn't really want Mario's advice; rather, they wanted to make the Elbans feel that they were participating in the liberation — a ruse they were all willing to accept.

It was a quiet consultation that would have reached a quick conclusion if they hadn't been interrupted by Luisa's exclamation — "Madonna!" — at the sight of Ulisse, who had appeared in the kitchen and stood there with his hand pressed on the hilt of the hunting knife strapped to his belt. The robes of the soldiers wafted as they raised their guns. One of the officers gestured with his open palm, ordering them to wait.

Hearing the soldiers in the courtyard, Ulisse had locked himself and his family in the cantina, and since no one had come to find him, he'd finally ventured out to offer Signora Nardi aid. But he couldn't bring himself to offer anyone anything while he was staring into the barrel of a gun. The soldiers, taking him for a German, were ready to kill him. They might have gone ahead and killed him. But when Luisa dropped the bread she'd been carrying, a loaf the size of a melon, so hard and hollow that it bounced with a clatter across the tile floor, the men burst into laughter. Did Elbans make their bread with sand instead of flour? they wanted to know. Did they bake it in one of their smelting furnaces?

"He is my gardener," Giulia said of Ulisse, taking advantage of the laughter to offer information. "He and his family are staying here with us."

How many in his family? one of the officers asked.

"Cinque," Mario said.

"Sei," Ulisse corrected him. There were six in his family, of course — three children, his wife, and his mother. Six, including Ulisse. An officer ordered two of his men to go count the members of Ulisse's family, though he asked for permission from Signora Nardi first. If it wouldn't be an imposition . . .

"Prego," she said, gesturing to Ulisse to take the soldiers over to the cantina.

The officers studied the map while the others waited tensely. Giulia listened for gunfire but heard nothing, not even the baby's restless wail, and within an unexpectedly brief time the soldiers returned, having left Ulisse in the cantina and indicating only by saying nothing that they'd deemed the family harmless.

Now the mood in the kitchen was a shared anticipation of relief that even the soldiers seemed to feel. While the officers continued to study the map, one of the men idly turned the faucet on and off, and for a moment Giulia forgot that Adriana was not in the cabinet below. Her thoughts narrowed into a warning to her daughter: silenzio. What a good girl, quiet as a statue. No one suspected that she was there. But she wasn't there. She was somewhere else being a good quiet girl, and when the soldiers left she would come home.

She could come home very soon, for after a polite exchange — the officers' French-inflected grazie, Mario's prego, an exchange of handshakes, Giulia's regal nod — the men were leaving, clacking in their boots through the villa and out the open door leading to the courtyard, one of the officers climbing into his jeep to join the driver, who must have been waiting the entire time the men were inside and was wriggling to alertness after having been caught dozing, while the other officer led his soldiers down the drive toward Portoferraio, their easy manner suggesting that their intrusion had been a deception from start to finish, a clever maneuver designed for the purpose of surveillance.

But at least they had left, and it was safe for Adriana to come home. "Adriana!" A daughter like a little song. Where was she? "Adriana!" A child who knew how to stay alive during a war. "Adriana!" And here she was, the clever girl, bursting through the opening in the hedge, running up the steps and into her mother's arms.

Why Adriana didn't tell her mother about the soldier in the garden, she couldn't have explained. She should have told her mother about him. She had a good story to tell. Mamma, listen! There was a soldier in the garden, un negro, and he had grabbed her when the shooting started and dragged her — no, he didn't hurt her — he'd led her into the olive grove. He'd been kind to her, and, yes, he was a good man. He believed in peace, didn't he? He wasn't carrying a gun. Actually, he wasn't wearing a shirt. But he had been wearing a silver cross on a chain around his neck, she recalled.

For some reason she didn't say this. She didn't say that she'd seen the man climbing over the seawall, she'd sensed his presence in the boathouse, and she'd played "Non M'Ama Più" for him on the piano. She didn't say any of this. Instead, she let her mother cover her with kisses and accepted her praise with wordless pleasure. What a good, clever girl to keep out of the way of the soldiers until her mother called for her. She was so very brave, the bravest girl on the island. She admitted that she felt ashamed for having run away when the soldiers arrived. No, she mustn't feel ashamed, her mother said. She'd done the right thing. She was safe now and could forget about the soldiers. They wouldn't be back. How did her mother know this? She just knew, she said.

Adriana settled between her uncle and her mother on the sofa. By then it was too late to tell them about her soldier. They were already deep into their own account, their earlier argument forgotten. The Allied troops had come and gone. La Chiatta had lost only one plate, and high up in the entrance hall there was a bullet hole, and another bullet had shattered the plaster in the corner. The officers had promised reimbursement for the damage — an empty promise, obviously, but it was reassuring to know that the Allied forces were not planning to punish Italians, and whatever atrocities had been committed in the midst of the offensive would be viewed by commanders as crimes.

Adriana understood this to mean that the soldier in the garden was trustworthy. And more than that, he and his comrades were fighting on behalf of the Elbans to rid the island of the occupying army. She offered her own opinion: she liked Africans much better than Germans.

What did she really know about Africans? her uncle demanded. Did she know what they did to little Elban girls? Did she know what would happen if she were caught by an African?

Adriana was shaken by her uncle's challenge — she knew something about what the soldiers had done to Sofia Canuti, though she wanted to say that her own soldier was different. Her own soldier was kind. But there wasn't a chance for her to speak, since her mother was replying in her place. "And what of the Germans?" Giulia demanded in a strained voice, though still speaking clearly, precisely. The Germans who massacred the boys at Montemaggio and Istia d'Ombrone . . . the Germans who appeared with a white flag one day and the next day dropped their bombs on Porto-ferraio . . . the Germans who arrested brave General Gilardi and sent him to a lager . . . "i tedeschi brutti . . . i tedeschi che mangiano minestra d'ebrei" — the Germans who ate soup made of Jews.

"Mamma!" Adriana had never heard her mother say some-thing so ugly. And neither had Mario, apparently, for he grunted in disgust and picked himself up off the sofa and marched from the room. A moment later they heard the engine of his Fiat revving. Adriana listened with her mother as the engine sputtered and died, then revved again . . . and died, revved and died. Uncle Mario must have been out there pumping the clutch and cursing. Adriana held her mother's arm in response. She wanted her uncle to come back inside and apologize for his abrupt exit. She wanted him to stay on good terms with her mother so he would continue to invite his niece onto his sailboat and take her to explore the is-lands of Cerboli and Montecristo when the war was over. She wanted to hear what he really thought about the Germans.

But the engine finally came to life, Mario drove off, and before Adriana could ask her mother if it was true about the soup, Luisa appeared in the room with Paolo.

"Paolo!" Giulia stood up to greet him. She admitted that she'd forgotten about Paolo, who'd been asleep all afternoon and had managed to continue sleeping through the soldiers' visit, waking only at Luisa's firm prodding. Frowsy, sloppy Paolo, who, Adri-ana was convinced, would grow up to be one of those men who every morning perform some brief but important task and do nothing for the rest of the day.

"Stupido Paolo," Adriana taunted as she brushed past him.

"Stupida Adriana," Paolo said, shoving her with his elbow.

"Bimbi!" This was not a time to misbehave. It was a time to be quiet and pious and thankful to be alive, Luisa said. And it was time to eat. Hungry children must eat.

Adriana hadn't been aware that she was hungry until Luisa introduced the notion. Yes, she was hungry, and this reminded her that the soldier in the olive grove was hungry, too — and thirsty. After running away from Germans, of course he was thirsty. He'd been too polite to ask her for anything. But she could help. She could bring her soldier bread and cheese, an onion, and water, filling Paolo's knapsack while Luisa had her back turned, her mother was over at the cantina checking on Ulisse and his family, and Paolo was in the toilet.

She did not tell Luisa where she was going. She just kept moving backward as she feigned idleness, then she turned and ran through the pantry and into the courtyard, into the night.

She was surprised by the darkness. Daylight had seemed capable of lasting forever while she'd waited behind the hedge for the danger to pass. Between then and now the moon had risen, its light tinged brown from the smoke of burning forests. The fighting must have been continuing in the hills. Germans were cooking Africans alive, or Africans were cooking Germans. Everything that could happen was happening somewhere. But now that the soldiers had come and gone from La Chiatta, Adriana felt that the peace her own soldier had spoken of was beginning.

Surely he wanted to go home, back to his own country. First, though, he needed nourishment. "Soldato!" Her voice strained to break out of its whisper. "Soldato!" What was his name? He hadn't told her. It wasn't polite to address him as soldato. "Monsieur," she whispered. Whoever you are. Wherever you are. In the hazy moonlight she couldn't have seen if he were crossing the olive grove, approaching her. She listened for the sound of his footsteps but heard only the rustle of leaves in the breeze. She waited. How could she let him know that she wanted to return his good deed and was bringing him his supper? "Monsieur!"

But maybe he wasn't in the olive grove anymore. He'd been running toward the wall and might have scaled it, climbing out of the Nardi property just as he'd climbed into it. Maybe he'd been captured by Germans — the same Germans who ate soup made of Jews. Maybe he was already dead. Or maybe, probably, he had found someone who could offer more than she could — someone who spoke better French than Adriana did and who would treat him with the respect due a good partisan. Surely he was as worthy as a partisan. For this, Adriana understood from her mother, was the secret story of the war: the story of the partisans, their leaders and their benefactors and the courage of resistance.

In her own small way, she was playing a part in that good story, a story that would be worth remembering. By helping the soldier who had helped her, she was aligning herself with those who were fighting to end the war. Further involvement might put her at risk, she sensed, but risk was a small price to pay for an exciting adventure. She found the idea of her potential consequence astonishing, even if she was confused about the difference between good and evil, allies and enemies. History could be trusted to sort out the sides. In history, she wanted to be remembered as a heroine. And her soldato, with his silver cross and bit of dirty cloth twisted around his arm, would be a hero. She may not have understood the exact nature of his ambition, but she was sure that he deserved to succeed.

Although she couldn't know whether her soldier was still on the property, she left the knapsack just beyond the opening in the hedge and she went back inside to her room. She lay on her bed savoring the memory of what she'd done. She was filled with an intoxicating sense of power — this in the midst of the worst fighting the island of Elba had ever known. She felt as if she had commanded the war to leave her alone. Nothing could harm her. She was the bravest girl on the island and exceptionally clever. And there was more that she could do to help. After supper, after her mother had finally given in to fatigue and fallen asleep on the sofa, Adriana stripped a blanket from her bed, crept downstairs, and carried the bundle outside, to the edge of the terrace. At first she was disappointed to find the knapsack in the same place she'd left it. But she was pleased to see that the sack was empty, the contents gratefully received, she hoped, by the person who needed them most.

Cover
of
Darkness

To explain why a young Senegalese soldier was lying in a ravine on the southeast edge of the Nardi estate in the middle of the night, June 18, 1944, the second night of the liberation of Elba, it is helpful to consider the different views among the members of the Allied Command regarding the Italian theater. The objection had been raised that "Anvil," the amphibious attack planned against southern France, was in danger of being weakened if major divisions were diverted for the offensive against Italy. Some of the Allied commanders argued that their forces should be concentrated against France. Others believed that Rome was the ultimate prize and insisted that the invasion of Italy required a maximum effort.

General John Harding and his staff members devised the detailed plan for the spring offensive that was finally approved, with some altering, by the Supreme Allied Headquarters. Harding predicted that the enemy would not be driven northward to the Pisa-Rimini Line, as was hoped; instead, the German resistance would continue — to the Allies' advantage, paradoxically, if they, in conjunction with a push from the south, launched a major offensive up the Liri Valley. With a strategic regrouping of forces, the Allies could encircle and destroy a large part of the German army in Italy.

The success of the plan depended upon a complex deception. Harding proposed regrouping the Fifth Army in such a way as to give the Germans the impression that the French Expeditionary Corps were preparing to return to their homeland to launch a new offensive. The attack against southern France, then, would serve as a cover operation.

The Chiefs of Staff resisted Harding's plan at first. They did not want France sacrificed to Italy. But in the last week of February, Eisenhower was persuaded that Italy should have priority, and the Mediterranean offensive, code-named "Diadem," was set in motion.

When the Eighth Army had finally broken through Cassino and the Fifth Army was advancing to Rome, supporting Allied forces were working to strangle German supply lines and push through their blockades. It was at this time that the island of Elba began to take on new strategic importance. In an attempt to reinforce the general success of Diadem immediately following the fall of Rome, the Allied Command sent French and British forces from Corsica to Elba in a tactical left-hook operation. The invasion, launched under cover of darkness, caught the Germans by surprise.

But Amdu wouldn't have been where he was if in 1916 France hadn't formally adopted military conscription for its West African territories, expanding the ranks of the Tirailleurs, along with the community of Frenchmen commissioned as officers and their Senegalese wives. Amdu's great-grandfather had been a Frenchman who chose to stay in Senegal when the other officers returned to France. Conscription into the Tirailleurs continued through the early phase of World War II. In 1940, after aligning itself with Pétain, French West Africa endured unprecedented exploitation under the Vichy government, which cut off imports from France and at the same time assigned African farmers excessive quotas for exportable crops. Following the Allied landing in North Africa in November of 1942, Governor General Boisson joined the Allied side. The Senegalese fought in North Africa and Corsica with the Free French Forces. Many would go on to southern France. But first, those under the command of General De Lattre de Tassigny had to complete their mission on Elba.

War is war is war — this was Amdu Diop's explanation for what happened on Elba. Though he had been trained to follow orders and was unprepared for the chaos of liberation, he wouldn't have been surprised to learn that while Operation Brassard was deteriorating, crazed German paratroopers under the command of Colonel Trettner were brutalizing the Italian contadini as they retreated across Val d'Orcia on the mainland, and Moroccan soldiers were systematically raping the women of the Ciociara as the

Allied forces moved through southern Italy. War is war is war, and in the midst of it anything goes. If anything goes, the logical connection between cause and consequence is broken. What happens happens by accident.

Amdu Diop, at his father's insistence, had enlisted in the army in the summer of 1943. The war had seemed so far away then, its reality diminished by distance, and Amdu, the sole volunteer among a group of conscripts, hadn't expected ever to have to leave the fort near Saint-Louis, where he had gone for basic training. But by the spring of 1944 he was in Tunisia, by the end of May he was in Corsica, and by the night of June 18 he was lying in a ravine, shivering inside a blanket, praying for a vision from God.

That he had a fever hadn't occurred to him. He was shivering because of the cool night air, he thought, and he was damp with sweat because of the blanket. He was too hot and too cold at the same time. Mostly he was tired. He'd eaten enough to ease his hunger cramps, though not enough to satisfy. But he had drunk plenty of water — the water in the knapsack plus the brackish, cold water from a little spring. Tomorrow would be better now that he had a friend in the little princess. He'd meant to leave her and make his way somewhere else, but when he'd reached the wall he'd found that either he had grown shorter or the wall had grown taller since he'd scaled it to enter the property. So he had wandered back through the fields south of the villa, through moonlight that transformed the hard little olives into nuggets of gold. Imagine if the olives really were gold, along with all the grapes in the vineyard. Then these people would have too much wealth and not enough to eat, and they would be forced to pick up and go elsewhere, to a land where they could raise their children in peace, leaving their island to be plundered by mercenaries and then forgotten.

Amdu would prefer to forget. Not the June rains falling in the fields of Casamance — this was good to remember. Or the sound of a drill at a construction site in Dakar. He liked that sound, too. And he liked the sound of his mother's voice, even when she was scolding him, telling him he must be serious about his studies and get his nose out of that book, *La Dictionaire des Miracles,* that listed every sanctified miracle since the birth of our Lord Jesus, including exorcism and stigmata.

He'd been taught at the mission school to understand life as the preparation for eternity. But he considered himself an exceptional thinker, and after thinking and thinking and thinking, he had decided that he could choose to mix profound optimism with the doctrines of catechism as they were translated by an efficient group of Senegalese nuns, resulting for Amdu in a peculiar, combustive faith, a mix of folklore and papal doctrine, Koranic law, and his own vivid imagination, that resisted all accusations of error. Beginning when he was a wise thirteen years old, he had remained steadfast against skeptics, undeterred in his journey. And though he'd faltered on this island, he had been guided back to the path, the only path that led to God, to be deposited by this trickling spring, where he would rest and recover his strength and dream and forget what he had seen.

A girl lying in a shed in a neglected orchard. Was it possible to know how she had suffered? But suffering was one of the challenges of life. Much could be learned from suffering — unless you were one of the unlucky ones who didn't make it through the night.

Forget it.

How do you forget what you can only presume, having witnessed the aftermath?

Would they really cut out his tongue if they caught him? Who put this idea into his head?

Run, Amdu! But he didn't want to run anymore. He was too tired.

A proper Tirailleur Sénégalais. He wanted a cigarette. But he didn't smoke. Attention!

He wondered: to what extent did accident play a role in the expulsion from paradise? And at what point did the men in the shed know what they were going to do to the girl, how they would proceed, how it would end?

Forget it. Just tell yourself to think of something else, okay? Oui, d'accord.

Smoke trailed from burning stars. From the hills came the crackle of gunfire. But not here. Amdu, being blessed, would keep the place that was *here* safe. Miracles were possible again. He'd saved at least one girl from the clutches of his comrades, hadn't he? The girl named Adriana. Perhaps in the history of his life this would constitute a new beginning. There would be other miracles. And it was clear to him now what the culmination would be: at the moment when he finally had earned the ability to hear the voice of God and follow directions, he would turn today into yesterday and prevent an act of savagery that had already been committed.

The nuns would say that he was confusing the illusion of magic with the possibility of divine intervention. But the nuns were wrong and he was right to believe that a reconstitution of reality was possible. He might even say that miracles were the point of faith.

He that believeth and is baptized shall be saved, Mark promised. *In my name shall they cast out devils; they shall speak with new tongues; they shall take up serpents; and if they drink any deadly thing, it shall not hurt them; they shall lay hands on the sick.* Such things happened to the righteous. The challenge, then, was to achieve a purity of faith sufficient to earn the right to such abilities.

He was not unaware of the fact that he was, as his commanding officer liked to say in English, very much strange. He had yet to read a book about someone like him. Even the stories he'd heard the griots tell didn't illustrate the capacity of the world to contain such an odd singularity as Amdu Diop. But he hadn't lost his sense of humor. Sometimes he just wanted to laugh at himself. At home he was like a monkey gabbling in French, making promises to please his parents. Yes, Maman, he would become a doctor. Yes, Papa, he would serve in the military. Eventually his parents would find him a good wife to marry, and he would father many children — without, of course, losing sight of his great purpose. He would be everything he was expected to be, and much more. Corporal-Doctor-Saint Amdu. But until then he would remain a very much strange Tirailleur Sénégalais who didn't feel so well, wrapped in a blanket that smelled of soap, lying among the rocks beside a spring on an island where the dead were accumulating with each far-off rattle of machine-gun fire, ten plus two plus twelve.

On the night of June 18, the second night of the liberation of Elba, additional Allied forces landed not on the beach at Bagnaia, as the officers in the kitchen of La Chiatta had suggested they would, but at Marciana Marina, to the east, coming in under heavy shelling from German defenses but successfully taking control of the port. Having already seized control of Marina di Campo, Porto Azzurro, and Portoferraio, the Allies pushed into the center of the island's eastern end, isolating German troops in the mountainous region around and above the village of Marciana Alta.

Although La Chiatta and its neighbors were quiet, soldiers were dying in the forests and fields to the west. By sunset on the eighteenth it was clear to all sides that German resistance was failing, but their high command had not yet ordered evacuation of the island, and the Germans continued to fight in a suicidal frenzy.

Some might say that the Germans' desperation infected the West African forces. It could no longer be called a proper war, this battle for a useless island. It was violence without purpose or restraint, and in the mountain village of Marciana Alta, young men whose brothers had been blown apart by German shells hours earlier went from house to house looking for girls to rape, while on Monte Capanne an Elban shepherd, enlisted to help carry supplies for an Allied platoon, watched soldiers chop off the hands of a wounded German before shooting him in the head.

The German batteries inland were unexpectedly resistant — some put up such strong opposition that they were killed by their own guns. Who was killing whom? Rumors spread through the Allied troops that the Elbans were firing on the Africans. The supposition behind this whole offensive — the idea of liberation — became uncertain. These were the people for whom the young Allied soldiers were sacrificing themselves? This bauble in the sea was the island where their lives would end?

Who was killing whom? Amdu wondered, shivering in his ravine. Who had tried to kill him last night when he was standing with a gray toad beside a well? He wished God would talk to him. But God wouldn't talk to him as long as his head was full of visions of what soldiers did to the girl in the shed before they killed her, two of the men opening their trousers while the others held the girl down. And when it was over, the bayonets shining, coated with blood. No: if Amdu had his way, today would be the day before yesterday, and the girl would run from the house after fighting with her brother. She would find a secret passageway leading deep into the earth, and she would follow this to a cavern three stories tall, where she would wait out the war.

It was a fine alternative, but Amdu needed a long period of convalescence before he performed a miracle. Truthfully, he didn't feel very well at all. His arm ached, his head ached, he wanted to sleep but couldn't sleep, and there was a faint vile stink clinging to him even after he'd washed his face and hands in the spring. That smell had a meaning he could guess. But he'd rather think about something else. Not the war. Not himself. How about the songs Princess Adriana had played and the improvement possible if she would only practice? Being spoiled, she would expect everything to come easily. Yet Amdu had to admit that he liked her. He liked the soapy smell of her, which was the same smell as this blanket. He liked the way she'd thrown herself into his arms on the terrace. She was a good girl, though she cried too quickly and believed him too readily when he said they must wait for reinforcements. There was a sloppiness about her that would have aroused the disapproval of his sisters. And they'd notice that her French was less than adequate. She'd told him that he had a nose! He smiled to himself, remembering, and the smile made him sleepy, but the good feeling of sleepiness was interrupted by his shivering, and he gripped the blanket tighter.

He'd wanted to help her. He had helped her. Now he would let the girl named Adriana do the helping. She'd brought him his supper, leaving it in the field. And then the blanket had appeared. Tomorrow she would bring him his breakfast.

Measured against ordinary life, it was boggling that he, a

seventeen-year-old Senegalese rifleman, had come to depend upon a young Italian girl who played the piano poorly. Yet to Amdu it made complete sense. The situation was exceptional because he was exceptional. He needed help in order to return to the important journey of his life. Help was being provided. It was right that he hadn't been shot in the head or crushed by an ejected fuel tank. It was right that he was lying at the bottom of a ravine, where his enemy would never find him.

Enemy was the wrong word. Amdu Diop had no enemies. At worst, there existed people who would find it useful to make a martyr of him. But please consider this: not all saints were martyrs. Amdu was prepared to offer as an example the case of the girl called Bernadette who encountered the Virgin of the Immaculate Conception in a grotto in Lourdes. Bernadette wasn't a martyr. She wasn't fed to the lions or thrust into a fiery furnace or beheaded. After her series of miraculous visions, she became Sister Marie-Bernarde. She lived a quiet life in the sanctuary at Nevers and died a quiet death.

Also, not all martyrs became saints. The girl in the orchard shed, for instance. She could be considered a martyr, but she wouldn't be canonized. And add to her example the martyrs who in this war were dying for their nation rather than their god. What would happen to them at the Universal Judgment?

In the story of Amdu's life, he was going to be a saint but not a martyr. He would learn the tricks of medicine in order to heal the sick, and when medicine failed, Amdu would ask God to step in. One miracle would follow another; his reputation would spread to distant lands; he would grow ancient, white-bearded and frail but still happily devout; and at the age of 109 he would fall peacefully into his final sleep — in his own bed in his own home.

But first Amdu had to make his way back to Dakar. He imagined his mother waiting at the front gate and from a distance mistaking every approaching young man for her son. He imagined his father writing a letter to General De Lattre de Tassigny. He thought about the motorbike he would own. He pictured an anatomy textbook open on his desk. He tried to remember things he knew. For no clear reason, the first thing that came to mind was something he'd once heard about how the juice of henbane root would drive a man mad. He wondered if this was true.

The night wore on. The explosions in the distance reminded him of cannon firing at the training camp near Saint-Louis. The stars reminded him of the desert sky. The smell of the earth re-minded him of digging graves in a meadow in Corsica.

He remembered overhearing men at a wresting match talking about his father, calling him a black Frenchman. Also, he remem-bered poking at a beetle, flipping it over from its back to its feet. Was the beetle really as big as the palm of his hand? Or was he confusing the beetle with a tortoise? And after his uncle died from a tumor in his throat, what had happened to his vast fields of groundnuts?

Monsieur Diop!

Oui?

Que désirez-vous?

He wanted God to talk to him. He wanted to see the blood of Saint Januarius redden and froth. He wanted to hear his mother scold his sisters and tell them not to disturb their brother — Amdu needed to rest. He ached all over. Still, he wanted to prove that his faith was unflagging. When he felt he was absolutely ready, puri-fied of doubt, he would set out walking from the beach across the sea. He would walk back to Dakar over water that would have the buoyancy of thick aspic. His mother would be waiting at the gate. His father would be working in his study. Waves would spread in gentle ripples while on a distant island shrapnel flew through the air at three hundred meters per second.

WHEN UNCLE MARIO LEFT La Chiatta in disgust at his sister-in-law's demonic exaggeration of German conduct, he did not return directly to Portoferraio, as Adriana and her mother had assumed he would. After passing Allied convoys heading east, he could only assume that the port was still unsafe for civilians, so he went instead to visit his cousin in Bivio Boni. But he found the little enclave of Bivio Boni deserted. Except for the hens pecking at the dirt and a gaunt dog that beat its tail wildly and whined for food, he saw no sign of life, and no one answered when he called to the second-story window from the courtyard.

He drove on to San Giuseppe, to the home of his friend Corrado. Corrado was a notary and usually the first to hear the important unofficial news. But Corrado's house was deserted as well, and broken pieces of singed wood lay scattered around the yard, as though the contents of the stove had been dumped there.

With Bivio Boni and San Giuseppe empty, Mario could only think to return to La Chiatta. But he didn't want to return to La Chiatta, where his sister-in-law was waiting with her barbed tongue to tell Mario just what she thought about his affiliation with the Germans. Wasn't that just like a woman, to offer insult only when it was safe to do so? And to think that when he was a young man, before he'd married her sister, he'd fancied Giulia Nardi.

She had always been able to twist him this way and that. Hadn't she implicitly approved of his associations during the months of occupation? He didn't remember her ever refusing the German's gift of meat, after all. She had readily accepted the advantages that came from having a brother-in-law in good standing with the Germans, though he was far from being that insidious thing called a collaborator — the accusation that was heard in mutters during the occupation and afterward would be directed with predictable derision at whomever someone wanted to blacklist. No, Mario Tonietti couldn't be accused of having been a collaborator. He'd merely answered questions put to him by the German officers, who sought him out not only because of his fluency in German but also because, as the publisher of the local newspaper, he had influence across the island.

He had been one of the few civilians consulted on September 1 of the previous year, when a group of German officers had arrived on Elba under a white flag to negotiate with the Italian command for a surrender. And when sixteen German aircraft dropped their bombs on the center of Portoferraio in a surprise attack the next day, killing more than one hundred civilians, Mario Tonietti was already safely at La Chiatta, far from the havoc.

He would remind anyone who cared to wonder at his well-timed absence that he had urged the Italian military command to resist the Germans. His loyalty to the island of Elba had remained steadfast. He would only ever recommend what he thought to be in the best interest of his people. Before the war began he'd been planning to run for mayor of Portoferraio. He would make a bid when the war was over. His friends were expecting it. Mario Tonietti was born to be a leader, they all agreed. Mario Tonietti, il prossimo sindaco.

Giulia Nardi knew about his honest ambitions. Why, then, was her hospitality increasingly infected with contempt? Or was it? She had never directly accused him. Nor did she look at him with the side-eyed glance that people direct toward someone they secretly consider guilty. But when she talked about the Germans as though they were worse than the Russians — this, she certainly understood, was a subtle way of suggesting to her brother-in-law that he was complicit.

Un collaborazionista, Signor Tonietti? Non c'è nessuna ragione per crederci. . . . If there was a time when he'd been persuaded by Il Duce's early apologia for individualism, if as a younger man he had been an ardent supporter of Mussolini, it was not because he shared any aspiration toward world domination. No — Mario Tonietti might have been an important man on Elba, but he never lost a sense of perspective. His island was very small, easily ignored. He preferred to keep it that way. He had never been foolish enough to think that a great empire could be born out of the seeds of social unrest. It wasn't the militarism that appealed to him. Rather, Mario had been attracted by Mussolini's early declaration that he and his cohorts had "torn up all the revealed truths . . . spat on all the dogmas, rejected all the paradises, mocked all the charlatans. . . ." In contrast with the fatalism of the Socialists, the early Fascists — in Mario Tonietti's opinion — offered a freshness of vision.

But Mario had never condoned the alliance with the führer and in fact had grown so disillusioned with the war that just days before the British had pierced the Mareth Line between Libya and Tunisia, he had drafted an editorial making the case for a withdrawal of all Italian forces from North Africa. Though he'd never gotten around to printing it, events had proved that his argument was sound. Mussolini's hopes for a new Roman Empire had dissolved in blood when Tunis fell, and now Italians were paying the heavy price for their leader's arrogance.

That the war would eventually reach Elba, Mario had never doubted. The Allied forces had moved through Sicily and Sardinia. On the mainland, they were pushing inexorably north. Everywhere, German resistance would fail. The abbey at Cassino had been destroyed. Vesuvius had erupted. Fascist guards were ripping off their insignia, replacing them with the king's stellette. Tunnels had been cut into quarries outside of Rome and filled with the bodies of executed prisoners. Mussolini, wherever he was hiding, had nothing to say. The Allies had landed in Normandy. And in Piazza Repubblicà in Portoferraio on the little island of Elba, the Africans were making themselves at home.

Mario Tonietti felt inclined to make himself at home here in Corrado's residence, since he could think of nowhere else to go. Soon night would fall, and in the darkness the rules of war would be suspended again. He thought of Sofia Canuti. He wondered whom he could ask to get an accurate account of the dead. The challenge of accuracy made him wonder if his assistant, Dino, had returned to his desk. Dino, a young man with a right leg shorter than his left, feared boredom more than anything else. If anyone could succeed in gathering information amid the chaos of the past day, it was Dino. Mario wouldn't have been surprised to learn that Dino had never left Portoferraio.

Mario, unlike Dino, was not reckless. But envy was easily stirred in him, and the possibility that at the war's end his assistant would be the one lauded for his heroic journalism was enough incentive for Mario to return to his Fiat, where he sat clutching the wheel while he tried to talk himself into an acceptance of his obvious duty. As publisher of *La Voce dell'Elba* and the future mayor of Portoferraio, he really should head back to town.

Ambition had incited him to return to his car. Maybe ambition saved his life. He certainly was better off inside the Fiat than out in the yard when the area suddenly erupted with the cross fire between invisible troops in the eastern hills and in an old stone warehouse to the west. An errant shell burst nearby, filling the yard with flying rock fragments. The Fiat tipped to one side and then the other, seemingly in slow motion, and the driver's-side window exploded in shards. Mario dove across the seat, hiding his head between his arms. He felt certain that the next sensation would be one of falling, that the earth would open up and the car would drop into a bottomless hole. But nothing like that happened. A period of calm followed the assault, a pause that could have meant the soldiers were reloading.

He pulled himself upright, but his hand was trembling too violently to turn the key in the ignition. All he could do was wait for the next round of firing. But there was no next round. Instead, the voices of men calling to one another in the distance broke into the silence. The sound was hollow, the language indistinguishable.

They were approaching the warehouse. If they reached it, they would advance to Corrado's house. If they came to Corrado's house, they would find Mario cowering in the Fiat, they would drag him out of the car, and they would beat him. That's what he found himself envisioning right then, his speculation fueled by the stories he had heard during the past day and the past year: stories of innocent civilians who, for the crime of being in the wrong place at the wrong time, were stripped and flogged to a bloody pulp by soldiers wielding army-issued belts. The prospect was enough to give Mario the fortitude to depress the clutch and steady his hand, successfully connecting with the ignition system. The chassis rattled from the force of the motor. Mario, his back drenched in sweat, was able to steer in a U out of the yard and down the drive, half expecting the car to be battered by gunfire as he continued down the hill and half expecting to hear the laughing taunts of soldiers who believed they had exposed a coward.

Not until he'd come to the paved extension of the Portoferraio road did he lift a hand to smooth his soaked shirt against his side, realizing only after he'd wiped his arm across his parched mouth that the sweat soaking him was mixed with blood. He couldn't locate any wound, but the blood on his hand was a bright red. The color was enough to rouse in him a new, focused urgency. He was wounded. He'd never been wounded in war before. Now, at last, he had an objective. He must get himself to the hospital in Portoferraio. It was only minutes away. He'd show up bleeding, with a tale to tell about a brutal assault, how he had resisted, how he had survived. This would be enough to make him a hero. Mario Tonietti, the future mayor of Portoferraio.

The car bounced over rubble in the deserted streets. In front of the broken dockyard gate, one of the front wheels popped. Mario kept going, the one wheel rim knocking angrily along the paving stones as he turned into a side street. He parked the car snug against a building, opening the door to the roar of an explosion somewhere to the northeast. Even from this distance it felt like a fist thudding against his chest.

Over the old port the smoke that hung in the air didn't smell just of burning wood and oil; it had that sharp, peculiar stink of singed hair, reminding him of the time when as a young boy he had leaned too close to a candle flame and burned his hair. The smell was unforgettable.

He made his way over shattered stones in front of an apartment building that had been bombed back in September, its facade shattered, and last night had been bombed again, the structure pulverized, reduced to the broken walls of its foundation. The street beside it was deserted. Or Mario was expecting it to be deserted, and he wasn't prepared to notice a boy kicking a chunk of plaster into crumbs as he exited a bar. Mario walked past the bar and at the open window caught sight of a flicker of movement as the barista wiped the counter. At the opposite end of the street he saw a carabiniere lighting a cigarette. Only as an afterthought did Mario decide to talk to him, but by then the man had disappeared around the corner.

It was dusk, and the green shutters, closed tight along the street, gleamed as if freshly painted. Mario couldn't decide whether it was odd that at this hour of the passeggiata there were so few people on the streets, or that in the midst of an invasion there were any people out at all, or that no one came up to him to ask if he needed help. Of course he needed help. Didn't anyone care that the shirt of the next mayor of Portoferraio was soaked in blood?

He walked on past the Municipio, which so far had survived undamaged. As he continued toward the hospital he found himself picturing something he'd only heard about: the arduous approach through the great hall in Palazzo Venezia in Rome, from the end with the doorway to the desk where Mussolini sat. He recalled a story he'd heard about a man from San Remo — a magistrate, the cousin of a friend of a friend — who had killed himself with a revolver simply because he'd been asked to appear before Il Duce.

How do we know for what, precisely, we will be held accountable? One thing Mario Tonietti had learned from life was that as he grew older it became more difficult to tell right from wrong. And it became even more difficult to make a distinction during wartime. He had tried to please all sides and leave behind no record of corruption or treachery that could be used against him. But still he had to wonder about certain indiscretions — for instance, conversations with Rosa, his mistress. Rather, his former mistress. He'd grown tired of her and hadn't visited her in months. He wondered how much of what she could say about him would be believed.

Where was Rosa now? If she was at her home in via del Paradiso, he could visit her. He didn't want to visit her. He wanted to take a bath and change his shirt.

As he neared the hospital he noticed a new flurry of activity — an empty ambulance waiting with its motor running, a small crowd gathered in the piazzetta, and French Colonial soldiers standing listlessly beside the entrance, their rifles cradled in their arms. To Mario's surprise, they didn't bother to interrogate him; they didn't seem to care that he was there or that they had come to fight a war.

Inside the hospital he was greeted by the same nun who had helped care for his wife, but before he could acknowledge her, she had disappeared into the crowd.

Nearby, a woman on a gurney prayed to the ceiling. "Grazie, O Gesù Cristo, grazie O Gesù, per tutte le grazie di purità, per tutte le forti virtù che questa . . ."

A priest murmured beside an unconscious man: "Domandiamogli perdono delle nostre negligenze. . . ."

All around the hall, voices were raised in protest, in anguish, in appeal, all of them, even the most pious, marked by the shrillness of impatience. These were civilians — residents of Portoferraio who hadn't managed to flee to the hills. The nurses moved quietly among the wounded, who were lying on gurneys if they were lucky, or who were simply lying where they had fallen from exhaustion. Though the generator was running, the room was poorly lit, and Mario found himself squinting to find someone he recognized. He was Signor Tonietti. And where was anyone he knew?

Everyone in the room was busy — busy dying, busy healing, busy saving souls. Only Mario had nothing to do. He wasn't even suffering any ill effects from loss of blood. In fact, he felt stronger than ever and had the impression that he'd taken a wrong turn somewhere and ended up in the hospital by accident.

The man with a bandage taped on his forehead, the blood seeping through the gauze to make a pink X — he looked like he belonged. Mario's gaze settled on this man, who was carrying a jug and offering cups of water to the injured, limping through the crowd, his face serene, his patience infinite. This great, calm man . . . why, it was Dino!

Of course it was Dino. Naturalmente. The most purposeful man there — of course it was Dino. And Mario was sufficiently clearheaded to stand there for long enough to calculate the effects of Dino's public service and then to devise a strategy of his own.

"Dino!" Staggering, he put a bloody hand on the younger man's shoulder as he passed.

"Mario! Mio Dio!"

"Let me assist you," Mario offered, lifting the stack of paper cups from Dino's hands.

"You're injured," Dino said. Mario signaled acknowledgment with a smile. Yes. Dino was injured, too, but Mario was worse. He should sit. No. Pour the water, Dino, and look at Mario Tonietti, a wounded man moving among the wounded, handing the thirsty, battered civilians of Elba cups of fresh water.

He saved the last cup for himself, gulped the water so fast he choked. Dino bloodied himself trying to steady Mario. Miraculously, an empty chair appeared — a wooden chair with a woven bottom that had a little split in the middle, Mario noticed as he sat down. But if it would support him, it would do. Indeed, it was as good as a throne. Mario Tonietti sat while a nurse, summoned by Dino, lifted his shirt to examine his wounds. He felt the welcome coolness of wet gauze on his back, then the painful sizzle of antiseptic. The nurse held up a small splinter of glass in her tweezers for Mario to see, then dropped it in a nearby bucket. She kept working, digging gently into his skin with the tweezers, while Dino stood nearby, staring stupidly, helplessly, his hands pressed together in front of his lips.

"Now, tell me," Mario began, but he didn't know how to continue. Tell me what happened? Tell me what I don't know? Just tell me.

Dino opened his hands. "Corrado is dead," he said.

Mario gasped, and the spasm caught the nurse by surprise, causing her hand with the tweezers to jerk forward against his shoulder.

"Basta!" Mario cried.

The din in the room subsided for a moment as everyone turned to see the man who couldn't endure the poke of tweezers: the future mayor of Portoferraio. Mario apologized quietly, earning from the nurse a winsome smile and a pat on his wrist.

"He was caught in his yard," continued Dino in a low voice, the voice that a sober man might use with a drunk. "The Germans shot him in the stomach. But he didn't die."

"Ma che! He's dead or no?"

"Corrado is dead. Fernanda left him there in the yard —"

Fernanda, Corrado's wife — "She left him to die?"

"She had been hiding in her closet in the house. When the Germans were gone, she came out and found Corrado bleeding. She ran for help. While she was gone the Africans arrived. They found Corrado. They soaked him in petrol and tossed a match on him. Fernanda ran all the way to Bernardo's — by the time they returned to the yard, the soldiers had moved on." Dino looked inside the jug as though hoping to find water there, but it was empty. "Bernardo put Corrado in the car," he said. "He started to drive him to the hospital. Then he changed his mind and drove him to the morgue. I went to see him there this morning."

What did you see? Mario wanted to ask. Corrado's skin must have been as black as charcoal. As black as the burned wood scattered around his yard. Freedom has a cost, the French would say. The cost is too dear, Mario would have wanted to argue. For a lesser price we choose the Germans. This would have been the advice offered by the future mayor of Portoferraio if there had been time to consider the options.

"O Cuore di Gesù, pieno di bontà e di amore, io credo nell'amor tuo per me!"

Someone called for a basin because her child was vomiting. Someone wanted morphine. Someone else wanted water. Dino, more water — quick! A nun stamped papers at the desk. A doctor appeared from nowhere and whispered to the priest. The priest nodded and went on praying. The doctor disappeared again.

The dimness of the light together with the heat of the room had the effect of muting reality, giving it the distance of a motion picture on the screen at the Cinema Moderno, though without the deliberateness of rehearsed actions, rather with an abrupt spontaneity, like images of crowds on a newsreel. But the smell was not the smell of a theater. It was the same stink Mario had smelled out in the street. It was the smell of his friend Corrado, and Mario imagined that such an odor would cling to his own skin forever.

The nurse squeezed him on the hand to indicate that she had finished her work. She hadn't said a word to him the entire time, and as he watched her walk away he wondered what she really thought of him.

He was becoming aware of his fatigue. He closed his eyes and let himself imagine diving from his sailboat into the clear water off Pomonte. Would the sea wash away the lingering effects of this war? He had promised to take his niece sailing again this summer. But now they must wait for this final offensive of the war to come to an end. After the armistice, Mario and his little niece would go for a sail and take turns diving into the sea. This had become their custom: spending long, languorous Saturdays in August together. She would tell him stupid jokes, and he would pretend to laugh, and sometimes he would forget that he was just pretending and he really would laugh.

This adopted child of his dead wife's sister — she was as beloved as a daughter to him. That's why he'd left Portoferraio last night after the first wave of the surprise invasion: not to protect himself but to protect his niece. Amazingly, he'd succeeded. When the soldiers did finally arrive at La Chiatta, Mario had managed to distract them, first with grappa, then with talk of harbors and beaches and roadways. Giulia should consider how the visit of the soldiers would have gone differently had Mario not been present. Giulia should consider what Mario had done for her and her daughter.

Pride had a sedating effect. With some astonishment, Mario calculated that he hadn't slept for over thirty-six hours. Even here, surrounded by the results of an ill-planned, unjust invasion, he enjoyed the feeling of accomplishment. He hadn't managed to save Corrado — how could he have? All he could do for Corrado at this point was avenge him. But he had saved his niece, and come August he would watch her balance on the rail of his sailboat, lift herself on her toes, and dive, disappearing with barely a splash. It was pleasant to imagine.

WHEN ADRIANA WOKE on the morning of the third day of the liberation of Elba, she felt as if she'd slept for twenty years. The fact that her mother had let her stay in her own bed was enough evidence that the world she'd woken to was fundamentally different from the world she'd left behind the night before. She wasn't sure what, exactly, had changed. But had things remained the same, she would have been tumbling out of the cabinet right about now, aching and hungry and annoyed by the inconvenience of it all.

Her first impression of the morning was that the veins in the tile floor, lit by cracks of daylight shining through the shutters, had a reddish tint, indicating that the rising sun was veiled by clouds. It would rain before the day was over. How disappointing. Rain was almost always disappointing, except on a hot August afternoon. Today was only the nineteenth of June.

Disappointment sharpened her consciousness. She remembered that there was a war going on. Yet somehow she sensed that the worst was over. Whoever was dead was dead, and whoever had survived would stay alive.

The pleasant coolness of her pillowcase against her cheek accompanied the transformation of disappointment into blissful relief. She was still alive. And without confirming it, she knew that her mother was alive. And Luisa and Paolo and Uncle Mario and Ulisse and his family and Signor Lorenzo and his household —

they were all still alive. Everyone familiar to Adriana was still alive.

Feeling happy and lazy, she became aware of the fragrance of caffè. To heat the water for caffè, the charcoal must have been burning in the stove, and if the charcoal had been lit, then the invasion must be over. Either the Germans or the Allies had surrendered. The skies were quiet. All over the island, people were lighting their stoves, heating water, and flinging open shutters to let in the cool morning air.

Adriana felt too comfortable to open her shutters. She wanted to lie there and think about peace. It hardly mattered if the day's weather turned bad. A good soaking rain might even be welcome. The sound of the drops splashing on the palm fronds was a nice sound. And the scent of the vineyard after a storm was a nice scent.

She just wished she didn't have to enjoy this new serenity all by herself. If only she had a sister. Or a pet. Someday, she promised herself, she would have her own dog, one as gentle as Pippa, to keep in her room. And she would keep other pets: goldfish, parakeets, a baby goat, and a cricket. And she would keep a kitten just like the one in the boathouse.

The boathouse made her think of her soldier. He was somewhere in the olive grove, perhaps still asleep. But when he did wake he would be ravenous. The bread and cheese she'd left him for his supper had hardly been sufficient. This morning she would bring him figs and plums, along with bread. Or better, she would invite him to come inside and eat his breakfast in proper fashion at the table. She would find him clothes to wear, and she would introduce him to her mother and Luisa.

She dressed slowly, stepping into her skirt as though it were a ball gown, and buttoned her shirt, then unbuttoned it when she noticed a stain on the front. She put on a half-sleeved cotton sweater instead and slipped her feet into straw sandals. Unable to locate her brush, she smoothed her tangled hair with her fingers, twisting it into a single braid.

Paolo's voice was the first she heard as she descended the stairs. He was imitating a dog yelping in pain, and when she entered the kitchen, Adriana found him hopping around with his forefinger in his mouth.

"Buongiorno, Paolo," Adriana said.

"Ahi," he moaned.

What a silly dance. But where was her mamma? "Mamma, dove sei?" She was not in the kitchen; neither was Luisa. But the shutters and windows were open, and Paolo was here to welcome Adriana to this new era of tranquillity.

"Mamma, where are you? Mamma!" She grabbed a plum from the bowl, gripped it in her palm to test its ripeness, then sank her teeth into the fruit. Casting the sophisticated half-lidded glance that in the past year she'd perfected, she asked, "Isn't it time for you to go home, Paolo?"

"Ahi," he repeated, holding his finger up to examine it before slipping it back into his mouth.

"Tu sei un' idiota, Paolo!"

"E tu . . . e anche tu, Adriana!"

Certainly Paolo wouldn't be acting so stupid if life had not returned to normal. Adriana wiped her hands with a dish towel. She found another towel in a drawer, knotted it to form a little sack, and filled it with plums and a thick slice of bread — provisions that were precious during war and yet still in abundance in the kitchen of La Chiatta.

With her back turned to Paolo, she asked him if he'd hurt himself. Certo! Couldn't she see? He'd burned his finger trying to stir the charcoal in the stove!

Adriana offered him a shrug. Too bad, Paolo. Ciao! She headed out of the kitchen, following the smell of coffee up the stairs and into the salotto, where she found her mother sitting with Lorenzo and his wife, the three of them absorbed in a whispered conversation. They fell silent when she appeared in the doorway.

Tucking the sack of food around the corner, she offered "Salve" to the visitors and took her place on the sofa, snuggling beside her mother, who greeted her in her usual serene voice but whose haggard face suggested that the night had indeed been twenty years long and now Giulia Nardi was twenty years older, her eyes framed in muddy pockets, her hair glittering with gray strands that Adriana hadn't noticed before.

"Is it over?" she asked.

Yes, her mother assured her. The fighting was over. The Germans had hoisted the white flag at Marciana Marina. The Allies had taken command of the island and had promised to deliver fresh supplies within the week. The guns were silent. No more bombs would fall on Elba.

"Never again?"

"Never again."

Her mother's tone of voice when she said never again, *mai più,* suggested that she wasn't inclined to offer proof. She was too tired to offer anything more than the assurance they all wanted to hear. Never again. It was the first thing her mother had ever told her that Adriana didn't believe.

Never again was an unconvincing promise. *Never again* didn't protect against surprise. Given that the worst usually happened unexpectedly, any protection Giulia Nardi had tried to provide for her daughter during the recent days had been superficial. That soldiers had come and gone without incident, the fires had burned elsewhere, and the bombs had fallen to the east and west was no more than good luck for the residents of La Chiatta. And good luck was only one possible outcome. *Never again* had no relevance.

And now Adriana's mother and the Signori Ambrogi thought they were protecting Adriana by keeping her from hearing their exchange of information. Didn't they realize that ignorance was an inadequate defense? Adriana wanted to compare what she'd imagined with the facts of the past few days. But in this immediate aftermath, facts were thought to be dangerous. The adults didn't realize that imagining was almost equal to knowing. They assumed that a ten-year-old girl — almost eleven — mustn't hear about any form of death: not the deaths of children or the deaths of grandparents, not the deaths of Germans or Africans or Frenchmen or Italians, and not the deaths of partisans or Fascists or Jews.

Lorenzo had been holding an unlit cigarette and a wooden match. During the pause in conversation, he struck the match and lit the cigarette. But when he shook the match it kept burning. He shook it more forcefully, and the flame flared and jumped down the stem before it went out. His wife exchanged a look with Giulia that seemed to communicate some mysterious understanding. Confused, Adriana pressed closer to her mother, finding some comfort in what was now only a remembered impression of her mother's indomitable strength.

The adults had nothing to say in Adriana's presence. While Lorenzo smoked, his wife unclasped and clasped her watch. Giulia turned the saucer beneath her demitasse as if turning the face of a clock. Adriana heard Luisa bustle down the stairs and into the kitchen, where she spoke sharply to her nephew. She heard

Paolo's peevish reply of sì, sì, sì. She heard the distant crying of Ulisse's infant son. And out in the courtyard she heard a dog barking and Ulisse's older boys, Aldo and Marco, calling to each other.

Rather than sneak outside again without permission, Adriana looked toward the windows and back at her mother with an expression meant to indicate her desire. "Posso?" May I? The war is over, Mamma! Adriana wanted to remind her. Ulisse's boys were playing in the courtyard, where they had played hundreds of times before.

Yes, she would have to be allowed to go outside again after her mother had promised that the bombs would never again fall on Elba. Mai più.

D'accordo, Adriana, go play.

What Giulia Nardi really said was "Sì, vai," yes, go. But she warned her not to make trouble. "Do not wander, Adriana."

"Mamma . . ."

"No farther than the courtyard."

"Sì, Mamma, sì."

Outside, Pippa leaped toward her as she jumped from the bottom step, almost knocking Adriana off her feet. She rubbed the furrow between the dog's ears. Sensing her mother watching from the window, she bided time tossing sticks. With the two boys, she threw the sticks far into the field, and while she waited for Pippa to lope back with her prize, she pulled weeds from between the courtyard stones.

Eventually her mother moved from the window. A few minutes later, Adriana returned inside, calling out a greeting from the hall. She wanted her mother to hear that she was inside. But she was there just to fetch the supplies she'd gathered for her soldier, and when she went outside again, her mother didn't need to know.

She was sorry to have wasted time. By this hour her soldier was sure to be awake. He'd wonder where his breakfast was. He'd worry that he'd been forgotten. But Adriana would never forget him. To prove that she was fond of him, she stopped in at the cantina, entering quietly so as not to disturb Ulisse's wife and baby and Signora Fausta upstairs. She filled a bottle with wine from the cask, plugging the neck with the only thing on hand — a rag stinking of turpentine. But she was confident that her soldier wouldn't mind if his meal was less than perfect. Surely he would appreciate the effort.

From the terrace she had a better view and could see the edge of the cloud bed to the west and the blue sky behind the peak of Volterraio. The wind mixed the scent of lavender from the meadows below Santo Stefano with the smell of the choppy sea and the faint scent that the dog's fur had left on her hands. A blackbird in the box hedge whistled angrily as Pippa led the way through the opening to the field. In the distance, a spray of dust followed a jeep winding its way along the road toward Rio nell'Elba.

Just as she'd hoped, the blanket she'd left the night before was gone. After scanning the area for some sign that her soldier had been there, she set off through the olive grove in search of him. This time she didn't call out. She tried to walk as quietly as possible over the crumbled soil and clumps of stiff-leafed grass, for she'd decided that her soldier was a timid fellow and her pursuit might frighten him.

She had left the villa shortly after nine in the morning. For the next half hour she and Pippa searched the olive grove and vineyard. Aldo and Marco followed her from a distance but eventually grew bored. After they'd returned to the cantina, she went to search the boathouse. She reminded herself that there was nothing to fear as long as the shutters at La Chiatta were open and the stove was lit. She would keep looking for her soldier until she found him.

Pippa dashed ahead of her through the gate to the little pebble beach. While the dog splashed in the water, Adriana wandered along the shore. Two seagulls landed and briefly ran along on either side of her before they took flight again.

Though she didn't find any African soldiers on the beach, she did see a gray toad tangled in seaweed and lying spread-eagled on its back, its pale belly covered with minute black specks. It was floating in the shallow water between the reeds and the rocks, with one of its legs snagged on a submerged stick that held it in place against the current of a small estuary stream. Impulsively, she reached toward the toad, intending to turn it right side up. Not until the carcass bobbed at the touch of her finger did she realize that the toad was dead.

A dead toad was a repugnant sight, and it was enough to make Adriana consider the possibility that her soldier had died during the night. If he had died, she coldly wished that he had first dragged himself at least as far as the Ambrogi fields — then Adriana would only have to hear about what Lorenzo's gardener, Nino, had found. She didn't want to be the one to find a dead soldier floating in shallow water. She didn't want to experience something she didn't want to remember.

Returning through the gate with Pippa, shifting the sack of food to her left hand, the bottle of wine to her right, she paused at the wooden step of the boathouse, too fearful to enter, and headed on through the vineyard. She reassured herself as she continued her search by imagining how if she did find the soldier alive she would invite him to stay at La Chiatta until the fighting had ended, and then, with her mother's help, she would book him a passage home to his own country. Thanks to Signora Nardi and her daughter, he wouldn't have to go back to the war. Never again.

Pippa ran ahead, disappearing into a small, dense pineta. Adriana walked along the edge of the grove to the point where the land started to slope upward, the trees giving way to scrub grass and big scallop-shaped pieces of slate. By then, midmorning, the grass was shimmering below the gray sky, whipped by the wind. Patches of fog leaked from the clouds. Beyond the tip of the Portoferraio peninsula, the sea was dark with the front sheet of approaching rain.

Thousands of years ago this land had been terraced for iron mines, crisscrossed with mule tracks, and crumbled stone walls still extended in strips along successive levels. When Adriana reached the top terrace at the edge of La Chiatta's land, she called for Pippa. But the dog was nowhere in sight and didn't answer with a bark. The silence was ominous, Adriana thought at first, until she heard the quiet sounds that filled the air — the brush of wind, the rattle of a motorbike heading toward La Lampara, and a low, steady trickling, like the sound of water running through the pipe below the kitchen sink

Ahead of her, the land dipped in a jagged descent to a ravine overgrown with ivy and woodbine. When she was a small child, no more than six or seven years old, Adriana had come to this ravine with Ulisse and his eldest son, and she'd been stung on her hand by a bee. She remembered it as a dark, damp place that hummed with the buzzing of thousands of angry insects, and she'd had no inclination to return.

She didn't want to go down there now. Clutching the sack and the bottle of wine, she decided that she'd been gone from home long enough. She would head back before the storm moved inland.

She glanced at the ground, preparing to take a step, and was momentarily jolted by the absence of her shadow before remembering that the sun was hidden by the clouds. The air seemed to hold remnants of last night's darkness, and it felt to Adriana that time had blended, putting her at once inside the cabinet below the sink, on the beach, and in the northwest corner of the Nardi estate, where she took a step toward the ravine instead of away from it, drawn by what she thought was a faint light, barely perceptible, glowing from below the edge of the grassy shelf.

As she climbed into the ravine, the light faded, giving the impression that someone holding a torch was withdrawing as she descended. The air, sweetened by the flowering woodbines, had the graininess of dusk. Pebbles rolled ahead of her feet along the rough path. Somewhere quite close to her a thrush started piping but was silenced when Pippa, waiting down at the bottom of the ravine, barked happily at Adriana's approach.

By the time she reached the spring, she became aware of knowing what she would find before she actually found it: a dead soldier wrapped in the blanket. And though it took her a few minutes, she did find something close to what she was expecting: the sausage of his bundled legs extending from between two rocks.

The sight was too terrible to contemplate, so she turned from it, calling Pippa to her side, intending to run as fast as she could back home and tell her mother what she'd seen. But she hadn't gone far when the dead man spoke: "Où allez-vous, madamoiselle?"

She tried to stop. Her knees buckled and she fell forward, scattering the food and listening helplessly as the bottle bounced twice and shattered on a piece of slate. "Merda!" she said. It was the first time she'd ever spoken the profanity aloud. She was surprised by its immediate rejuvenating effect, and she let herself say it again in a more studied way. "Merda!"

From behind a boulder came the sound of the dead man's laugh. "La petite princesse," he said to her. "Why didn't you come sooner?"

"Me?"

"All this time, I have been waiting for you to find me."

She wanted to explain her mistake, but she couldn't summon the rules for the tense in French. "I think you are dead" was the best she could manage.

He laughed again, pushing himself up to a sitting position so Adriana could see the whole of him wrapped in the blanket, which he'd hooded over his head and pinched closed beneath his chin. His top teeth, she noticed, were perfectly even, but the bottom teeth looked like pebbles stuck haphazardly in the gum. His lips were cracked with a brown that was either dirt or dried blood. Only his right cheek dimpled when he smiled. His dark face gleamed with the brilliance of polished steel, and because magic seemed inevitable in this place where dead men came to life, she let herself conclude that the soldier's face was the source of the glow she thought she'd seen from the top of the ravine.

Pippa sat beside him, panting lightly, grinning a grin of lazy pleasure. Adriana found her own pleasure growing. She was pleased to be in the soldier's company, pleased to be having this adventure, pleased to offer whatever help she could. Spilled wine didn't matter. She could bring more.

The soldier's voice faded from a chuckle into a contemplative silence. She watched him watching her. He was studying her eyes, gazing at her with frank interest. She suspected that he was judging her age. She tried to estimate his. He was eighteen or nineteen. No, he must have been seventeen, or even fifteen or sixteen. He was just a boy! She could see his youth in his eyes and his silly dimple. He had the round, smooth chin of a boy, the flat hairline of a boy, the blunt fingernails of a boy. He was too young to be a soldier. He should have been in school. Or if he wasn't in school, he should have been delivering messages and doing chores, like Paolo.

If he was Paolo's age, then Adriana could let herself feel some measure of condescension. The African soldier was more than a little ridiculous. She found all boys ridiculous. And here was one stupidissimo ragazzo who must have lied about his age in order to be accepted into the military. There were plenty of Elban boys who had done the same thing just so they could wear uniforms — boys who found their heroes in stories about the rough Italian Arditi and who waved their rifles and sang crude songs all the way to the front. A noi, a noi, a noi! Here was their African equivalent, a boy who couldn't even grow a mustache and who smelled like an ox!

Yet she didn't have to persuade herself that there was more to him than to most boys his age. It was his helplessness that mattered most. He was lost and alone, with a shine on his face that Adriana began to perceive as evidence of sickliness. He might need a doctor. This was a concern worth expressing. Forgetting that he couldn't understand her, she asked him in Italian if he wanted her to take him to Doctor Grini. He shrugged. She decided he should eat something, and she began gathering the fruit and bread to arrange in front of him. "Marocchino?" she asked him. Was he Moroccan? But she must speak in French, she remembered. "Marochine?" She knew there were Moroccans fighting with the Allies. Moroccans wore white robes and red scarves, and for no reason they fired bullets into the walls of villas — or worse. But he wasn't a Moroccan. He was a Senegalese, he said. He repeated the word: "Sénégalais."

And what was his name? She could say that in French: "Comment vous appelez-vous?"

"Amdu," he replied, his tone polite, even a little shy. As she started to ponder the name, wondering what it indicated about its bearer, she saw him blink in a sleepy way that reminded her of a cat lying in the sun. She thought that he must be filled with trust if he was allowing himself to give in to fatigue in her presence, and his trust made her proud of her own steadfast attention. Any other girl would have been afraid. Not Adriana. Che coraggio! Any other girl would have stayed at home.

She wanted to be sure the soldier named Amdu knew that she was different from other girls her age. She hoped he would come to Viticcio to watch her dive. Having concluded that he was a nice boy, better than most, she wanted to earn his admiration. She'd already earned his trust. Come along, then, Amdu, and Adriana will introduce you to her mother and Luisa and Paolo and Ulisse. Come to La Chiatta and sleep in a proper bed, and before you go back to your home, Adriana will take you to Viticcio, where, to impress you, she will leap from the highest rock and twist backward into the sea.

But while she was trying to think of some way to prove that she was worthy of admiration, Amdu sank into the tent of his blanket, slumping forward onto the ground, his head tilted so only the fuzz of his hair was visible. Adriana didn't know whether to feel offended or concerned. She had thought they were in the middle of a conversation, but he'd gone and fallen asleep on her! Didn't he know there was a difference between blinking and actually falling asleep? Even if he was exhausted by his ordeal, there was no excuse for just falling asleep in the middle of a nice conversation! Except he wasn't asleep — not completely. His body twitched beneath the blanket, rousing Pippa, who started to bark excitedly. No, Pippa, stop! The barking was confusing Adriana. Or maybe the soldier named Amdu was the source of confusion. Maybe he wanted to fool her into thinking that he was dying. Or maybe he really was dying.

Wake up! He was supposed to live, not die. "Amdu!" His bundled body jerked in tremors. "Amdu!" She wished Pippa would stop barking. She wished Amdu would sit up and tell her that he was only joking. Boys played awful, stupid jokes sometimes. They lied; they snuck up on you and pulled your hair; they pretended they were dying. Stop pretending, Amdu!

The whole point of the adventure was to keep this boy alive, not to watch him die and certainly not to hear what sounded like the rattling of gunfire resume up in the fields. The war was supposed to be over. Was it possible that the war had just begun — or was beginning all over again, as wars will do? A boy was dying. Someone was spraying the field with a machine gun. And was that the faint crackling of fire? Maybe. Possibly. Most likely. Where there was war, there would be fire. The fields were burning and would always be burning.

With some bitterness she recalled her mother's promise of *never again*, though she felt betrayed not by her mother's exaggeration but by her own vanity. She had only herself to blame. She had come to the ravine simply to prove how wonderful she was. And now she had to decide either to stay or to leave. Weren't those always the two choices? She would stay if the soldier named Amdu chose to live. But she didn't want to stand there waiting for him to die. If she couldn't do anything for him, she wanted to be someplace else, someplace far enough away so she wouldn't be expected to save him.

Halfway up the path she ripped her skirt trying to free it from a patch of thorns, and as she struggled on she found herself looking forward to her mother's annoyance and Luisa's scolding. Even as she pushed herself over the lip of level ground into the battle that could have been the beginning of the end of the world, she imagined the eloquence of her apology. And though she'd offer to repair the skirt, she knew that Luisa would insist on doing it herself.

It felt good to predict the effects that would likely follow a particular cause, just as it felt good to feel the rain on her face. A predictable future meant that any previous change had not been too severe. And the rain meant that she'd mistaken the sound of a storm for war. There was no battle raging around her — no spray of a machine gun or bazooka blasts or pinging of mortar. There were only thick gray clouds overhead and rain falling in sheets that churned like metal blades across the grass.

SHE'S STILL HERE, though she's not doing much thinking. The ventricles of the heart are still contracting, the valves are working properly, and blood is being pumped. But somewhere between the right ventricle of the heart and the capillaries in the lungs, midway along the pulmonary artery, a clot has formed, impeding the circulation of blood and the diffusion of oxygen into Mrs. Rundel's needy tissues, causing the third cranial optic nerve to weaken and at the same time disrupting the signals from the vagus nerve to the thoracic cavity, so after the last exhalation the intercostal muscles don't contract, and the lungs don't expand.

The train is five minutes from Penn Station, and the other passengers are gathering their belongings in preparation for arrival. Ordinarily, Mrs. Rundel would do the same. She would glance at the ghost of her reflection in the window, smooth her hair, and take her place in the aisle. When the doors opened and she joined the crowd on the platform, she would consider the tasks awaiting her.

With her vision registering only the absence of light and her brain focused on the breach of contract between her lungs and her heart, Mrs. Rundel hasn't even had a chance to admit once and for all that she has reason to panic. But somewhere within her is the awareness that she's Ma to her grown son and daughter, and *Ma*, however coarse the sound, is the person her body wants to protect. Along with her desire to fall into her husband's arms, she feels an urge to continue the conversation begun the night before and say what deserves to be said. Even if she can't articulate it, her body senses that she has unfinished business. When the family is gathered again around the dinner table, Mrs. Rundel will pick up where she left off.

Not that any recounting of events is ever sufficient. For instance, she likes to tell her children about how she and Robert met in Paris in 1956. But she has never adequately explained why she left Elba. Or why in 1971, following her mother's death, she sold the estate of La Chiatta for far less than it was worth. Or why on a summer's day when she was forty years old, alone one afternoon in her house in Rahway, she stared with eyes clouded by useless tears at a Formica counter upon which sat a yellow felt marker missing its top, a bent lid ripped from a cereal box, a plastic pony, a plate spotted with dried ketchup, a list of phone numbers for her daughter's classmates, and the comics from the local newspaper. And then the banging of doors, children squabbling, her husband's mediating voice, Mrs. Rundel reaching for the ringing phone, holding it up so whoever was on the other end could hear the chaos in her home, and then hanging up the phone without even saying hello while her family stared at her, appalled.

They've never understood why she hung up the phone, though she tried to explain — that and more. Why she is who she is, mother, wife, daughter, bouncing from island to mainland to a kitchen with a television on the counter. They know her opinion of American talk shows. They know her likes and dislikes, her habits, her dreams. Over the course of her long life, she has said everything that deserves to be said. And yet she feels that she wants to say it all over again, to say it correctly. In the face of the possibility of an everlasting silence, everything deserves to be repeated and refined, beginning with whatever she's just been thinking. But she can't remember what she's been thinking until her body receives an adequate supply of oxygen. And she can't get adequate oxygen without medical help — which depends upon the ability of the other passengers to act decisively.

The man beside her, no longer absorbed in financial reports, is already standing in the aisle behind the student with the brown-bag lunch. The woman who refreshed her lipstick is waiting for the woman who's been reading about water resources to put away her report and close her briefcase. The man who absorbed himself and his companion in his complaints about his flight is quiet, except when he offers a pert *geʒundheit* in response to his friend's sneeze.

Mrs. Rundel has slumped in her seat, her head falling over the armrest that she shared with the financial adviser, who glances down at her with impatience. His first conclusion is that the old woman is in distress. His second conclusion, which he prefers, is that she's drunk. There are plenty like her on the streets and subways of New York. It's a pity — the waste of potential. But a drunken woman can be expected to take care of herself.

He takes a step forward, bumping against the student, who rotates his shoulders to reclaim the space around him. But just then the train jerks to a halt on its approach to the station, and at the same time that the financial adviser stumbles, shoving the student forward, Mrs. Rundel rolls from her seat.

The student, looking back at the financial adviser in annoyance, is the first to notice the old woman on the floor and the first to exclaim. Closest to the student is the husband who's been talking on his cell phone to his lover's answering machine — he's cupping the closed phone in his hand, holding it like a stone he wants to throw through the window. Startled by the student's voice, he drops the phone and immediately bends over to retrieve it. The student, watching him go down, assumes the man is collapsing, following the example of the woman behind him, and he stands there staring helplessly at the top of the man's head.

Meanwhile, the financial adviser can't ignore the fact that the old woman who might be drunk has fallen from her seat. Moving to help her, he notices that her skirt has ridden up above the dark line of her pantyhose. He feels embarrassed for her — or, more precisely, he is embarrassed by his proximity to this scene, and though he has already started to reach for her, his effort is slowed by his reluctance to get involved.

The Polish woman, having heard the student's exclamation, snaps her report closed right at the point when she's been mulling over the section about basic water requirements — including agricultural needs as well as sanitation, quantified at fifty liters per person per day. Seeing a woman's arm extending across the floor of the aisle, she quickly rises from her seat but is blocked by the financial adviser, who is trying to position himself on straddled legs so he will have enough leverage to set Mrs. Rundel upright. But her body is jammed in the narrow space between the seats, and the financial adviser can't lift her on his own.

The lawyer who's been sitting behind Mrs. Rundel springs into action. But he can't reach the aisle unless his companion moves. The companion, confused, is looking past the financial adviser at the face of the Polish woman. His confusion is matched by hers, though the difference between them is that the software designer tends to wait for an opportunity to present itself to him and the Polish woman is used to making quick decisions.

After inching forward along the track, the train is easing to a halt beside the platform. The student reaches for the man who dropped his cell phone. When he gently lifts him by the elbow, the man pulls away, clearly disgusted by the contact. Behind them, the financial adviser stumbles again and grabs the nearest headrest. The lawyer pushes his way into the aisle past the software designer, who makes an effort to get up but falls back into his seat with the jerking motion of the train.

At the same time, the Polish woman manages to slip into the aisle under the arm of the financial adviser. Having dealt with many crises in her life, she is confident that she can deal with this one. Feeling awkwardly for the carotid pulse, she concludes — wrongly — that Mrs. Rundel is in cardiac arrest, which stirs in her a jolting recognition of her inadequacy. This is the second time in the past decade that she's been unable to help someone because she doesn't know how to perform CPR. The first time involved a Sudanese child who had fallen into an irrigation ditch.

"Is there — is anyone a doctor here?" she calls. Her raised

voice silences the chatter among passengers in the rear seats. When no one replies, she says more urgently, "This woman needs help."

The train has stopped at the platform, but the doors don't open. This infuriates the lawyer, who manages to pull Mrs. Rundel from the floor. Though she isn't a large woman, she flops into his arms with unexpected heaviness. The financial adviser, comprehending all at once that the situation calls for a heroic response, sets his briefcase on the seat vacated by the Polish woman and helps the lawyer steady Mrs. Rundel in an upright position.

After understanding that the man with the cell phone does not need his help, the student whirls to face Mrs. Rundel, whose grayish lips abruptly call to mind the memory of a twenty-nine-year-old man pulled from Salt Pond last summer. The man, who didn't know how to swim, had gone in after his nephew, who he thought was struggling to stay afloat in deep water. But the boy had swum to shore while the uncle disappeared beneath the surface. The student, working as the sole lifeguard at the time, had jumped in with his rope and life preserver, but he hadn't been able to locate the man in the murky water. It took forty-five minutes and two divers to bring the body back to the beach.

The student turns to face the door at the head of the aisle. He wants to believe that there's nothing he can do. But there's always something he can do. At the very least, he can summon help. He moves into the compartment between cars and waits for the door to the platform to open. He waits and waits, knowing that his worthlessness is increasing with every passing minute. But he can't bring himself to go back into the car, where he would have to press his mouth to an old woman's gray lips and breathe for her. And even this probably wouldn't do any good.

Meanwhile, the Polish woman tends to Mrs. Rundel, pushing the hair from her face while the financial adviser and the lawyer keep her from flopping forward. Her eyes are only half-closed, with the bottom rim of the pupils barely visible. A thread of drool is drying on her lips. The Polish woman thinks of the wish she's wished a thousand times during her travels: when she dies, she wants to be in the privacy of her own home, surrounded by her family.

Mrs. Rundel is dying in public. But she doesn't have to die. If she could be kept alive long enough for an able doctor to free the pulmonary artery of its embolism, she could go on to live for many happy years.

The doors to the train open with a swooshing sound, and the student leaps to the platform and heads toward two transit workers who have just entered the gate. Finally, he is doing something useful. He is setting the rescue into motion.

In the car with Mrs. Rundel, to everyone's surprise, the woman who was putting on lipstick has taken charge. All the time spent watching soap operas: here she is having some idea about what to do because of the schmaltz she's watched on television. She directs the lawyer and the financial adviser to lift Mrs. Rundel into the aisle. The lawyer curls his arms under Mrs. Rundel's, the financial adviser holds her ankles, and with great awkwardness they manage to lay her on her back, giving the woman the opportunity to begin performing a muddled resuscitation, breathing effectively into Mrs. Rundel's mouth, then giving a few tentative pushes on her sternum, which, though she can't know it, is preferable to a more accomplished technique, since though Mrs. Rundel's respirations have stopped, her heart is still beating.

It is the same heart that began beating on the island of Corsica seventy years ago, then beat on Elba through her childhood and continued beating in Paris, London, New York, and Rahway, New Jersey. The heart that has beat steadily every weekday morning on this commuter train for twenty years and elsewhere on holidays and vacations. Lub dub. The heart that has, on the whole, been rewarded with contentment and good health and has grown so used to ease that it doesn't willingly register distress. Lub dub.

It is a good, strong heart, but there's only confusion in the brain, without any conscious awareness of earlier concerns. And though Mrs. Rundel would be reluctant to agree, unconsciousness is a benefit right now, for if she were awake she would be mortified by the attention. One strange man at her head, another at her feet, her neat wool skirt riding up her thighs, a strange woman pressing her lips, moist with fresh color, against Mrs. Rundel's mouth, another woman tenderly holding her hand. On the platform two transit workers go in opposite directions, one accompanying the frantic college student, moving toward the train through the swell of disembarking passengers, while the other calls for an ambulance.

THE RAIN WAS A GIFT FROM HEAVEN, Luisa said — a sacred cleansing to wash away spilled blood. Ulisse's boys squealed happily in the courtyard, catching raindrops on their tongues while Pippa danced around them. Luisa ran through the villa closing shutters. Giulia Nardi followed Lorenzo to the loggia. She stood with him, looking out across her land. The neat rows of olive trees, unyielding in the wind, made her think of stone columns inside a basilica. Those sturdy trees had survived a century's worth of storms. And now she could add that they had survived a war.

Lorenzo speculated that the weather would slow the German evacuation. Giulia was certain that the storm wouldn't last long. And though the sea was frothing wildly in the distance, the military ships would still be able to make the passage to the mainland. Signora Ambrogi, who'd been standing inside the doorway, wondered aloud where the Germans would go.

"They will come to regret ever leaving Germany to begin with," Giulia said, her prediction saturated with relief.

The palms in the courtyard made their noisy protest — a comforting sound that seemed to express the personality of the wind. She could almost hear words embedded in the sound, the *shhh* of sirocco or sciroppo. The loud, syrupy, shushing wind that disturbed but never stole what belonged to her. A wind that bounced off the surface of the sea and dipped into the fields before curling up and over the mountains.

She looked toward the ancient ruins crowning Volterraio and wondered if fugitive Germans were hiding there. She wondered what would happen to them if they were caught.

The previous night had been oddly quiet, though she'd spent most of it awake, repeatedly propelling herself from the snare of sleep until her body had given up fatigue entirely and she'd sat on the sofa, the knife Luisa used to quarter chickens hidden beneath the cushions by Luisa herself, who believed, unlike Giulia Nardi, that sooner or later the soldiers would return to La Chiatta.

But Giulia had been persuaded by the French officers that the soldiers had a mandate to protect the citizens of Elba, especially the aristocrazia. Whether or not the soldiers had finished shooting

open doors locked against them, they had been made to understand by their superiors that the villas were not to be disturbed.
The wealth that Giulia Nardi secretly considered a burdensome
responsibility during times of peace — an inheritance that had
made her too fiercely suspicious to accept suitors when she was a
young woman — proved to be a far more effective defense than a
kitchen knife during a time of war. At least during this war. From
the start, households like La Chiatta had been spared the deprivations that so many others suffered, and because of the bounty of
their gardens and the black-market trade with the military, no one
on the island had gone hungry. The provisions of rich Elbans
were substantial enough to share with anyone who needed help. It
was Giulia's good luck that she was rich. And a baptized Catholic.
And a mother without a son of military age.

The Signori Ambrogi had come over this morning to share the
news that the Germans were retreating. But whether or not the Allied rampage had truly ended was still a question that she couldn't
bring herself to ask. Nor was she ready to hear what had been lost
during the second night of the liberation.

After fifty hours without more than a few minutes of broken
sleep, Giulia Nardi felt herself floating somewhere between the
past and the future, in a present moment but not in full presence,
fully aware but not fully feeling emotion or physical sensation.
She couldn't even say for sure that she was tired. And she couldn't
entirely understand anything that was told to her. Elba had been
liberated. Grosseto had been liberated. Rome had been liberated.
What did any of this mean? Not what she'd said to her daughter —
mai più, a promise much worse than an outright lie. The Germans
were retreating? The occupation was over? What, exactly, had
they occupied, besides beds and rooms and lavatories?

The sky was already brightening; soon the rain would let up.

Spilled blood had been washed away. Ulisse's boys were shouting with pleasure. Kestrels were wheeling through the mist. Somewhere nearby, her daughter was humming. On the other side of the villa, Adriana was running across the meadow bordering the Ambrogi land and humming loudly. She had always loved to hum. Even her cry when she was a baby had sounded like phrases of a melody. Adriana was humming, the storm was moving back out to sea, and the liberation of Elba was complete.

Long ago, when Giulia Nardi was a child, her father had found an injured nightingale fledgling and given it to her to nurse back to health. Giulia had kept it inside for weeks, until it took to dipping its claws in her inkwell and leaving prints around the villa, at which point her mother had exiled the bird to a box in the court-yard, where it died three days later after eating a scorpion.

She found herself thinking of the nightingale as Adriana's voice grew louder. It used to perch on a high shelf in the library and sing. Why she remembered this now, she couldn't say. Adriana wasn't singing. She was screaming — "Mamma! Luisa! Dottore!" — as if she wanted to be heard across the island. She was calling for a doctor? Giulia thought with sluggish detachment that if her daughter needed a doctor, she'd already done something foolish. And she wanted her mamma and Luisa as well. She wanted someone, anyone, who could help her.

She wanted her mother to come to the ravine, she said between gulps of breath, her wet hair hanging like a cap of seaweed, her clothes drenched from the rain. And Luisa, too, must come help. And the Signori Ambrogi — come with Adriana, per cortesia. Paolo, you come, too. No; Adriana changed her mind. Paolo must go find Doctor Grini and bring him here. Go, Paolo! "Subito!" Straightaway!

The adults were gathered around her, urging her to calm down. Stop shouting, Adriana. Explain yourself, start at the beginning.

Instead she'd start at the end. There was a soldier in the ravine, she said.

A soldier, Giulia heard. A scorpion, she thought.

Adriana told them that the soldier was very sick. He was lying there in a blanket in the ravine and he was dying.

A trap, Giulia said to herself, feeling as sly as the soldier she was imagining. A dying soldier. A clever disguise.

The soldier was dying, Adriana repeated.

Poison, Giulia thought.

"Italiano?" Lorenzo asked.

"No."

"Tedesco?" Signora Ambrogi ventured.

"No."

What, then? Who was he?

"Un senegalese."

Giulia remembered that it had been her sister who had seen the nightingale gulping down the scorpion as though it were a cricket. Foolish bird. But Giulia shouldn't have tried to keep the nightingale as a pet. Foolish girl. And now she was the foolish mother who had let her daughter wander when there were still soldiers prowling the island. Why did she think that anyone with the name of Nardi was invulnerable? Because she wanted to believe it. Foolish woman. She who was supposed to be available always, sempre, upon whom others could rely. Now, because of her neglect, she'd let a Senegalese soldier poison her daughter. That was her vague conclusion. And how could a young girl survive a soldier's poison?

"How could you, Adriana!"

What had she done? "Cosa?"

What? What does *what* mean? A soldier lay dying in the ravine. The war was almost over. In this case, *almost* was an important word. Paolo was already on his bicycle, creaking up the drive. Luisa stood by, twisting her hands in her apron and muttering, "Madonna mia." Signora Ambrogi brought Adriana a glass of water.

Lorenzo took it upon himself to clarify the point: Adriana had found a wounded Senegalese soldier in the ravine. He was alone, yes?

"Sì."

"Nessun'altro?"

"No."

If it wasn't a trap, then what was it? Giulia wondered. Once, her nightingale swallowed a scorpion. Now a wounded, solitary Senegalese soldier lay dying on her property. What would Signora Nardi do about it?

She would order Luisa to find Ulisse and bring him here — that's what she'd do.

Giulia's direction seemed to give everyone a purpose. Signora Ambrogi took Adriana's empty glass and headed down to the kitchen. Luisa left to find Ulisse. Lorenzo untucked his shirt, lifted his revolver from the hidden holster, and checked the magazine and the back sight. He went to intercept Ulisse, and when Adriana started to follow him, he gestured toward the salotto with the barrel of his revolver, unintentionally turning his direction into a threat and drawing an exclamation of reproach from the girl.

Signor Ambrogi!

He offered a grunt of apology and tucked the pistol back into the holster. Adriana, pleased to have had such a powerful effect, insisted on coming with him. He turned to Giulia — the child must stay inside, he said. He was wrong, Giulia thought. Adriana should lead them to the soldier. It would be easier that way. Yet she couldn't bring herself to say this. "Ulisse will accompany Signor Ambrogi," she said. The men would go and bring the soldier back while Adriana waited with the women inside.

"No!" Adriana protested.

"Sì!"

"No, no, no!"

"Adriana, Lorenzo and Ulisse will bring the soldier to us. They will carry him here."

"They will kill him."

"They will help him."

He will be brought to La Chiatta dead or alive, Giulia wanted to say. But she managed to add in a gentle voice, "We will wait."

Lorenzo exited just as Luisa returned, and the three women waited with Adriana for the men to bring the dying soldier into the house and for Paolo to return with Doctor Grini. Luisa put a pot of water on to boil, Adriana threw open the shutters, and Signora Ambrogi and Giulia shared a cigarette.

This war had introduced Giulia Nardi to three important pleasures: the pleasure of smoking, which she'd avoided these many years, the pleasure of simple food during a time of scarcity, and a newly heightened sense of what it meant to feel relieved. This morning, though, she'd been too exhausted to eat anything. And now she'd lost the feeling of relief. But at least the pleasure of smoking remained. She drew the cool smoke into her lungs, the sensation making her feel that the inhalation offered a spiritual sustenance, as if she were drawing into her body the ghost of the capable woman she used to be. She'd been waiting so long for the war to end. She could wait a little longer.

Adriana, pacing around the room, muttered something about how she knew, she knew, she knew.

What did she know? Giulia demanded.

She knew, she said sullenly, that she should have kept her soldier a secret!

Her soldier? Giulia thought. Her own, like a sweater or a dog or a fiancé! Like a daughter. Giulia's daughter. Didn't Adriana know what the African soldiers had done to Sergio Canuti's daughter? Of course she didn't know, because Giulia had refused to tell her. Her daughter's ignorance was her mother's fault. Her daughter's kindness was her mother's fault. That her daughter still hadn't learned to be cautious with strangers was her mother's fault.

The good feeling of smoke filling the lungs. The bittersweet memory after the world had complicated the feeling of pure relief. Who was this soldier, anyway? Why had he wandered onto Giulia Nardi's land? Where was his commanding officer?

Rather than reprimand Adriana, Giulia tried to offer reassurance. Her daughter had been right to seek help. If the young man needed medical care, he would receive it under the roof of La Chiatta. Paolo had gone to find a doctor. Lorenzo and Ulisse had gone to find the soldier. Why wasn't anyone returning? And where had her brother-in-law ended up? Giulia wondered. When would Mario give up his fondness for the Germans?

They waited and waited. Adriana stomped her foot and insisted on going to the ravine herself, but Giulia forbade her to leave the room. Signora Ambrogi watched their arguments with obvious disapproval but said nothing. In the kitchen, Luisa took advantage of the boiling water and cooked eggs.

After more than two long hours, Paolo returned without Doctor Grini, who was busy at the hospital and would not be able to come to La Chiatta any time soon. But Paolo had important news to share: rogue battalions were still fighting on Monte Capanne, the port of Marciana Marina was still burning, and twelve hundred Germans had been taken prisoner. And there was more. "Listen to this," he said, lowering his voice as he described how he'd heard a man report that his brother had watched African soldiers roast a German over an open fire and then eat him on the beach at Le Ghiaie! Adriana snorted in disbelief. Giulia shook her head. It was true, Paolo insisted defensively. The man said that the soldiers had made his brother bury the German's bones on the beach. It was true!

What was true? Retold stories changed shape, gained details, lost facts. War was a time when you had to choose: either you believed everything or nothing. What was the name of the man who had told Paolo this story? Paolo didn't know. What was the name of the man's brother? Paolo didn't know.

But consider, Signora Nardi did not say, that in this war the most unbelievable facts were the most likely to be verifiable: more than a quarter million listed on a burial roll for a single city, thousands imprisoned, thousands firebombed, thousands disappearing overnight, their fates mentioned briefly in a newspaper that could be purchased for less than a lira. Giulia, in peacetime a skeptic, believed that the more unbelievable the story, the more probable it was. So many bodies buried in shallow graves that the explosion of gases polluted nearby villages. War spreading like a chain combustion following an original flawed chemical reaction. Bang, bang. Cover your head with your arms. A lot of good that would do. Not even an island was safe anymore. The foolishness of women, the way they gathered the young and the old and the impotent around them, closed the shutters, locked the doors, and waited for the danger to pass.

So far, La Chiatta had been spared. But that was about to change. Signora Nardi couldn't bring a dying soldier into her home without expecting consequences.

Terra Pax

H E BLINKED. AND WHEN HE OPENED HIS EYES HE FOUND himself surrounded by a fog so thick he couldn't see the rail of the ship. He assumed that he was back on his ship. Or maybe he was a prisoner on a spirit ship. He couldn't dismiss this possibility. Somehow he'd known he wasn't heading home. He was heading out to sea — forever out to the sea of purgatory on a ship pirated by spirits. Perhaps he was a spirit. And so was his companion. If he had a companion. He wouldn't have seen the colorless rainbow if his companion hadn't pointed it out to him. Or had Amdu pointed it out to his companion? An arch of pure light pouring through a hole in the foggy canvas. The only clear form in a world of mist. Was it a good sign or a bad sign? Rainbows meant the end of rain. Was this a good thing or a bad thing? And what about a rainbow that had no color?

If he wasn't so tired, he'd have felt perplexed. After the rainbow faded, all he wanted to do was sleep. He did sleep. And later, when he was roused by voices nearby, he pretended to stay asleep. But he wasn't really pretending. He couldn't have opened his eyes even if he'd cared to try, even when whoever-they-were lifted him under his arms and by his ankles and carried him over a surface so uneven that they kept stumbling and dropping him onto the sharp stones. Mon Dieu!

What did any of this have to do with God? Who was God, anyway? Amdu thought about this question while he swung like a goat on a bamboo pole. Had God been the origin of the bright arch? Or had the bright arch been his Embodiment? Either way, the vision must have been a message of some sort. Was it a message of hope or a message of doom? Was a bright arch penetrating the mist a clue to the mystery of the future or to the past? And if the rain ended early, what would happen to the groundnuts?

But truthfully, he enjoyed being carried uphill like a goat on its way to a wedding feast. Unlike the goat, he looked forward to wedding feasts. The most recent marriage, he recalled, was of his youngest uncle, Alfonse Diop, to the daughter of his uncle's second cousin. Amdu had more uncles than he could count. His youngest uncle now had a cousin who was also his mother-in-law. Irèna, who prayed five times a day and distributed half of every animal her husband slaughtered to the poor — pious Irèna, a follower of Cherif Hamallah, had tried to convince Amdu to be a Muslim in his heart. It was his fate, she insisted. A boy with his contemplative nature, his goodness, his purity . . . and didn't he believe in the equality of all souls? Of course he did. But by then, Amdu already had a different plan for himself.

To be carried by two strong men out of the place where he had almost died seemed to him a logical part of the plan. To feel somewhere deep inside him the pleasant jiggling of silent laughter in response to the two grunting, stumbling men. To find himself treated to charitable but imperfect intentions. Not yet worthy of being worshipped, but worthy enough to be delivered from peril.

He blinked. And then he really was awake, swaying once again between the two men. They were white men, if the dry-riverbed color of their skin could be called white. Amdu sneaked searching glances through a squint. As long as they thought he was still without consciousness, they would continue to carry him. He would let them carry him, though from time to time they dropped him and left him on the ground while they took the opportunity to rest. With the grass tickling his face, Amdu heard the gurgling of an upended canteen and foreign speech that was clearly full of complaints. But if they considered themselves superior to the task of carrying a foreign soldier, they were still willing to pick him up again.

On they went across a meadow that smelled smoky and sweet, like a candle flame sputtering out in liquid wax. It must have been early morning, Amdu thought. Or late afternoon. Or it could very well have been midday, with the sun still hidden by the heavy clouds. They could have been walking in place or around in circles. They walked until the clouds finally opened, revealing the blue vault of sky and the sun. They walked from one lifetime into another. And just when Amdu was thinking he should speak, he felt himself moving feet-first up a step. Somehow he knew he was passing through a door. He entered an interior as clear and cool as springwater and was lowered roughly onto a blanket on the floor — a blanket saturated with a fragrance he recognized. He blinked and saw what the fragrance had led him to expect.

"Bonjour, monsieur," said the girl.

"Bonjour, mademoiselle," he replied, which prompted an eruption of curses from the men, who had carried him all the way from the ravine when in fact it appeared that he could have walked on his own perfectly well.

Amid the uproar, the girl smiled at him, and Amdu lazily returned her smile with his own. And then he closed his eyes. When he blinked again, the white mist had returned.

The fresh water was intoxicating. The hens out in the yard chortled a beautiful melody. The clean white cotton sheets shone in the light reflecting off the tile floor. Puffs of clouds floating in the infinite blue outside his open window disappeared into the darkness behind his eyelids. A pungent liquid burned into the wound on his shoulder. Waiting for the pain to reach his fingertips felt like waiting in a cave for the echo of his name.

It didn't occur to him to ask whether the cleanser being used was preferable to simple soap and water. He could endure the pain. It was enough to know that if he was alive now, he would probably be alive tomorrow.

When he sat up, it was evening, the shutters had been closed, and the floor tipped like the rolling deck of his ship. He knew for sure that he wasn't on his ship. But sooner or later he would have to go back. Not until he regained his strength, though. For no clear reason, he felt entitled to take his time recuperating.

He stretched out his legs, noticing only then that he was wearing a striped cotton nightshirt, with nothing beneath. Someone had changed him from his clothes into the nightshirt, bathed him, and properly bandaged the wound on his arm. He no longer stank like the rancid juices of a slaughtered sheep. He felt fresh and clean, privileged, grateful, and awkward.

How long had he been asleep? He tried to piece together the sequence of events. First he'd lost his comrades shortly after disembarking in the marina, then he'd been shot at, then he'd run and run, then he'd met the spoiled princess named Adriana, then he'd run again, then he'd blinked and plunged into a fog so thick he hadn't been able to see his hands.

The wind had risen, dispersing the fog. Now the wind was murmuring from behind the door. "Ssss, Monsieur Amdu. Ssss. Silence. Ssss." Amdu blinked, and the wind appeared in the form of the barefoot girl named Adriana, who'd sneaked inside the room and pressed herself against the wall to keep hidden from anyone passing by.

"Monsieur Amdu, you stay well?" she asked in French.

"I feel better," he said. Watching her, he was struck by two possibilities: the girl had been present when he had been bathed, and she had saved his life.

"Good," she said, and after staring at him for a long moment, studying him in the way that she might have studied a sheet of music before she attempted to play, she slipped from the room again, leaving him alone in the place that seemed unaccountably strange and yet perfect.

And then he woke again to a sound out in the yard that reminded him of watching a laobé in the market in Dakar whittling the end of a wooden stick. He pulled himself upright, stood on wobbly feet, and pushed open the shutter. Beside his window, a stout woman was sweeping the steps leading to the courtyard. He called a greeting to her, "Bonjour," causing her to exclaim and clutch her hand to her throat. She looked as though she'd just swallowed a fly. "Pardon," Amdu said, thinking that he'd lost track of time and mistaken evening for morning and this was why she was surprised. "Bonsoir," he corrected himself. The woman said nothing in reply. She just stared up at Amdu as if she were watching him rise from his grave. Unable to assure her in her own language that he hadn't yet been treated to the joy of resurrection and had merely woken from a long nap, he shrugged and retreated back into his room.

Without the sound of the broom, the sound of humming could be heard coming from another corner of the villa. It was a girl's voice, sweet like pomegranate juice, and it made Amdu want to pluck the string of a molo and dance across the room. Despite the disorienting effects of his fever and the apprehension of the woman in the courtyard, he felt carefree, just as he'd felt walking home from the last day of school holding his Certificat d'Études.

God had been gracious. It was pleasant to acknowledge this and to take pride in having survived not just the dangers of war but the temptation of doubt as well. He had fought his way out of despair and caused no harm to anyone. He had lived before God in all good conscience up to this day. Feeling strengthened by his faith, he gulped the fresh water in the glass that had been left on the table beside his bed. But the deck began to tip again, and he vomited into the chamber pot.

•　　•　　•

He blinked and saw his handsome face reflected in the eyes of the woman he'd seen sweeping the steps. Having offered the wrong greeting earlier, he kept his mouth closed and enjoyed the damp cloth she was pressing against his forehead.

He could tell from her expression that she'd forgiven him for having startled her. Between then and now, she'd grown fond of him. Everyone who came to know Amdu grew fond of him. He couldn't help it. He was like the beer his father made at home — the more you drank, the better it tasted.

Sometimes Amdu worried that he was too handsome for his own good. He had to consider the examples of such devout beauties as Saint Angadrema, who, to avoid marriage, prayed to be made hideous and was bestowed with the gift of leprosy. Or Saint Angela, a pretty young girl who washed her hair with soot. Of course, feminine beauty was the more dangerous kind. Amdu's sisters were too beautiful, and their beauty made them vain. Amdu, in contrast, did not suffer from an excess of vanity. If pressed to divulge his plans, he'd say he intended to use his advantages for the benefit of humanity.

At some point, having nothing else to do, he sang softly to himself, *Kyrie eleison kyrie eleison kyrie eleison et in terra pax* . . .

He blinked, expecting to be surrounded by the sea. But instead he was surprised to find himself in bed, alone in the room where he had gone to sleep, with the shutters open and the sun shining and voices raised in what he interpreted as happy excitement.

He stood on weak legs and made his way out of his room and down a short hallway. Here the floor was a polished blond wood that gleamed beneath his feet. He came to a closed door. Telling himself that when there is happiness on the other side, a closed door deserves to be open, Amdu carefully unlatched and pushed open the door. Through a pantry he saw the hunched shoulders and back of the woman who earlier had been cooling his burning skin with a damp cloth, the same woman who'd been sweeping the steps. Now she was vigorously shaking salt over something laid out on the table — some kind of fish, Amdu guessed from the smell — and behind her the voices of men and other women in the kitchen expressed surprise and joy that the fish had been acquired.

Amdu would have liked to propose that the family's unexpected bounty and their kind treatment of a wounded soldier might have something to do with each other.

"Monsieur Amdu."

He blinked.

"Monsieur Amdu, bonjour. You to wake, please. I am prohibited here. My mother says to me it is not safe in a room with a stranger. But I tell her you are a nice stranger. How do I know this? my mother asks. I do not tell her I know you from the yesterday before the yesterday. Excuse me for not to speak very good French. I study French in school. I like to learn to be more good to speak French. Do you understand me?"

"Oui, bien sur."

"Please you do not tell my mother you meet me yesterday before yesterday. If you tell her, she wants to know why not I say I meet you the first time yesterday. Do you understand me?"

"Oui."

"We have a secret."

"D'accord."

"And maybe you tell me of you, yes? Good. But now, no. Later is possible. Now I must go. I am content you to be better. Au revoir, Monsieur Amdu."

"Au revoir, mademoiselle."

At some point over the course of the day he heard a man out in the courtyard exclaim, "Che bel' mar' oggi!" He wondered whether these words, whatever they meant, had something to do with the war.

How long had he been drifting in and out of fever? Amdu had lost track of time. When had the girl named Adriana said they'd met? The yesterday before yesterday, which would make today the to-morrow after tomorrow. Something like that. And why was a bald man with a thick black mustache tipped with gray suddenly stand-ing in his room and lifting his water glass, peering at it as if he didn't believe that the liquid was just water? What was he telling Amdu when he said, "Scemo!"?

"Bonjour, monsieur."

At the sound of Amdu's voice, the man slammed the glass onto the table, splashing water over the rim. "Che cazzo —" he hissed, then whirled around and strode from the room.

Apparently, he didn't yet know Amdu well enough to like and trust him.

"Monsieur Amdu?"

"Oui? Bonjour, Adriana."

"Do you like pignoli? Ecco. I bring you good pignoli from our island. You are hungry, yes? Very well. Eat pignoli, and then I bring you more. Maybe the little fish we name acciughe also. We have acciughe now. It is war, you know, and we have not much to eat. But we have more good fortune than someone other. We are a house with good fortune. It is good fortune for you to find us. Someone other would not be good fortune. You be better, yes? My mother says to me you go back to your, how do you say, soldiers all together? Pow, pow. When you be better you go back. Do not be better very fast. The war is still a war, and the peace is not completely arrived. You be very happy here instead of in the war. You stay as much time as you want. Oh, someone comes."

"Wait!"

"I go. Au revoir."

His head ached, and he was alone again. He remembered once overhearing his comrades report that when Italians were sick, they drank as medicine a soup made from an eel found in the body of a drowned person. He remembered reading in a textbook about how Italians didn't like to give up their dead, so they mummified bodies by brushing them with arsenic. Lying in the heavy darkness, feeling newly dazed by the unfamiliarity of his situation and temporarily uninterested in prayer, he wondered at the oddity of this country. And then he wondered what he would say if he ever had an audience with the pope.

Yet however unlikely the circumstances in which he'd found himself, he had only to insist that it was true, and it would be true. It was true that a wounded Senegalese rifleman had sought refuge on the estate of a family who ate salted fish. It was true that a young man named Amdu Diop had interrupted his education in order to serve in the military under French command, following the example of his grandfather, who had attained the rank of general. And it was true that Amdu knew himself to be blessed with at least the potential ability to repair the world through the action of miracles.

Put all these truths together and you got the absolute truth of what Amdu knew to be ongoing experience, which included, besides his own self in its present condition, an Elban princess named Adriana, a man with a graying mustache, and a stout woman who tied the laces of her apron in a bow beneath her bosom.

"Excuse me, what is this?" he asked, holding his spoon poised above the bowl. Pale tentacles, yawning seashells, and green shoots like grass gone to seed floated in the broth. Amdu was reminded of what he might find if he'd overturned a rock on the bank of the Felu.

"Cacciucco," the woman said. This regal woman, who spoke French perfectly and wore her hair in a tight glossed bun, was new to him. The big-bosomed woman in the apron stood beside her.

"The soup is made with eel?" he asked gently. He didn't want to be rude, but he also felt a need to identify the ingredients in the soup that was being offered as nourishment.

"You don't like eel?"

"Pardon me, please. Where did you find the eel for this soup?"

"Where does anyone find an eel, my dear boy? At the top of a tree, of course." Then the woman said something in Italian to the stout woman, who cupped her hand over her mouth and snorted with laughter.

Based upon this knowledge, Amdu could only conclude that

the people of Elba did not deserve to be blamed for their oddity. Rather, he would blame this island itself — a cursed place where toads grew as big as warthogs, princesses were poorly educated, and eels lived at the tops of trees, unless they lived inside corpses that didn't rot because they'd been brushed with arsenic.

As grateful as he was to be welcomed as a guest inside this grand palace, Amdu felt a private yearning to be back in familiar surroundings, in his own bed in his own room.

"Eat, monsieur. Our soup will make you strong. Eat."

"Oui, madame. Merci."

"Eau. Acqua."

"Acqua."

"Homme. Uomo."

"Uomo."

"Ciao."

"Chow."

"Voi visitare la Villa Demidoff?"

"Pardon?"

"Niente. Rien."

"Niente."

"Tu parli bene, Amdu."

"Tooporlybenné, moi."

"Sì."

"Arrivederci."

"Arrivadarsee, signorina."

He could say that he was born in 1927 in Dakar, into a privileged métis family. His great-grandfather had been a French commissioner under Governor Louis Faidherbe. His grandfather had been an officer in the Tirailleurs. His father was a surgeon. His mother was an educated woman who had lived for three years in Paris. Amdu was the eldest child, with two younger sisters. A brother had died in infancy. Unlike most Senegalese, the family spoke French at home. Following the completion of his elementary education at a French Catholic school, Amdu had attended a three-year course of studies at the Lycée Van Vollenhover. He planned to continue his studies in medicine at the university in Cairo.

Or he could say that on his thirteenth birthday, he went fishing with his uncle, who owned a fleet of dugout canoes. They fished for mullet in the shallow water south of the port of Dakar. Afterward, Amdu rode in the truck that was transporting the entire dugout catch to the wharves in Dakar. The truck broke down. Having been encouraged by his mother through his early childhood to fashion faith into a belief that had practical uses, Amdu prayed to God to preserve the fish. His prayer was heard. After sitting in the back of a truck in the hot sun for seven hours, the fish did not spoil. This was when Amdu first became aware of his potential holiness.

Or he could cite his age, his height in centimeters, and his weight in kilos just to prove that he existed in a time and place.

"You are feeling better, Monsieur Amdu?"

It was the woman who had told him that the eels of Elba lived at the tops of trees. She sat in a chair beside his bed. He wondered how long she had been sitting there. Putting aside her embroidery, she poured fresh water into his glass.

"Oui, madame. I feel better."

"You have a fever still. But it is much improved. The infection has been contained, we think."

"How long have I been here? A long time, I suppose. You have been very kind to me."

"You arrived yesterday and stayed through the night. And now today. We will make you strong again. And when you are strong we will take you to your post. We have made inquiries and understand that you serve with the French forces."

"They know I am here?"

"Monsieur Amdu, don't worry, they do not know yet that you are here with us. But why shouldn't they know? Have you done something wrong? Are you in trouble?"

"Pardon me for telling you this — they are not all heroes, my comrades."

"I understand. But you should not let them abandon you."

"They are leaving the island?"

"Soon."

"The war is over?"

"The Germans have been defeated."

"That is good."

"It is good. Now you must eat and drink to strengthen yourself. Luisa will bring you a bowl of her persata."

"What is it, persata? Is it another soup made with eels?"

"No — there are no eels in persata, Monsieur Amdu. Are you afraid of eels?"

"I am afraid of eels only when they live outside the sea, madame."

She smiled and picked up her needlework. In the silence that followed he heard the sound of the piano.

"The girl — she is your daughter, yes? She plays the piano." It was a fact meant to stand as appreciation. Even though she played the piano poorly, at least she played. That was better than Amdu could say about himself.

"She plays the piano," the woman agreed.

As Amdu watched her thin hands working at the embroidery, he was reminded of watching his mother string beads onto a loom. It amused him to think that someday in the future he would be watching his mother string beads again, and he would be reminded of this Elban woman pressing a needle through cloth.

His white shirt, bunched into his belted trousers, billowed like a sail. His hair smelled of pine, his skin of lavender. As inexplicably as it had peaked, his fever had abated; the wound on his arm was healing with unbelievable speed. Despite the unfamiliarity of his surroundings, he needed no assurances that everything was connected. He felt like a man who'd been shipwrecked on an island where each element, however strange in itself, was essential to the whole. *See one, say one, know one,* as the poet Shaykh Mahmud Shabistari sang centuries ago.

"Viens," the girl directed. "Come with me please, Monsieur Amdu."

"D'accord, madamoiselle." Barefoot, he followed her across the room to the window. "Guarda," she directed, pointing to the end of the sill. "Eccola." Between the rainspout and the wooden ledge, brown doves had built a nest, and now the female roosted while the male looked on, perched on the top edge of the shutter.

"Oiseux."

"Uccelli."

She said something about how the birds had built their nest the night before Amdu had been brought to La Chiatta. She spoke with rising excitement and at one point touched his wrist to be certain that she had his attention, then she reached along the sill, shooing away the bird, and scooped one of the little cream eggs from the nest, displaying it in her palm like a valuable gem. "Regards," she whispered.

Amdu couldn't contain his amusement at the girl's wonder. All it took was a bird's egg to delight her. Her future husband would find her easy to please. He laughed aloud at the thought, and the sound of his voice startled the girl, causing her to jerk and let the egg roll from her hand.

Her gasp contained sorrow and innocence and anger and impatience and guilt. A dove's egg was falling to the ground — an ordinary event to anyone else, but in this girl's privileged life a dove's egg had an exceptional value, which was about to be reduced to nothing. Amdu sensed the future in an instant. The girl would collapse in tears, blaming herself for the loss, then blaming him, demanding that Amdu match her unhappiness with his own.

As Amdu blinked, he told himself that the egg must not crack. Unhappiness must be avoided. Closing his eyes to the egg plunging toward the cobble, he murmured a prayer for it to survive intact. With absolute faith, he requested the exchange of what would happen with what should happen — life instead of death — a request as sensible as it was impossible or, perhaps, as possible as it was ridiculous.

He opened his eyes, and what he saw he couldn't immediately comprehend. Did the velocity of the egg decrease, so a fall that should have been almost instantaneous now was stretching over several seconds? Did the egg actually hover above the stone and then lower gently, as though being set down by an invisible hand? Had time slowed? Did the girl look at the egg, then look at Amdu's startled face, then look at the egg, then look again at Amdu? Before she ran outside to pick up the egg and return it to its nest, did she whisper urgently, "Merci, Amdu," as though she really believed that what she'd just seen had not followed the laws of nature and Amdu Diop of the Ninth French Colonial Division was responsible for a miracle?

WHEN MARIO TONIETTI RETURNED to La Chiatta, he was comforted to see that the routines of the estate had resumed. Driving toward the villa in a car he'd borrowed from Dino, he caught sight of Ulisse and one of his boys turning over the soil around the olive trees. On the hill to the west, he saw two of Lorenzo's cows pegged out to graze. And after he stepped from the car into the courtyard, he smelled the good, garlicky fragrance of a broth left to simmer for hours.

Giulia greeted him at the door, offering her stony face for him to kiss. Mario hoped she'd be the one to initiate some sort of reparation, if not an apology, then at least a mild expression of concern for him. But instead she asked for confirmation that the entirety of the German troops had either been taken prisoner or retreated from the island — a question that Mario perceived was filled with resentment.

But there was more to her resentment than a political disagreement. There was the shared memory of their brief courtship, enjoyed in their youth, and the rupture that remained unresolved. Without any apparent cause, Giulia had become suspicious and broken off the romance, expelling Mario from her life with such indifference that he could only assume her earlier love for him had been no more than a performance — artful, confident, and false.

Though he'd gone on to marry her younger sister, his anger

toward Giulia never disappeared entirely. Neither did his love for her, though he wouldn't speak of it. His manner with her was brisk and formal — as artful a performance as hers had been, and Mario succeeded in perfecting it over the years, convincing everyone, except himself, that Giulia Nardi meant nothing to him.

He did not bother to hide his affection for his niece, however, especially after Teresa's death, when his solitude became a burden. And it was the thought of Adriana — her innocence and vulnerability disguised by her stubborn pride — that stirred him to outrage after Giulia told him that a Senegalese soldier was asleep in one of La Chiatta's beds.

"An African! What are you thinking, Giulia? We are still at war!"

"He has a fever."

"He could have a bullet in his heart for all we should care. He must leave immediately!"

"Please do not interfere, Mario. I have invited him to stay with us. He will leave when he is ready to leave."

They were still standing in the front hall; a rustling around the corner indicated that someone, probably Adriana, was listening to their conversation. Mario lowered his voice but formed his words slowly, precisely, so Adriana would be able to hear.

"If you haven't yet heard the news, Corrado is dead. My friend Corrado. Do you want to know how he died? Of course you don't want to know, but I will tell you anyway. Those Africans, they drenched him in petrol and threw a match on him. Corrado is dead. Maybe your invalid soldier had something to do with the bonfire in Corrado's yard? No? Yes? You cannot say for sure one way or the other. What are you thinking, Giulia? You are putting your daughter at terrible risk by playing nurse to an African. These soldiers who have come in the name of liberation — they despise us."

"I am very sorry about Corrado." She said this gently, with a tinge of pity in her voice.

"And yet you will continue to defend his murderers!"

"I don't defend their crimes. But that they have reason to doubt the purpose of their sacrifice . . ."

"Sacrifice, you call it!"

"They can see for themselves that we have not resisted German rule. They can see that there is a fine line between occupation and collaboration."

"In your eyes, only in your eyes, Giulia, to survive one's enemies is the same as collaborating with them." Mario wanted to rip off his shirt and show her his bandages as proof that he was no collaborator. The Germans had done this to him. Or the British had done this to him. Or the French Colonials had done this to him. It didn't much matter who had hurt him. What mattered was that he could have died. If he had died, Giulia Nardi would have been obliged to join the many Elbans who would praise Mario Tonietti for his heroism, his charity, and his famous honesty.

"Mario." Giulia said his name with some tenor of affection — real affection, he believed. "You have tried to help. But in this war, kindness has an affiliation. Don't worry" — she silenced him before he could speak — "I don't blame you. And I don't blame the Senegalese boy sleeping under this roof. He is a good boy, Mario. I am sure of it. He is well-educated and well-mannered. He intends no harm. But how could he harm us? He has no weapon. He is weak from his ordeal. Anyway, soon he will leave us, and you can forget him. Now, come in, sit down. Tell me about Corrado."

Following her around the corner, he only pretended to be surprised to find Adriana standing by a table, brushing brown petals into her hand. The roses were over a week old, but no one had thought to throw them out.

"Adriana, my vain little owl," Mario said, drawing her into his embrace.

"Uncle." Her voice was muffled by his shirt. "Uncle!" As she pushed herself free, the petals fell to the floor.

"Good morning, beautiful girl."

"Uncle, what happened to your friend?"

"Corrado?"

"Yes."

"Corrado is with the angels."

"Why was he killed?"

"Mario . . ." Giulia spoke his name to caution him against saying anything more in Adriana's presence.

"There is an African under this roof, yes? Why don't you ask him what happened to Corrado?"

"Mario, please, that's enough."

Mario and Giulia exchanged icy stares. Then Mario shrugged in concession. "Little owl, you shouldn't be listening to talk about death. You should be concerned with life. Thank God nothing happened to you. But you are not safe as long as you have to share your home with a soldier. Come stay with me in town. There will be a dance tonight in Piazza Repubblicà. La Gargotta has opened its doors again. Will you dance with me? My clever girl. Just like your mother, you will make all the boys miserable."

With a glance, he saw that his last comment earned the twitch of a smile from Giulia, a woman who ordinarily existed in her body as though it were a uniform, with every action an expression of duty. She had grown rigid, uncompromising in her goodness. But Mario was pleased to find that even she liked to be reminded of her beauty.

"I'm glad the Germans are gone," Adriana declared.

"Everyone is glad," Mario agreed, taking his niece by the wrist and leading her across the room. "Each day the war moves closer to its end," he said, "one liberation after another. We can say to ourselves, We are free again. We will return to work, and you will return to school. And someday soon, Adriana Nardi will be famous!"

"Why will I be famous?"

"Because you will be the niece of the mayor! Now I would like to hear your music. Play something for me, little owl. I will sit here and listen. That will be pure happiness for me. Dear Giulia, sit beside me and listen to your daughter play. We are alive and well. This is reason to celebrate."

Later, he found the soldier lying with closed eyes on his bed in a guest room, breathing softly through slightly parted lips. He looked too young to be a soldier — too naive and tranquil. Only his knotted forehead suggested deeper thought, as if he were working through some endless calculation in his sleep. Or maybe — more likely — he was dreaming about the crimes he'd committed, the girls he'd raped and the men he'd set on fire. Mario waited, listening carefully in case the soldier whispered something revealing or incriminating. He thought for a moment that he recognized him — a startling, inexplicable mistake. Mario couldn't have recognized the boy, for he was the first Senegalese infantryman he'd ever seen up close.

The liberation of Elba was over, two thousand Germans and a few hundred Italian Fascists were either in retreat or in captivity, and the French Colonials would be deployed to the mainland soon enough. But here in a sunny room in La Chiatta, one of the liberators was taking his time recovering from a scratch on his arm while he enjoyed the unearned luxuries of clean sheets, a bright, clean room, and fresh springwater. Clearly, he considered himself deserving, and he was too innocent to consider how vulnerable he was, alone and unarmed. How easy it would have been to clamp a pillow over his face and suffocate him. Even easier: stirring poison into the water in his drinking glass.

Mario picked up the glass and studied it in the sunlight. It hadn't occurred to him that the soldier was only pretending to sleep. But when the boy suddenly opened his eyes and said with startling ease, "Bonjour, monsieur," Mario knew that his distrust had been warranted. The soldier was a charlatan, taking advantage of Giulia Nardi's wealth. Maybe all he wanted was the experience of luxury. Or maybe he wanted something more. Perfectly capable of getting up and walking out of La Chiatta back to his regiment, the soldier preferred to take his time and enjoy himself while he persuaded others that he wouldn't survive without their help.

Mario wasn't fooled by the soldier's deception, no more than he'd been fooled by the false reasoning that had gotten the world into its current predicament. All along he'd been convinced that power succeeded in maintaining itself only when it resisted the temptation to expand. Mussolini had understood this best when he'd put the emphasis on order rather than on conquest. "In a certain sense," he had famously propounded, "one might say that the policeman preceded the professor." Mario would have liked to remind him of this now: his police agencies had been assigned to watch over the nation, and even if Il Duce had spent a good portion of his day lying on his bed leafing through old magazines, as rumors suggested, he'd given the impression that he never slept and never wavered in his ability to govern absolutely.

The mistake for all sides came with the ambition to expand the domain of power, an ambition that a native Elban like Mario Tonietti, who rarely traveled to the mainland, couldn't share. An island was its own empire, and the inhabitants who prospered were the ones who accepted the confinement. A little island, and the sea surrounding. Wasn't this enough?

It was more than enough — more than Elbans deserved, according to the Germans, who had dared to claim the island for themselves. And now the Allies had arrived, posing as saviors. But the Elbans didn't need to be saved. They simply needed to be left alone.

After securing a promise from his niece that she wouldn't go anywhere near the African soldier, Mario set out to see for himself the damage in Marciana Marina, where, according to Dino's report, the fires had been brought under control. As he drove west, he told himself that he'd return to La Chiatta and send the African packing before the day was over.

WHEN SOMEONE EXACTS FROM YOU a promise you don't intend to keep, you shouldn't just cross the fingers of your left hand behind your back. You should cross the fingers of both hands, and your toes, as well — the big toe overlapping like a cat's paw over a mouse. And you should make sure you open your eyes wide when you nod.

Mi 'spiace, Zio Mario. Sorry. Adriana was not innocent, and she was not telling the truth when she promised to stay away from the African. Why would she stay away from him when she considered the soldier named Amdu a friend? Better than a friend. He was as good as a long-lost brother, as interesting and deserving and sometimes just as annoying, like when he had pretended to be dying after she'd found him in the ravine. Brothers played all sorts of dirty tricks. Maybe he was her actual brother — her birth mother's child by another man, born on the continent of Africa and adopted by Senegalese parents who never bothered to tell him about his origins.

This freedom to concoct relations was the best thing about being a foundling. Adriana could pretend to be related to a Russian czar. Or to the exiled emperor Napoleon. Or to the African soldier who had fallen into the vineyard on June 18, the second day of the liberation. It was possible that Amdu and Adriana were related. And if something was even slightly possible, then she could imagine a case for it as a probable fact.

Yet she wouldn't necessarily have chosen Amdu to be her brother. He was très gentil, but he was also molto strano — very strange indeed. The way he'd sparkled in the distance when Adriana had first seen him tumble from the top of the wall. The influence he'd had over her since she'd met him, as if he could control her thoughts. Why hadn't she been terrified of him? A foreigner, a soldier, a black man — he would have frightened any other Elban girl. But Adriana wasn't like other Elban girls. Che coraggio! She'd have a story of her own to tell when the war was over, though first she needed to know more about one of its main characters. Who was he? Why had he run away from his regiment? And what had really been the source of the glow emanating from the ravine?

Adriana waited for her uncle's car to disappear up the drive before she went to the pantry to fill a bowl with pine nuts. Luisa, who was conferring with Ulisse at the kitchen table, saw her with the bowl but didn't bother to question her. Only Paolo interfered. He stopped her in the hall and reminded her of the promise she'd made just moments earlier.

She didn't say that she had already visited the soldier alone, in secret. Instead, she pointed out that her mother had concluded that their Senegalese guest was not to be feared — she'd said as much to Mario — and so she wouldn't mind if Adriana took him a few pignoli to nibble.

Paolo tried to block her way. When he frowned, his thick eyebrows met, like two hedgehogs nuzzling, Adriana thought, and she laughed aloud.

"Why do you always laugh at me?" he demanded.

"Because you are ridiculous," she replied, pushing past him.

"And you are, you are . . ." His inability to complete the sentence amused her, but this time she stifled her laugh, for she was realizing the meaning of his anger. Luisa's nephew, Paolo, the son of a fisherman, was jealous of Adriana's attention to Amdu!

"Tu sei . . ." Adriana echoed. You are . . . jealous. She couldn't bring herself to say it. But she knew that Paolo must have heard the echo as pure mockery. You are, you are. You are ridiculous, Paolo. You are a fisherman's son and the nephew of the cook. You are ordinary.

Whatever the soldier named Amdu was, whatever his origins and affiliations, he was not ordinary. It didn't take any unaccountable phenomena to convince Adriana of this.

Later, after she'd dropped the dove's egg and Amdu had murmured some hocus-pocus in French and the egg, which should have shattered, had settled intact on the cobblestone, Adriana came to a conclusion about her soldier. He was a stregone — a witch doctor. Un buon stregone, hopefully. A stregone who wanted to help rather than harm.

She had never before met anyone who combined opposite qualities in such a serene demeanor. He was young and old at the same time, robust and frail, apprehensible and mysterious, earthy and sophisticated. He could, when necessary, suspend the law of gravity. He could radiate a soothing light. He could perform any magic that suited the occasion.

Adriana's willingness to believe that the soldier was a witch doctor had nothing to do with her belief in God. Nor did she equate Amdu's strangeness with exoticism. There was something quite familiar about him, as though he were someone she'd long ago prepared herself to meet — not just a brother but a twin, a mixed-up version of herself, related to her in spirit if not in blood. Thinking back to the moment when she'd first met him, when he'd grabbed her and kept her from running home when La Chiatta was full of angry soldiers, she remembered feeling surprised at herself for so quickly relenting, as if even before she knew him she sensed that she had reason to trust him.

But though she liked to imagine a connection, in the long run she preferred the more logical explanation: she trusted the soldier because he was obviously trustworthy. His goodness was indicated in his radiance, his gentle voice, the graceful way he nodded. On an island full of all sorts of coarse, common minerals, he was as rare as the small diamond a German soldier claimed to have found on Volterraio back in February.

Adriana felt brave and justified in her affection for the African. But she wasn't without some reservations. A soldier from the Allied forces had wandered uninvited onto the Nardi estate and needed rest and nourishment before he returned to the war. Everyone else at La Chiatta treated this as no more than a temporary inconvenience. But in Adriana's estimation, Amdu wasn't an ordinary soldier, and his effect would be profound.

Even when she'd been aware of no more than a shadow in the boathouse, she had been drawn to him. Without reason, she had become progressively convinced that some element of her destiny involved him. And in the hours since he'd arrived at La Chiatta, Adriana had come to believe that her guest had magical abilities. But this same belief stirred in her confusion and doubt. Why did she care so much about this stranger? Had he cast a spell on her? What did he want?

It wasn't enough that he had saved an egg from smashing. She wanted him to prove himself in other ways, to demonstrate once and for all that he was as much as or more than she believed him to be. She wanted to be sure about the nature of his magic and know that she was right to trust him.

The egg had dropped through the thick pudding of air onto the stones below Amdu's window, and that's where Adriana found it. Cupping it in her hands, she was surprised by its warmth, like the deep warmth of a cat that had been sleeping all afternoon in the sun. She thought for a moment that she would like to keep the egg for her collection. But Amdu was already leaning over the sill, stretching his arm to her, so she handed him the egg and watched as he carefully returned it to the nest.

What more could she ask of him? She had so many questions — she didn't know where to begin. She wanted to know more about his past, his family, his education, and, most of all, the nature of his magic. She wanted him to assure her that she shouldn't doubt him.

She wandered back inside and found her mother going over accounts at her desk in the library. Adriana picked up a book and tried to read, but she was too restless. She took a seat on the piano bench and began to play with her right hand the opening measures of a simple march. It was the only portion of the piece she could remember, and rather than find the music and play the whole piece, she kept playing the same notes over again until she grew bored. As she played, she wondered what memories were passing through the soldier's mind right then. How could she know what he was thinking?

She stopped playing and wandered downstairs to the kitchen, expecting to be waylaid there by Paolo. But the kitchen was deserted, so Adriana continued through the pantry and along the hall to Amdu's room.

From behind the door, left slightly ajar, she heard the rasping sound of her soldier clearing his throat. Once he regained his voice, he began to hum. It took a few moments for Adriana to recognize that the melody he hummed was the march she'd just played, the same tune note for note, beat for beat, as though in echo. It was her song, and he was humming it — surely this counted for something. She peeked around the edge of the door and was pleased to see that instead of lying lazily in bed he was standing at the window. His shirt — one of the fine cotton relics that had once belonged to her grandfather — puffed around his slender body as he extended a handful of pine nuts and beckoned to the doves to come eat.

Here, then, was the opportunity for the soldier named Amdu to prove himself once and for all. If he was as pure and good as Adriana wanted to believe, the doves would eat from his hand. If there was reason to be suspicious, the birds would refuse him.

She waited quietly. The male bird perched on the edge of the sill, cocking its head anxiously. Its neck swelled, and it made a purring sound, almost in response to Amdu's humming. It hopped closer to his cupped hand.

With the late-afternoon sun lighting the room, the marble floor shining, the world silent except for Amdu's soft humming and the bird's reply, it seemed to Adriana that she had accidentally entered a place where she didn't belong, her own home made new and strangely beautiful. Even more than she wanted to know the result of Amdu's effort, she found herself longing to stand there forever, outside of time. The sound of humming, the bird hopping forward centimeter by centimeter, the temptation of pine nuts, everything within the room in a perfect arrangement, everything as it should be, as if all of history were culminating in this quiet moment, the wars throughout the world were over, and spring would never end.

But she was wise enough to know even in the midst of it that the scene was too delicate to last. Although the pop of a jeep backfiring on the drive startled her, she wasn't really surprised — unlike Amdu, who jumped into the air, bumping the bowl of pine nuts and spilling it onto the floor. The bird flapped away. Adriana rushed into the room. She had to be quick about it or whatever was about to happen would prevent her from receiving an adequate answer to the one question she wanted to ask.

"Why have you come here?" Pourquoi? Perché?

Voices rumbling in an indistinguishable language filled the courtyard. Doors opened and closed throughout the villa while fists pounded on wood. The war had returned to La Chiatta.

Looking baffled, Amdu said, "I was trying to feed the birds."

Adriana had thought she needed proof that she could trust this foreign soldier. But she didn't need proof to know that she wanted to be near him, to belong where he belonged, not to adore him in any familiar way, not to have actual contact with him — she was too independent, too haughty, too disdainful of common infatuation, and, despite her estimation of her own intelligence and her great maturity, too much of a child — but to exist within an approximate space, this would have been enough, to take up space near him, in sight of him, or at least within hearing distance, to watch him, to listen to him, to be close enough to assume that he was listening to her.

PEOPLE STEP BACK from the curb to let the ambulance pass. Taxis sidle into adjacent lanes. A bus slows to a standstill and then remains unmoving at the light. The ambulance edges around it, the siren echoed by a police car traveling uptown a block away.

To the medic calling in the details over the radio, Mrs. Rundel is just another nameless female who may or may not survive respiratory arrest. But she would be pleased to hear that he estimates her age at sixty. Though her blood pressure is falling and her pulse is weak and rapid, Mrs. Rundel is thought to be a mere sixty years old!

In the time it has taken for her to be strapped in and the ambulance to start on its way to the hospital, the strangers who collected around Mrs. Rundel on the train have dispersed. The financial adviser, who didn't linger at the scene, is already entering his office building on Thirty-seventh Street. The woman who performed CPR is in the restroom in Penn Station, splashing water on her face. The lawyer and the software designer are shaking hands outside the east exit of Madison Square Garden. The student is in the coffee shop at the end of the lower-level corridor leading to the Long Island Railway. When asked what he wants, he shrugs, and the woman in line behind him calls out her own order. The man who was talking on his cell phone to an answering machine is standing in the waiting area, staring at the knuckles of his fists. Only the Polish woman has stayed behind on the platform to help the transit police with their report, describing to them in thorough detail all that she witnessed on the train regarding Mrs. Rundel's collapse, though she's unable to help the police with the important matter of identification and is unaware that Mrs. Rundel's purse was stolen.

No one saw the thief making off with the purse, though because of the dominating fragrance of her Chanel perfume, many passengers noticed her when she boarded the train in Newark. She is a short woman, under five feet tall but raised a couple of inches by the heels of her pumps, in her late twenties, carrying a bulky lambskin shoulder bag and wearing a knee-length skirt and brown jacket — a drab but expensive suit suggesting that she is a young attorney or perhaps a novice associate in a consulting firm.

She'd been among the passengers standing at the end of the crowded car on the short stretch between Newark and Penn Station. She appeared confident and cheery, and whenever her eyes happened to meet the glance of another passenger, man or woman, she immediately smiled. She seemed eager — too eager — to start up a conversation, and yet when the man beside her asked her where she'd bought her handsome bag, she turned away without replying, the smile frozen on her face, her eyes containing a hint of fear but her poise indicating that she was contemptuous of anyone who dared even the mildest come-on.

As the train pulled into Penn Station, passengers began to wonder about the confusion at the other end of the car. Word spread that a woman was having a heart attack. But since the aisle was clogged with the people who immediately gathered around Mrs. Rundel, most of the other passengers realized they would only get in the way if they tried to help, and they began filing out the opposite door.

The woman in the brown suit, however, squeezed backward through the line of passengers and found a position between two seats where she could observe the action. Looking down at the woman bent over Mrs. Rundel, she saw the pronounced black roots at the dye mark in her hair. She observed that one of the men standing nearby was wearing a Rolex watch. Across the aisle, she noticed the red corner of a wallet peeking out of a purse that had been left open on the seat. She started to move in that direction. But then she felt her right shoe kick against a strap and with a glance saw another purse — a fatter, more promising purse — on the floor.

Squatting nimbly on legs thin and strong from years of ballet classes, the woman in the brown suit swooped down, lifted the purse, bunched it between her bag and her chest, and slipped away, following the other passengers out of the train and onto the platform, joining the crowd funneling up the narrow staircase.

Now, locked in a stall in the lower-level women's bathroom, she examines the contents of the purse item by item, depositing what she doesn't want in the box for used sanitary napkins. She is disappointed to find only forty-three dollars in the wallet. But it is thrilling to run her forefinger along the embossed print of the credit card.

She stuffs the purse itself into her own bag and exits the stall. The sinks are in use, and while she waits her turn, she tries and fails to look at her reflection in the mirror over the shoulder of a woman who is vigorously washing her face. Staring at the back of the woman's head, the thief notices with distaste the black roots. She is shocked to recognize the woman from the train who was trying to revive the woman who'd collapsed.

The thief leaves the restroom without washing her hands. While the ambulance carrying Mrs. Rundel is nudging through the intersection at Twenty-ninth Street, the woman in the brown suit is clacking in her pumps toward the subway and the line that will take her over to Bloomingdale's on Lexington.

Later, Mrs. Rundel will share the disbelief of family and friends at the thought of a stranger who was desperate enough, or maybe just sufficiently coldhearted, to steal a purse from an old woman who'd passed out on a train. But she will also feel a sharp regret that she would never know the other individuals, the ones she'd ignored or chosen to avoid, who tried to save her life.

In fact, they did save her life. Although the aid they offered was not entirely appropriate for her condition, their intentions have left an impression. Even without full awareness, she continues to feel the effects of their fumbling attempts to revive her. They pushed and pounded and breathed for her. They did what they could to help — the memory of this is perceived by her body as a physical fact, like a surge of adrenaline prompted by astonishment. At a time when she needed help, they tried to help her. And though when she wakes she'll have no memory of their efforts, somehow she understands that they've challenged her to help herself.

Bracing herself, Mrs. Rundel prepares to cough. In order to cough she needs to breathe on her own. She takes a deep breath. She doesn't need or want to cough, but she coughs nonetheless. She breathes again. She coughs again. She keeps coughing. And though in the netherworld of nerve impulses and sensory signals she can't yet tell whether the action will be productive, she is pleased to sense the determination.

Mrs. Rundel keeps coughing simply so she can keep hearing the sound. She coughs out the airway. The medic lifts off the oxygen mask. Taking her for a Latina, he begins speaking gently to the old woman in Spanish, explaining to her where she is.

Welcome

MONSIEUR LIEUTENANT — YOUR INFORMANT MUST BE MIS-taken. There are no renegade soldiers hiding in my home. What would I want with a renegade soldier? How would I feed him? I hardly have enough food for my own household. We are nine altogether, counting the gardener and his family. Imagine adding a soldier to the group. Impossible! If it weren't for the bounty of the sea outside our back gate, the residents of La Chiatta would be eating nothing but bread. Even bread is a luxury during a time of war. We're lucky to have a sufficient provision of flour. And wine — it's true that there is plenty of wine. When you live in the middle of a vineyard, there is always wine. And the early crop from the fruit trees. Sour peaches and plums, wine and bread. There was a wheel of pecorino as well, but it's almost down to the rind. You can't feed a renegade soldier with a cheese rind.

Anyway, why would a member of the liberating army want to hide from his comrades? The struggle has been successful, even if it hasn't gone exactly according to the plan. Although the war isn't over yet, the end is in sight. The Germans are on the defensive, their supply lines strangled. Their occupied territories are shrinking and their propaganda campaigns are faltering. The Allied forces are celebrating in Palermo, in Naples, in Rome, and in Portoferraio's Piazza Repubblicà. Now it's just a matter of following the effort to its inevitable conclusion. If you're a soldier on the winning side, you'll be going home soon. Surely the French Colonials understand this. Why would a soldier want to run away from a war when the war is almost over?

But really, Monsieur Lieutenant, what does a woman know about war? I may know a great deal about such diverse subjects as embroidery, geology, and the cultivation of vines. I can speak three languages with fluency. And I know something about the history of this island, as well. For instance, I can tell you that the emperor Napoleon once dined at La Chiatta. Apparently, he ate nothing but a small piece of beef and a bowl of boiled peas, and he brought his own claret to drink! But the wars in Europe and Asia — I don't pretend to understand these wars, Monsieur Lieutenant. Or even how the island of Elba figures in the scheme. Why does anyone bother with this little bauble? It's said that Elba was formed with the rest of the surrounding archipelago when Venus's necklace broke and the jewels scattered in the sea. Will the victors gather up the jewels and string them together again? Is this what they intend? And then what? What do the Allied forces want with a pretty necklace?

Monsieur Lieutenant, you have come looking for one of your own. Go ahead, order your men to search the villa. I keep everything of value on shelves in full view. I have no need for secrets. Secrets leave a map of wrinkles upon a face. Please observe, if you will, how at ease I am, with my forehead as smooth as the inside of a seashell. Pardon my vanity, but I want to be sure that Monsieur Lieutenant believes me when I say that I have nothing to hide.

A soldier is missing. There is evidence that he has deliberately run away. Why has he run away? And what is the basis of the charge? Who advised Monsieur Lieutenant to come to La Chiatta in the first place? Does he know that he's not the first officer to come to La Chiatta to gather up errant troops? It's hardly worth commenting upon the fact that the Ninth French Colonial Division is not a model of military discipline.

There are so many stories circulating about the Allied forces, so many witnesses offering contradictory testimony that I'm not sure what to believe. Did the soldiers douse a wounded man in petrol and light him on fire? Did they murder the daughter of Sergio Canuti? Did they cook and eat a German prisoner on the beach at Le Ghiaie? The more lurid the story, the easier it is to concoct. But if some things are easily invented as fantasies, doesn't it follow that they are easily enacted, especially during a time of war?

Monsieur Lieutenant has not come to La Chiatta to ponder unanswerable questions. He has come to verify the whereabouts of one of his men. Va bene. I will lead my guest myself through the villa that has been my family's home for more than two hundred years. If you listen closely, you might hear ghosts whispering. The air is saturated with history. Think of it, Monsieur Lieutenant: Napoleon Bonaparte once stood where you are standing. Perhaps he thrust his pale hand inside his jacket and extolled the merits of his little kingdom of Elba while he privately calculated the details of his escape from exile. Perhaps he wiped his boots on a worsted mat just like the one on the floor of the front hall. Perhaps he sat in the high-backed chair at the head of the dining-room table. The chair, by the way, like the two oak cassoni against the wall, dates from the seventeenth century. And those puzzling fine-meshed trays once held the eggs of silkworms that the family used to raise. Entire bedrooms were filled with branches of tree heather and given over to the silkworms when they were ready to spin. Monsieur Lieutenant is welcome to visit the bedrooms. Or would he prefer to sit and sip Chartreuse from a Venetian glass?

Come then, Monsieur Lieutenant, and sit beside me. I will tell you about Napoleon. I will tell you about the Etruscans and the Turks and Barbarossa and Mussolini. You couldn't have known that Mussolini earned the resentment of Elbans years ago for doing nothing to save all the jobs lost when the first ironworks closed. He visited the island on several occasions and he was warmly welcomed, it's true. Elbans lined the streets and cheered. But cheers for a dictator don't necessarily indicate the true feelings of the people. A dictator's subjects tend to keep their true feelings to themselves. Is this cowardice or self-defense? Sometimes it's hard to tell the difference. Don't think I'm unwilling to hold my countrymen accountable. But I have also learned that sympathy is a clarifying influence, especially during a time of war. You can see more clearly when you imagine seeing through someone else's eyes. Also, it helps to read widely. Did you know that I was educated at the university in Pisa? I can recite poems by Manzoni, Carducci, Negri, and whole cantos out of Dante. I have read Austin and Eliot and Dickens in English. I have read Molière and Montaigne in French.

But isn't all this beside the point? The subject at hand is a renegade soldier. What will Monsieur Lieutenant do with the soldier when he's found? Will the soldier be punished? But why should he be punished if he merely ran away from slaughter that shouldn't have occurred in the first place? It's easy to imagine running away. Most of my dreams lately have involved running through the darkness from an enemy I haven't been able to identify. In some dreams I am followed by the sound of boots thumping over paving stones. In other dreams a Frenchman commands me to halt.

There are Elbans who believe that dreams seep from the dead, from their tombs into the island's soil, to grow in the vineyards and eventually to be crushed with the grapes and drunk by the living. They believe that the island contains a limited collection of dreams, with each dream available for borrowing, and that death comes when the dreams are due to be returned to the land. But it's just as likely that dreams are blown in by the sirocco. Or else dreams are memories left behind by the future.

I have taken to dreaming that I am being hunted. How strange, then, to wake and find that I am only a bystander in this war. I have done nothing to provoke it. But neither have I helped to prevent it. Maybe this is why I am running away in my dreams — like a renegade soldier, I am running from my duty.

My duty, I understand, is to provide Monsieur Lieutenant with useful information. First, though, I need to know what he means by *useful*. To some people, there is nothing more useful than a weather forecast. Typically on Elba, June is one of the driest months. But visitors need to be reminded that this is not a desert climate. Yes, in fact, it rains here. Yesterday's squall was not untypical. And though cacti thrive and flowers bloom year-round, in winter snow falls in the mountains. It is magical in the forests on Monte Capanne. When I was a young girl I used to climb with my father up to the snow line. Once we saw a pair of wild boars shuffling together across a frosted meadow. I still remember the way their breath puffed in the cold air like white smoke blown right from their tusks.

But this is probably not something Monsieur Lieutenant needs to know. As to the whereabouts of his soldier — why, it's possible, if not likely, that he has found a place to hide in La Chiatta. How easy it would be for an intruder to sneak into the villa and make himself at home. Even to me — and I have lived here all my life — the rooms seem joined by accordion folds, so that when I'm walking from one end to another, I'm not always sure what room I have left or entered. But I prefer it this way. I wouldn't want to live in a home where all the bedrooms were lined behind closed doors along a single corridor extending east to west. Really, I wouldn't want to live anywhere else. I am not alone among my countrymen in this regard. Foreigners will often comment on the fact that so many Italians never leave the village where they were born, and some, like me, don't even leave their childhood home. But don't think I have stayed because I am afraid of change. To the contrary, I welcome change and am known to have a supple mind when it comes to unexpected challenges.

I can't help Monsieur Lieutenant, however, until he clarifies his intentions. For instance, he could say something about the Allied forces' long-term plans. How will they choose representatives for an interim government council when most members of the Ninth French Colonial Division don't even speak Italian? When will they deliver basic supplies? When, exactly, will the war be over? Will one occupation be replaced with another? When will the accounting begin?

For the past few months the news from the mainland has been contradictory. Rome was liberated on June 4, but Florence remains under German control. Mussolini sent out a proclamation: "Workers and peasants, to your posts." But where is Mussolini now? He left Gargnano to meet Hitler at his headquarters in East Prussia. And then where did he go? Does Mussolini believe Hitler's assurance that victory is imminent? And what about the rumors of secret weapons powerful enough to split the earth in half?

I have listened to my brother-in-law arguing with his friends about the origin of this war. Did it begin at the end of the last war or with Franco's victory in Spain or when the first star was cut out of yellow cloth? To think that even after it's over those who survive will have to live with the possibility that the slaughter could have been prevented.

But Monsieur Lieutenant has many responsibilities and can't waste his time chatting with an ignorant Elban woman about this and that. I hope you've had a pleasant visit. Would you like to see the library before you go? La Chiatta is full of unusual treasures. A porcelain cup that belonged to Napoleon. Geographical surveys from the eighteenth century. Letters from counts and princesses. And on his way out Monsieur Lieutenant will see at the edge of the property a furnace built in the nineteenth century, following an Etruscan design.

Arrivederla, Monsieur Lieutenant. Be sure to visit again. And if I can help in any way . . . if I hear news of the renegade soldier . . . if I can offer suggestions for the interim council . . . if Monsieur

Lieutenant ever returns to Elba after the war, he shouldn't hesitate to visit. He will always be welcome at La Chiatta.

Having somehow succeeded in distracting the lieutenant from the purpose of his visit, Giulia Nardi accompanied him and his companions into the courtyard and wished them success. When the jeep reached the road, she returned inside. She found her daughter waiting in the kitchen, eager for a report. Giulia assured her that their Senegalese guest was out of danger. He could linger at La Chiatta until he was ready to return to active duty on his own. As long as he returned voluntarily and was prepared to offer a convincing story to explain his absence, he would be spared the consequences. At least, this was Giulia's reasoning. Without evidence, she concluded that the lieutenant who had come in search of Amdu would have treated him harshly if he'd discovered him lounging between white cotton sheets, freshly laundered and ironed, on a bed as wide as a boat. But Amdu hadn't said anything about punishment. He'd made it clear that he didn't want to rush back to his regiment, but he didn't say why.

Yes, he'd have to go back to his regiment. And later, much later, after the war, after the reconstruction, Giulia Nardi, who had proudly professed her ignorance to Monsieur Lieutenant, would begin to read about the war. Settling herself in the overstuffed chair in La Chiatta's library, she would prop her glasses on her nose and read about the incremental confusion that accompanied stages of awareness, and she would realize that she hadn't even known enough about what was happening to know what to ask. When she told Monsieur Lieutenant that she was ignorant about the subject of war, she had thought she was misleading him. Unlike some of her friends, who went out of their way to avoid learning more than they wanted to know, she'd read any newspaper she could get her hands on. Yet somehow the reality of the war had managed to elude her.

She would keep reading about the war in the years ahead until she seemed to be living half her life in other people's memories. She wouldn't be able to stop herself. From the liberation through to the end of her life, she would feel a driving need to grasp the truth. She wouldn't be able to say what she meant by the truth, but she'd know that she couldn't help but persist. Stupidly, ignorantly, she'd be drawn to a mystery that would forever evade her attempt to assess it. Her own life would grow murkier as she lost faith in her ability to measure and understand experience. And over time she would acquire a new tolerance for the uncertainty of the present, as if to make up for her earlier ignorance. As she read more and understood less of what she was reading, as she recognized the need for fostering a feeling of blankness to counterbalance horror, she would become more patient and permissive in her own life. Since she couldn't be sure what to think about the nature of war, she couldn't have unreasonable expectations. As she aged, she would give the impression that she was a regal, wise woman, more private than most others but at peace with herself and full of trusting love for her daughter. Even when the world gave her reason to be wildly anxious, Signora Nardi would appear ethereal in her serenity.

IN GENERAL, he had always found it easiest to see when he was wearing his mask topped with antelope horns. It was a real Diola mask made of woven matting, not one of the fake masks imported by Bambara traders from Mali. Everything became clear when he looked through the tubular eyes, especially when he was beating a tamas drum and his sisters were dancing. Everything became funny. He hadn't watched his sisters dance in sixteen months and thirteen days. He could have calculated the equivalent number of minutes if he'd had a pencil and paper. He remembered how not long before he left for the training camp in Saint-Louis he had tried to make a khalom with a gourd and a piece of leather, but he did not succeed. He promised his sisters he would try again with another gourd when he returned home after the war.

Music was one way to praise God. Who shall not fear and glorify thy name, O Lord? All nations shall come and worship thee. Amdu would play the song of the Lamb and do good work. This was how it should be. Those who keep the commandments of God in any faith will be blessed. Of course, he did not know what was meant by blessed, exactly. But he could safely assume that it was better to be blessed than not to be blessed. Here is a call for the endurance of the saints. Each of us is the expression of the Spirit on earth. The heart is the house of God, the abode of Divine Light. In this house we learn to love jamal and jalal, beauty and rigor. Also, it helps to acquire the wisdom of fear.

He remained where he was because he felt sure that he should be there. In this house he was learning to love beauty and rigor and to acquire the wisdom of fear. Everything was becoming clearer. The only thing missing was his mask. Also, his tamas drum. Thrump-a-chittuah, thrump-a-chittuah, choochoo, choochoo.

His room as he saw it without his mask: a bed the size of a garbage barge, layered above the board with a thin mattress and a plump feather duvet. At night the moonlight shone through the closed shutters, and the marble squares on the floor turned to bright, flashing waves. At dawn the shutters began to glow like the underside of a mushroom cap, reminding him that he'd seen plenty of mushrooms in the forest on Corsica, but he could not be persuaded to eat them. He didn't eat anything that grew in darkness.

There was no closet in this room and no case with drawers. There was only the bed, the window, a soldier named Amdu Diop, and the changing light. He was used to a different kind of light — a playful light that bounced between metal roofs and whitewashed surfaces. Here, light soaked the varied colors, making them full and pure, giving a soul to their solidity.

He could look northeast from his window across the courtyard, down the mowed strip between the vines, through the iron gate, to a patch of pure blue sea beneath the pure blue sky. They were different blues, separated by a thin transparent band, like a belt of visible wind. At sunset, the belt turned the same red that streaked the flesh of the peaches he was served every day after his bread and soup.

These colors made him wonder briefly if he had already passed through the mist to heaven. But he knew he was alive because all day he was aware of the varied fragrances from the kitchen, along with the smell of a slow burning in the fields. No one who lived in the house seemed worried that the fields were burning. The Germans had been defeated, and the island was at peace again. Still, Amdu had reason to worry. Hour by hour, he was learning the wisdom of fear. He had learned to fear the smell of smoldering scrub. He had learned to fear the taste of soup made of eels. He had learned to fear the sound of men speaking loudly in French. Most of all, he had learned to fear his own foolishness. Here in this house that was the mirror of his heart, he was becoming who he was meant to be, but he did not yet know how to be who he was. Surely his allotment of miracles was limited,

and he had already wasted one good miracle on a dove's egg —
this for the sake of a girl who played the piano badly and who
sounded as if her mouth were full of pebbles when she spoke
French.

Maybe this girl was a distraction. Or maybe she was the reason
Amdu's holiness was suddenly available to him. She was someone
he wouldn't have guessed he'd ever meet. Her skin reminded him
of the cream inside the éclairs his mother made for the feast of the
Epiphany. He couldn't stop staring. She couldn't stop chattering.
To this girl who knew nothing about the world beyond her island,
everything was interesting: pignoli and pigeons and rocks and
verb forms and even African soldiers. Especially African soldiers.

She earned the right to visit him more often. She'd arrive with
her mother and stay for an hour. She wanted to teach him Italian.
Her mother seemed to approve. At least she gave the impression
that she didn't want to discourage their efforts at communication.
If Amdu had been less trusting, he would have suspected that she
was trying to trap him into a promise of marriage, since that was
what most mothers did with rich, eligible young men in Dakar.
But not only did Amdu have no intention of marrying anyone
anytime soon, he also didn't think to attribute to the signora any
secret motives. Even if he still couldn't see everything with perfect clarity, he was confident in his interpretive abilities. Amdu
was Amdu. The signora was the signora. And the girl named
Adriana could say whatever she pleased.

She appreciated the fact that Monsieur Amdu could perform
small miracles. She probably hoped that his miracles would become ever more momentous. He hoped so, too, and didn't want to
disappoint her. Although he may not have been sure that he was
what he wanted to be, it helped to be admired by a young girl who
had no need for the wisdom of fear.

•   •   •

He recovered completely from his fever. By then, the lieutenant had come and gone; no one could say when he would return. The irritable man named Zio Mario brought news each day of the Allied forces: the British commandos had already left for another mission, but the warships that had brought the French Colonials to the island were still anchored in the harbors at Portoferraio and Marina di Campo. There was no sign that they would be leaving anytime soon, so Amdu could continue to enjoy his respite at La Chiatta. He'd wait until he received word that the general himself had given the order to embark. Then he would run all the way back to the place he'd been separated from his comrades. He'd arrive breathless and disheveled. To protect the family that had protected him, he would claim to have no memory of where he'd been. It would be a small but necessary deception, which God would surely forgive.

One bright morning, after he'd bathed and eaten, he was encouraged by the signora to go outside. He roamed alone around the courtyard, dressed in trousers that only reached his shins and a white shirt with long, ballooning sleeves. He hadn't been there for long when he felt the weight of someone's stare. Looking up, he saw Adriana watching him from an upper-floor window. She swished her open hand in a greeting, and he nodded solemnly in response. To provide her with something to admire, he moved across the cobbles with the half-stepping dignity of a prince who had decided to forget, momentarily, his important concerns.

The girl did admire him, didn't she? Maybe. Or maybe not. He surprised himself by worrying that she would grow bored with his company. Maybe she'd already grown bored now that Amdu wasn't a novelty anymore. Maybe she had better things to do than watch a Senegalese soldier doing nothing. He glanced up at the window. Just as he expected, the frame that had contained her was already empty.

One minute she had worshipped him. The next minute she didn't even find him worthy enough to keep watching. Unless he was performing a miracle, he was useless. Wasn't this typical of young girls? Their coy hints and fickle adorations. Give a girl a kerchief and she'd wrap it like a turban, signaling that from then on everything must revolve around her, and if the attention she received was less than she thought she deserved, she would go away.

Adriana had gone away, leaving Amdu to drift by himself in the same place where earlier he'd been skulking like a stray dog. He recognized the windows of the cantina, the stone wall surrounding the lemon garden, the trellis wrapped in roses, and the path cutting between the front of the villa and the thicket of junipers. Here was the place he'd hidden, waiting to be found. But the door that had sheltered him had been heaved into the bushes and lay upon the broken branches like a body that had fallen from a great height, stirring in Amdu a chilling apprehension, as if he were looking at what he would have been if he'd made other choices.

He wanted to believe that God had reason to keep sparing him for many years to come. But being spared did not necessarily assure happiness. He was wise enough to be able to think of many unhappy possibilities.

For instance, it was possible that in the future he would suffer a hunger as severe as the hunger suffered by the Peul and the Lebou every year during the soudure. It was possible that he would suffer a thirst as severe as the thirst suffered by the poor people in Grand Yoff outside Dakar when the fountains ran dry. It was possible that he would never see his sisters dance again.

In such a moment a young Senegalese man far from his home might be prone to misjudgment, and when he heard a girl's voice calling in the distance, he might assume that she was in danger. He might think it more than possible that this girl who didn't know the wisdom of fear needed him. In such a moment, he might remember another time not long ago when he had run toward a girl's screaming voice. In his disoriented state, he might even confuse the past with the present. As he ran around the corner of the villa and through the vineyard, he might think he was heading through a neglected orchard. He might predict that once again he would arrive too late.

But when he found Adriana in the boathouse, she wasn't afraid. She was smiling in a lazy, slightly taunting way, like a lizard basking on a rock. She'd been calling him to come and see for himself. Look, Monsieur Amdu.

No, don't look.

Yes, look. She expected him to look.

The sunlight made a second doorway on the floor. The girl stood at the far edge of the rectangle, and Amdu had to resist the impulse to throw himself against her, pushing her backward to keep her from falling through the light into another world.

"I forget the word in French," she said in a secretive voice.

"What word?"

"Micia."

"What does that mean — meecha?"

"Guarda, Monsieur Amdu." She indicated with a nod the direction he was supposed to look — into the emptiness beneath a tarp propped across two barrels. Following her gaze, Amdu heard a muffled hissing, a sound that prompted him to imagine that beneath the tarp a snake was preparing to strike.

Because it was the logical thing to do, Amdu gasped. The girl glanced at him with obvious puzzlement. Didn't she understand? There must have been a snake hiding under the tarp, a slender, quick snake, black and red and a full meter long in Amdu's imagination, its flat head sliding up from its coil, its tongue flickering. He didn't want anything to do with snakes, yet he felt he should take advantage of the opportunity and demonstrate his courage. With God's assistance, he would act before the snake could strike. He would kick the barrel and crush the snake.

Or else he would excuse himself from Adriana's company and run in the opposite direction. Though in fact he didn't have to run. He could walk. Like this, backward.

As it turned out, he wasn't going anywhere. The girl had another plan in mind. She gave him some incomprehensible direction in Italian and grabbed him by the wrist as she tugged the tarp off the barrels. Amdu had to lock his knees to maintain his balance, and he stood in a defensive stance, mirroring the cat that had been hiding beneath the tarp — a hissing, straddle-legged cat, her ears flat against her head, her fur bristling.

Una micia, Adriana had called it. A pussycat. Why, she asked Amdu in French, had he been so afraid of a mamma cat and her kittens?

"Quel horreur!" Amdu said, failing to steady his voice sufficiently to achieve a tone that was properly ironic.

Just a mother cat defending the mewing, wriggling mass behind her. Just a cat and her kittens in their den. The full extent of Amdu's stupidity had been revealed. But at least he had the chance to put something back in its proper place. After admiring the kittens, he stretched the tarp back across the barrels and smoothed the corners, an action meant to signify that the danger was over. And it was true, wasn't it? No one else would be hurt. The Germans remaining on the island had surrendered, the Allied forces would be moving on soon, and the girl named Adriana was melting into giggles.

And then he was alone again, having lost Adriana to the signora's voice calling her from an open window of La Chiatta. She had bid him a wry farewell and told him not to be late for his midday meal. Ciao, mademoiselle. He was alone and freshly startled to find himself where he was. A proper Tirailleur Sénégalais looking through an iron gate at the sea — the same sea that he had crossed to get here, though its blue seemed even bluer than he recalled, so blue that when a floating gull, appearing white in the distance, flapped off its surface, its wings were stained with the same tint.

The girl he'd come to save could only laugh at him. What would be his next test to fail? When would he have the chance to do the kind of work for which he wanted to be known? Until he had the faith and influence to perform miracles, he would have to wait patiently for something to happen.

He didn't have to wait long. In the midst of a war, anything could happen: snakes could turn into cats, and mice could turn into little boys hiding behind the corner of the boathouse. Amdu heard them before he saw them: the scratching of dry leaves beneath little feet, the muffled grunt when an elbow was shoved into a gut, the whispered curses. He'd heard the same boys earlier from his room — their hooting and scuffling as they played in the courtyard. He didn't know how many boys there were altogether, but he knew they had come to spy on him.

They would be disappointed that he had no rifle. To amuse them, he grabbed a wooden garden stake from a bundle propped against an empty stretch of wire. The pointed tip had broken off, but it would do. He crept forward, his new rifle tucked firmly under his arm, his finger ready on the trigger.

In Amdu's game, he was following the trail of a German barbarian. He walked with his shoulders hunched, eyes squinting, senses alert. Step by step toward destiny. What's that? A warthog's snuffle. And that? The tip of a lion's tail swishing above the grass. Branches crackling, pushed aside by the thick, filthy fingers of a man who has murdered many people. Don't ever doubt that he's the one responsible. Come along. Ever so quietly. Throaty protest of an invisible bird. Grape leaves stirred by the breeze. Where are we? Hard on the trail of the German barbarian. Step by step through the jungle, across the windswept veldt, into the mountains. Look sharp now. Up the rocky slope. Down the rocky slope and into the desert, to suffer courageously deprivations that would kill lesser men. Now is the time to justify our lives. To endure. God is watching. The soup is simmering on the stove at home. Our families are waiting for our triumphant return.

As he wound through the vineyards, Amdu kept glancing behind him to make sure the boys were following. There were two of them, both dressed in short pants held up by elastic straps, with light brown caps worn at a tilt. Whenever he turned his head, the boys ducked beneath the vines, so Amdu continued in pursuit of the German barbarian. At one point he heard a muffled argument behind him, and from their movements among the branches he could tell that the boys were looking for something. When one of them stood up bareheaded, Amdu guessed that they were searching for a lost cap. He was preparing to go back to them and offer to help when he saw the slightly smaller boy — the bareheaded one — push the other to the ground. A moment later the other stood up, waving the cap in a taunt. The boys grappled and collapsed in a tangle. Then they scrambled back to their feet, their caps planted back on their heads. The game continued. Amdu followed the trail of the German barbarian. The boys followed Amdu.

Three boys, including Amdu, playing at war. How long had it been since Amdu had been able to play at anything? Among the many qualities that gave him reason to boast was his talent for pretending. He had always been artful in his inventions, confident in his immersion in any odd game.

But wasn't he too old to play games? Amdu was a man — a proper Senegalese rifleman, the grandson of General Diop. Or else he was a boy pretending to be a man. Or else he was a man pretending to be a boy who was pretending to be a man. It hardly mattered, as long as the game absorbed him. There were three players. Then a fourth boy, perhaps a year or so younger than Amdu, with thin brown arms and a red face, came running across the field to join them. He was armed with a pocketful of stones, which he threw ahead of him in an arc over the top of the seawall as he approached.

The boy joined the two younger boys, drawing them together to confer. While Amdu waited for them a few meters away, he pointed the stick toward the sky and idly shot at the clouds.

The boys broke from their huddle with a loud whooping. Amdu didn't realize that now all three of them held rocks until they sent them flying in his direction. Two of the rocks missed him. One hit him sharply on the temple.

Why, those boys were making a terrible mistake! They had confused Amdu with the German barbarian. He wanted to explain to them that he was innocent. But then the boys threw a second round. One rock thudded hard against his back as he turned away from them. Another fell just to the right of him. The third hit his tender shoulder, sending a scorching pain from his neck to his fingertips.

No mistake had been made — the boys had chosen their target and aimed deliberately. Here on this estate he'd come to think of as the refuge he deserved, the boys he'd wanted to consider his friends were trying to hurt him. Maybe they were trying to kill him.

Run, Amdu!

Yes, he'd run, but first he needed to know why these boys hated him. Did they attribute to him the crimes committed by others during this war? Did they despise all members of his race? Or were they trying to destroy him because he was supposed to be destroyed? Was this a necessary part of the story?

These boys knew he was a welcome guest at La Chiatta. He'd given them no reason to hurt him. What new information had the older boy brought them to prompt this attack? Amdu turned back to them, prepared to ask for an explanation, but another rock, a pear-shaped piece of granite, came sailing through the air and struck him on his chest so forcefully that he staggered and fell.

Seen through his tears, the world became languorous. He watched the smallest boy prepare to throw another rock and then bring his arm down to his side, as if waiting for Amdu to stand up. He watched the older boy check his empty pockets. He watched the third boy strain his arm backward, as though pulling a slingshot, and then fling another rock at Amdu. He watched the rock soar like a bird riding an air current and drop a short distance from him. He watched the older boy scouring the area between the mounds of soil around the vines. The boy found a stone, weighed it in his hand, then turned to find his target. He was only a few meters from Amdu — close enough for a boy with good aim to do serious harm. Amdu watched as he readied himself for the throw. He wondered if the boy intended to throw the stone as straight and forcefully as possible. He wondered how long it would take the stone to reach him. He wondered how long it would take the dog named Pippa to lope across the field. Which would prove faster: the boy's throwing arm or the dog's running legs? He heard the dog growling, and the sound made him think of ocean surf sucked backward over pebbles. But that sound had always reminded him of people laughing. Remembering the sound of people laughing made him wonder what they found so funny. Then he knew. They were laughing at the dog. Dogs were funny, especially when they flew like a rock flies out of a boy's hand. Up into the air flew the dog named Pippa, with her teeth bared and her wet gums shining. Into the soft flesh of the boy's thigh sank the teeth of the dog named Pippa. Amdu watched without feeling much of anything as the howling boy pivoted in place, swinging the dog in a half-circle around him. He watched the younger boys watching, their jaws hanging in an expression that suggested both delight and terror.

If Amdu had learned to talk with animals, he would have told Pippa to let go of the boy's leg. Muddy brown blood was already seeping out the corner of the dog's lips. Amdu would have wagered that this was the animal's first taste of human blood. He could guess that a dog with its mouth clamped around a thick, bloody piece of human flesh for the first time would never want to let go.

Amdu Diop, a proper Senegalese rifleman, felt a sudden urge to prove that he could act heroically. With the stick he'd used as a rifle, he pushed himself to his feet. Using the same stick as a cane, he wobbled over to the boy and the dog. Raising that sturdy, useful stick high above his head, he brought it down hard against the back of the dog's neck.

The animal sprang backward as though from the force of an explosion and lay motionless in the grass. The boy sucked in his howl and stared. Amdu pushed the haunches of the dog, then shook his head in disbelief. The stick was intact in his hand, the sun was shining, and the dog named Pippa was dead. He hadn't meant to kill her. He had never killed anything in his life. Even mosquitoes he'd always blown from his arm with a gentle puff of breath. How was it possible that he'd killed a dog — the same dog that had befriended him under the door and then remained so fond of him?

The bitten boy ran in long, limping strides back toward the villa. The two smaller boys stared at Amdu. He raised his stick at them, meaning the gesture as a question: how had this stick in his hand killed a dog? The boys seemed to think that Amdu was threatening them and they ran off, shouting wildly as they overtook the older boy and continued toward the villa.

Leaving Amdu alone with the lifeless body of the dog named Pippa. He lowered himself to the dog's side and rested his cheek on her belly. She was still warm and soft between the outline of the ribs. She might have been sleeping. But she wasn't sleeping. Amdu had killed her with a single blow.

It wasn't right. It made no sense. He had not been born to be responsible for this. Without counsel, plans go wrong. Amdu had proved himself an abomination. He felt the eyes of the Lord watching him. Everyone was watching him, knowing him to be his father's ruin. And yet he was entirely alone. He had wandered away from understanding into the assembly of the dead. He who digs a pit will fall into it.

The end of the matter. All has been heard. Fear God, and keep his commandments, for he will bring every deed into judgment, with every secret thing, whether good or evil. The earth will be desolate because of its inhabitants.

Unless — could it be — the dog lay dead in order for God to be made manifest? However unlikely the possibility, it was tempting to believe. Why else had Amdu been born but to work the works of God? What would happen if he spit on the ground to make clay of the dirt? What would happen if he rubbed the clay into the place on the dog's neck where he'd struck her with the stick? Go, wash in the pool of Sio'am. What would happen if he prayed for the gift of one great miracle and promised, in return, to ask for nothing more?

Why, he'd put his hand on the dog's belly where he'd been resting his head, and in a moment he would feel the gentle rise and fall of her breath, of course. He would see the dog's moist snout glistening. He would wonder whether the dog had been breathing all along and he'd been mistaken. He would wait for the dog to open her eyes. Eventually she would roll upright and twist around to snap angrily at Amdu, the traitor who had tried to kill her while she was trying to save his life. Once she was fully awake and alert, she wouldn't let him touch her.

As he watched her trot home across the field, he gave up wondering whether the event deserved to be added to the registry of miracles. All that mattered was the foolish promise he'd offered in exchange for divine intervention. To revive a dog, he had relinquished all claim to his magnificent potential. He regretted making such a vast promise. He knew he'd regret it more and more as time went on. But above all, he was a man of his word. So be it. He was through with his good work before he'd properly begun. He could ask for nothing more.

SINCE THE BEGINNING of the war and especially through the hard months of the German occupation, Adriana had been comforted to see evidence of the land's persistence. As long as the island itself didn't change, she knew that the power of the occupying force was limited. Though they could blow up schools and make people disappear, they couldn't stop the sun from shining or the fruit from ripening, and when Adriana bit into a yellow pear, the juice would still dribble down her chin. It had always been this way. If the Germans burned one orchard, the trees would seed themselves elsewhere. The red blush of an orange would always taste sweet. Mounds of kelp would collect on the Magazzini beach. Buckets full of squid would be unloaded from fishing boats onto a dock. And if you weren't careful when you were wading in the shallow water at Bagnaia, you might set your bare foot on the spiny bubble of a sea urchin.

But now that the Germans were gone and the island was at peace again, it was time for everything to be transformed with simple wishes. For instance, today she might wish that the wind would change direction or that the moon would turn scarlet in an eclipse. Tomorrow she might wish that she could breathe under water. The next day she would impress her mother by walking on her hands across the room.

It was the morning of the sixth day of the liberation of Elba, the third day since the Germans had retreated, and Adriana Nardi felt silly and happy to be who she was — a girl who lived in a villa where a Senegalese soldier named Amdu had taken refuge.

She'd concluded once and for all that he wasn't a witch doctor. Witch doctors wouldn't tremble at the hissing of a little pussycat. And he wasn't the savage her uncle Mario had warned her about. He had no magical powers or dangerous motives. The truth was, she liked Amdu because he was perfectly alive, though how the quality manifested itself she couldn't have described. She just felt it, the way she felt the warmth of the sun. All he had to do was stroll across the courtyard with his head held high and his arms folded across his chest, and she wanted to laugh in delight. It wasn't that he was particularly handsome or noble. In truth, his forearms were too long and his elbows too bulby, his broad nose was dented on one side, and in six days his beard hadn't grown beyond a feeble scruff. Yet everything about him seemed right and worthy. And if he appeared comical, it was because he'd obviously been born for a grander world and proceeded in a manner that was always a little awkward or exaggerated.

In the simplest sense, Adriana enjoyed the company of a gentle young man who was so different from anyone she'd ever known. There was more to it, however — more pleasure, more hilarity. The good feeling of being inspired to a new responsiveness. She wanted to see outside what she felt inside. The clump of red pistachio berries, the lemons streaked with green, the feathery blue blossoms on the rosemary bush, the yellow fuchsia and red poppies — these were too familiar and ordinary to express what Adriana was feeling as she walked from the boathouse after showing the kittens to Amdu.

She'd heard Luisa talking with her mother about the many funerals that would occupy Elbans in the days to come. A boat carrying nothing but coffins was said to be on its way from France, due to arrive that afternoon. She'd overheard Mario describe how at the hospital in Portoferraio he'd watched a mother pulling out handfuls of her hair as she wept over the corpse of her young son. And yesterday she'd heard Signora Ambrogi say that she wanted to sink into a mud bath at San Giovanni and never come up for air again.

But to a ten-year-old girl, very nearly eleven, who was walking through a vineyard on a sparkling summer day, all the talk of suffering seemed to belong to a story that was only half real, like the stories of Barbarossa and the Turks and the pirate Martino — the one who slit the throats of two children he'd captured and threw their bodies into the sea off the coast of Montecristo. That was supposed to be actual history, though to Adriana the story seemed as unbelievable as the stories of gods and nymphs. Even if the story was true, she liked to imagine a better ending for herself. What would she do if she were taken captive by pirates? Why, she'd break free of their chains, dive into the sea, and swim home. And what would she do if an artillery shell exploded overhead? She'd flatten herself on the ground and watch the glowing shrapnel dropping around her.

Her uncle believed that La Chiatta's Senegalese guest was not to be trusted. He had warned Adriana to bolt her door at night. Or even better, she should come and live with him in Portoferraio until the soldier returned to his regiment. Adriana had politely declined. And though she failed to convince him that Amdu was harmless, she reminded her uncle how he used to say that there was nothing worse than a Bolshevik. Whatever else the soldier was, he wasn't a Bolshevik.

Could Adriana be certain of that? her uncle had asked. Could she be certain of anything? he had persisted.

Such was her uncle's relentless manner, always ending with a taunting lilt. Yet he was her only uncle, so she put up with him. She was even glad when she returned inside and heard his voice in the front hall. When he saw her he sent his hat the short distance across the hall to the hat rack, clearly trying to impress her, though the hat missed the hook and landed on the floor.

Adriana leaped ahead of her uncle and grabbed the hat, pulling it low over her forehead and cocking it at an angle. "Ciao, bello," she said. She took a deep suck on the end of the invisible cigarette she held delicately between two fingers. "Come va?"

"Accidenti," Mario muttered in despair and delight. His lips twitched into a grin. "Damela!" he ordered. Give it to me.

He'd have to catch her first! A dopo, Uncle! See you later.

She was a clever girl. But Luisa's nephew, Paolo, who had far overstayed his visit to La Chiatta, wanted to prove himself superior, and he sprang from behind a doorway, grabbed the hat from Adriana, and with an obsequious bow returned it to its owner.

Well, if Paolo wasn't superior, he was funny, at least. Wasn't he funny, Adriana?

She didn't know the word that would adequately describe how useless she considered him. "Paolo," she said, "ascolta" — listen, isn't that your mamma calling you home?

Of course she knew that Paolo's home was far away, in a little house on the reedy Bovalico. That's why he stank of marsh grass — which was just one more reason Adriana wanted nothing to do with him. She'd rather sit at the piano and muddle through the opening measures of a piece she'd never played before than spend time with Paolo. Stupido Paolo.

Half an hour later, Paolo was sitting on the kitchen table howling while Luisa cleaned the punctures on his leg. By the time Adriana arrived, the kitchen was already crowded with Ulisse's two boys, Uncle Mario, and Giulia Nardi, who was trying to draw from

Paolo an accurate account of what had happened. Paolo could do nothing more than curse the crazy African and sob loudly like a baby when Luisa wiped more liquid onto the wound. Ulisse's boys kept interrupting, though with both of them speaking at once it was difficult to make sense of their words. They were saying something about the dog — Signor Ambrogi's dog. Adriana tried to understand. It was Pippa, not Amdu, who had hurt Paolo. And now Pippa was hurt. No, Pippa was dead — "morta" was the word being repeated by one of the boys. La cane è morta! Paolo killed Pippa? The dog was dead, così, like this, the younger boy said, collapsing on the floor and lying there with his eyes closed. Paolo killed Pippa! No, no, no! The African killed the dog. Capito? The African killed the dog!

Adriana couldn't have heard correctly because what she heard wasn't possible. Pippa wasn't dead and Amdu didn't have anything to do with the chaos in the kitchen. Amdu was probably sitting outside the boathouse soaking in the sun. He was humming a marching song and waiting for Adriana to return.

She started to rush from the kitchen, intending to find Amdu and bring him back so he could tell the true story of what had happened. But her uncle caught her as she whirled past, his fingers pressing hard into the flesh of her upper arm, pressing even harder when she tried to pull away.

"Let me go!" The wicked man! She decided at that moment that even if he was her uncle, she couldn't stand him. She had always hated him. She had tried to amuse him over the years only because that was the best way to disguise her hatred. She hated Mario even more than she hated Paolo. And if her uncle wouldn't let her go, then she would demonstrate her strength by giving him a good strong kick in the shin.

Her uncle winced and released her. She was too shocked by what she'd done to move. Everyone was shocked. A severe, convicting hush immediately fell over the room. The boys stopped yammering. Even Paolo stopped howling. Everyone stared at Adriana in disbelief.

O Dio. Madonna mia.

"Adriana." It was her own name uttered in her mother's steady voice. Yes, that's right, that's her: Adriana the penitent. She hung her head in an exaggerated way to acknowledge her guilt, hoping to raise some feeling of sympathy among her witnesses. She had kicked her uncle in the shin, and under the seersucker a bruise was probably darkening already. She'd done that, amazingly. Forget about the dead dog and a soldier who'd been wrongly accused. Adriana Nardi was the real criminal. She had kicked a man more than twice her size and five times her age. She had kicked him hard.

"Apologize to your uncle."

She apologized.

"Now go to your room!"

"But Mamma . . ." Where is Pippa? she wanted to ask. Where is Amdu? Didn't anyone care?

"Go to your room."

There were many activities to occupy her in her room. She could read the book her mother had given her about Marie-Antoinette. She could sit at her desk and draw. She could braid and unbraid her hair. There was even a skein of scarlet wool and needles her mother had left in a basket under her bed in case Adriana ever wanted to practice knitting. But Adriana hated knitting almost as much as she hated her uncle.

She could unlatch the window, at least, and search the fields for some evidence of what had really happened. Pippa was dead, the boys had said. The African had killed the dog, they'd lied. Boys lied as readily as they complained about their hunger. Boys were always hungry. Except the soldier named Amdu. Although he ate whatever was brought to him, he never asked for anything. He was a courteous boy — un ragazzo gentile. Courteous boys didn't kill dogs. If Pippa was truly dead, then Paolo had killed her, and Ulisse's sons were trying to protect him by blaming Amdu, who couldn't come forward to defend himself.

She saw the speck of a ship in the distance heading into the Rada di Portoferraio, perhaps the coffin ship from France. The water was calm, the sky clear. The young green leaves of the vines glistened as if coated with oil. She saw no sign of Pippa — either Pippa alive or Pippa dead.

She'd have to ask Amdu for an accurate account of what had happened out in the vineyard when he returned home. Home — her home — it seemed natural to think of it as his home as well. She practiced the conversation she would have with him in her mind, in French. Monsieur Amdu, peut-tu raconter la vérité? Was that the best way to ask? La vérité sur la chien, la belle chien qui s'appelle Pippa?

Pippa had always liked La Chiatta better than her master's home of La Lampara. Almost every day she came next door to bark at the Nardis' rooster and fetch the sticks that Adriana and Ulisse's boys would throw for her. Adriana liked to call her la migliore — the best. Without a doubt, she was the best dog in the whole world and more than an adequate substitute for the pet that Adriana wasn't allowed to keep for herself.

The boys had said that Amdu had beaten Pippa with a stick and she'd fallen dead to the ground, così. As the hour passed, the possibility of Pippa's death began to sharpen into a likelihood in Adriana's mind. Somewhere in the grass lay Pippa's corpse. Adriana's eyes scanned the fields until her head ached. There was no way to fill the emptiness. Only this morning she'd felt as buoyant and carefree as she did when she swam in the sea, as though invisible particles in the air were shifting and swirling around her, lifting her off the ground. But as she went on waiting and her mood became drearier, the nothingness of the space outside her window seemed to thicken and become oppressive. Gravity itself exhausted hope. She would be confined to this ugly, desolate island for eternity, with nothing to do, nothing to notice that she hadn't noticed before, nothing to break the monotony now that Pippa was dead and the soldier named Amdu had gone away.

She didn't have to be told that he'd gone away. She sensed his absence in the sluggish air and the glassy sea. He was gone for good. As soon as she realized this, she found herself wondering whether he'd ever existed at all. She could remember him as a real being in real time, but the memory itself seemed no more than a kind of deceit — the same sort of trick her mind played on her in her dreams. She couldn't completely describe how she'd persuaded herself that the emptiness she couldn't stand to feel was inhabited by the perfect occupant. But she did know that she had never really known him. She didn't have to be older than ten to understand that she'd fooled herself into believing what she wanted to believe and had seen what she wanted to see. She didn't even have to be eleven years old to have some idea that she'd concocted for the foreign soldier the identity she thought best suited him.

He was gone forever. For the first time in her short life, Adriana felt the full impact of the notion — per sempre, for always — words describing the oblivion beyond the end of any possible correction. This was what it must feel like to turn into stone, she thought. He had gone away and wouldn't return. It was too late to acknowledge him as the stranger he was and experience the reality of him, to come to know him all at once and then in the incremental way she came to know anyone else. She could only imagine what it would have been like to really know him and in knowing him to become aware of the inaccessible parts of his identity, to know him and not know him at the same time, the way she knew and didn't know the whims and contradictions of the people she was closest to — her mother and Luisa and even her uncle.

Though she was too young and inexperienced to understand what she had missed in these exact terms, she was aware of having made a terrible mistake. She had pretended that the soldier named Amdu was someone he wasn't, and now he was gone. If she revised her perception of him, it would only be in hindsight. Her mistake was as permanent as his absence.

Whether the dog had been killed accidentally or intentionally, Amdu was responsible, and he couldn't return to La Chiatta after what he'd done. Adriana reminded herself that he would have gone away sooner or later. The French Colonials would be leaving any day now, and Amdu would accompany his comrades. It was inevitable. He couldn't have stayed on Elba, even if he'd wanted to. He was probably making his way to Portoferraio already, or to Marina di Campo, or to wherever he expected he'd find the ship that had brought him to the island.

She pictured him striding along the side of the road in his white shirt and undersized trousers, his brown shins shining above the tops of his boots. If he was lucky, a military jeep would stop, and the driver would offer him a ride. She pictured him sitting in the passenger seat like a colonel, resting his arm on the door and trailing his fingers in the wind.

He who once kept a dove's egg from smashing on the stones. Monsieur Amdu, in his radiant body. Adriana would always credit him with saving her life. But was he really afraid of eels? Was he afraid of cats? He came from Senegal. He came from the other side of the wall. He spoke a beautiful, musical French. Wolof was his second language. He was a soldier. At the military base in Saint-Louis he'd sworn an oath of loyalty. He had plans to save humanity. He had a mother and a father and two sisters in Dakar. He was a guest at La Chiatta. He had the confident manner of someone who considered himself trustworthy. He wanted to study to be a doctor. He stayed for a while. Then he went away and left behind the impression that he was no more than a fanciful invention, proving with his example that no one like Amdu Diop could ever really exist.

HE WAS A GOOD BOY, but he left without saying good-bye. When a good boy left without saying good-bye, there were only two possible explanations: either he was suddenly called away, or he didn't want to take responsibility for something he'd done wrong. Giulia was certain that the young soldier hadn't received any urgent message. Then what had he done wrong? He had killed Lorenzo's dog, the boys alleged. Giulia didn't believe it, and neither did her daughter. Adriana had immediately wanted to run off to search for him, but her uncle held her back. In a rage, she had kicked him in the shin. Secretly, Giulia thought Mario deserved it.

Everything was so confusing. And everything became even more confusing. Shortly after Adriana had gone to her room,

Ulisse entered the kitchen. His sons repeated their story. But Ulisse reported with a shrug that though he hadn't seen any sign of the soldier, he'd just seen Lorenzo's dog heading across the grassy border beyond the vines and through an opening in the hedge that separated the Nardi land from the Ambrogi estate.

Of course Amdu hadn't killed Pippa. Giulia was convinced that the boy who had been her guest for nearly a week would never willingly cause harm. She had confidence in her ability to judge human nature, and she believed that Amdu Diop was fundamentally good. But a good boy doesn't just run away without warning . . . unless — now here was a third possibility — he was running away from danger. Something had happened out in the vineyard. Why had the dog attacked Paolo in the first place? Paolo must have been taunting the animal. Did Amdu strike the dog in order to save Paolo? Giulia didn't bother to speak this proposition aloud because she knew that her brother-in-law would scoff. He believed that all African men were rapists and murderers. That's why Amdu had run away — because he refused to be held accountable. As far as Mario was concerned, everything came down to accountability, with each sin the equivalent of an entry in a debit column, to be balanced with sufficient retribution. Amdu, Mario would say, knew exactly what he'd done. Or else he sensed what others thought he'd done. Wasn't this more likely? Amdu was running from the punishment Mario and the boys were planning for him.

Amdu's absence was Mario's fault. Of course it was his fault. Giulia was used to blaming everything that went wrong on her brother-in-law. And to think that long ago she'd fancied herself in love with him. What a foolish girl she'd been. But aren't all girls foolish? Adriana was foolish for kicking her uncle in the shin, and she had to suffer the consequences alone in her room.

Mario, who liked to pose as a gallant man, offered to pursue Amdu in order to recover whatever the soldier had stolen. Giulia pointed out that there was nothing missing. How did she know that nothing was missing? Mario demanded. She didn't say that she could count up her most valuable possessions at a glance. Instead, she told him that he could go ahead and search for the soldier if that's how he wanted to spend his time, but she would wait for Amdu at home. She was confident that either he would soon return or he would send word explaining why he'd gone away.

Hours after Mario had left to look for him, Amdu was still missing, and no communication from either of them had reached La Chiatta. Luisa pointed out that the vigilanti were beginning to come back out of hiding now that the Allies were preparing to embark, and if they found a solitary French Colonial wandering around the island, they would kill him. Maybe Amdu already was dead and buried in a shallow grave along the side of the road.

No, he couldn't be dead. Good boys were ingenious survivors. Amdu Diop could stand in a bullet's path and come away with nothing worse than a scratch. He timed his sicknesses carefully, waiting until help was guaranteed before he fell seriously ill, and he was as quick to heal as he was quick to learn. After surviving a year of war, he would survive another day on the island of Elba. He still had some growing to do, after all. He was too alert to danger to let himself be caught by those who wanted to hurt him. It was hard to believe that anyone would want to hurt him, but this would explain why he'd run away from La Chiatta. He must have had reason to sense that he wasn't safe here any longer.

As the day wore on, Giulia convinced herself that Amdu was a capable boy who knew how to stay alive and who understood that the best way to defeat one's enemies was to run from them. No, he wasn't afraid to run. If he ran fast enough, he would never be caught. If he was never caught, he wouldn't have to explain why he was running away.

Shortly before sunset, Giulia heard an automobile rattling down the drive toward La Chiatta. At first she feared it might be the lieutenant who'd come looking for Amdu earlier. She was relieved to see Lorenzo Ambrogi step from the car.

"Lorenzo, buona sera!" Before he could return her greeting she asked about his dog. Had the dog returned home safely? Was it injured?

He didn't understand her concern. Why was Giulia Nardi asking about his dog? Pippa, that little scoundrel. "You know," he said, "this very afternoon she caught a rabbit and left it right on the step for someone to trip over!" Pippa was fine. But Lorenzo hadn't come to talk about the dog. He had come to tell Giulia about the celebration in Marina di Campo — two of the ships transporting the French Colonials were leaving, but first the soldiers were going to celebrate their victory with a feast and dancing. It will be something to see, Lorenzo promised. He was going there himself, and he offered to drive Giulia and Adriana and anyone else who wanted to come along.

And his wife? Where was she? Giulia asked. She preferred to stay at home, Lorenzo said, taking off his cap and pressing his fist inside to reshape the form. He shrugged. His wife was afraid of the Africans, he admitted. But what danger could there be at a victory celebration? Come along with me, he urged.

Giulia thanked Lorenzo for his invitation and declined. But Paolo, who'd been listening to the conversation, begged for a lift to Marina di Campo, showing his bandaged leg to explain why he couldn't ride his bicycle. Pippa did this, he said. Lorenzo rubbed the bristles on his chin and shook his head skeptically. It wasn't possible, he said. "It's the truth!" Paolo insisted, though he was quick to add that Pippa had been agitated by the presence of the soldier. The dog didn't like the soldier, and now that the soldier was gone, she would stop roaming the fields in search of boys to bite in the leg.

But Signor Ambrogi mustn't conclude that Paolo was afraid of Pippa. Paolo wasn't afraid of anything, and as proof he reminded everyone listening that he'd ridden his bicycle across the island on the second day of the Allied invasion. He'd ride back again if he didn't have a bandaged leg on account of Signor Ambrogi's dog.

Lorenzo nodded, obviously perplexed, but he offered an apology to Paolo on behalf of his dog, and he said he'd happily drive him to Marina di Campo. And yes, he could fit the bicycle into the car if they took off the wheels.

Luisa filled a sack with onions and focaccia and fruit, as though her nephew were going away for a month. In the courtyard, Lorenzo waited patiently while Paolo struggled with a wrench, trying to loosen the rusty bolts on the bicycle. Ulisse's boys ran around them whooping, and Ulisse's wife scolded them from the upper story of the cantina because their noise had woken the baby.

"What happened?" Adriana asked. After spending hours in her room, she had finally emerged. She could have come out much earlier — Giulia had invited her to come practice her music, but she'd said angrily that she wanted to be alone. Now she looked as though she'd just woken, or else she'd been crying. Her forehead was still knotted with lingering displeasure, and the many strands floating loose from her braid made a dark haze around her face. "Why is Signor Ambrogi here?" she asked.

"He's driving Paolo to Marina di Campo."

"Stupido Paolo."

"Adriana . . ."

"Mi dispiace, Mamma." She was sorry for speaking about Paolo like that in front of her mamma. But more than she was sorry, she was very hungry. Her mother was pleased to hear it. They would sit and eat their soup as soon as Signor Ambrogi and Paolo had left, and then Giulia would wash her daughter's hair. One hundred strokes with the comb, Giulia reminded her — that's the way to tame unruly hair and make it shine. And afterward, perhaps a game of chess? Her daughter was becoming a formidable opponent. Her poor, darling daughter. She looked as if she'd just tumbled out after spending the night inside the kitchen cabinet. But the war was over, and Elbans would soon have their island back to themselves. Remember what your mother promised, Adriana: mai più. Never again.

"Why is Signor Ambrogi driving to Marina di Campo?" Adriana asked her mother.

"I think . . . I do not know."

Adriana looked at her mother skeptically, finally drawing from her a better answer. "There is a celebration. The Africans are preparing to move on."

The girl's frown seemed to tighten, almost as though she were resisting a smile, but her eyes were shining with tears. She didn't say anything more — she just watched Paolo and Lorenzo load the bicycle into the car, and Giulia watched her, thinking about how she wished she could guide her daughter carefully through the years ahead, step by step. But the girl was too easily drawn to adventure, too reckless in her attachments to follow her mother's lead. She'd find her own way somehow, wouldn't she? Her strong, impetuous girl. Giulia once overheard Luisa telling Ulisse that Adriana must have Gypsy blood in her. Any girl who defied her mother's prohibition and kept returning to Viticcio to leap into the sea — to leap backward! — must have Gypsy blood in her. No doubt she'd give her mother plenty to worry about as she grew older.

But wasn't this worry a mother's necessary burden? It was one thing to allow yourself to feel a carefree optimism about the predicament of a foreign soldier who had been your guest for several days; it was something else entirely when your own child was involved. If Amdu had been Giulia's son, she wouldn't have cared that he was too good a boy to get into trouble — she would have been out scouring the island for him right then instead of leaving him to his fate.

She reminded herself: peace had returned to Elba, and her daughter was safely at her side. It was time to resume the life that had been interrupted by the bombs, to go backward and find the best route averting the reality of war, heading from the familiar past to the future — a future in which her daughter would grow up and soldiers would go home and letters would arrive explaining everything.

A fisherman told Ulisse, who told Luisa, who delivered the news to Signora Nardi and her daughter at supper: the African soldier had cut across the beach at Magazzini and later was seen on a road heading south.

"He was walking?" Adriana asked.

"He was flapping his wings," Luisa said over her shoulder as she returned to the kitchen.

"I don't know why he went away," Adriana said sullenly. "He just went away."

He was not some stray animal Adriana could claim as her own, Giulia reminded her daughter. He was a member of the military and had duties to resume.

"Duties," Adriana scoffed. "He carries a baton in parades!"

"That is something."

"He didn't even say good-bye." She turned her spoon over the bowl and dropped the beans back into the soup. Giulia thought she understood the reason for her daughter's anger. She had known a real Senegalese soldier and had been fearless in his company, but she'd lost him before she could show him off to her friends.

Adriana pointed out that it was easy enough to say Au revoir, mademoiselle, though he could have tried Arrivederci, signorina, or even Ciao. She had taught him many Italian words, but he didn't care. He didn't care that she'd brought him bread and pine nuts and springwater. He was selfish and ungrateful. He'd taken advantage of the family's generosity. Really, the week had been no more than a pleasant vacation for him. Uncle Mario had been right — he wasn't worthy of her trust. Though he'd pretended otherwise, she meant nothing to him. Nothing, she repeated, spitting out the word: Niente.

Giulia was taken aback by the force of her daughter's bitterness. Children shouldn't understand what it means to feel worthless, yet here was Adriana acting like a much older girl — like a girl spinning loose from a romance, a girl who had fancied herself in love. A ten-year-old girl acting heartsick.

"My birthday is on Wednesday," Adriana said, as if she'd read her mother's thoughts. "He won't be here for my birthday."

A ten-year-old girl, almost eleven. What did she know of love? She knew everything she needed to know. She knew what it meant to be loved — and to return love with love.

"Adriana —"

"Are you sure Pippa is not hurt?"

She loved strays and wanderers.

"I am sure. The boys were telling . . ."

"A lie."

She loved adventure.

"A story. Now eat."

"Paolo is stupid."

"Adriana, hush!"

"It isn't fair. Already I am losing the picture of him in my mind. I close my eyes and I try to see Amdu, but I can't see him the way I want to remember him. Mamma, you must find him and bring him back. Tell him he can't just leave us like this."

She loved anyone who loved her. Of course she did. She didn't have to be an adult to feel the ache of missing someone who belonged in her life forever. A girl can be infatuated at any age. Once the spell is cast, conviction is unshakable. Nothing can be done to prevent it. Lives will remain tangled together even at a distance, even through time. Wonderful, horrible love. You open up the cabinet door, and your daughter tumbles out. You've done all you can to protect her. And look what happens.

THIS TIME HE LET HIMSELF OUT through the iron gate instead of scaling the wall. He followed the coastline east, back in the roundabout direction he had come, across the shallow estuaries, along the rocky beach, over mounds of kelp, and into the hamlet of Magazzini, where a white-haired fisherman was dragging a fleet of beached caïques one by one across the sand. The fisherman stopped his work and stared at Amdu. The unlit cigar stub he'd been chewing fell from his lips into the sand. When Amdu said, "Bonjour, monsieur," the fisherman turned and hurried in awkward, limping strides up the beach, disappearing behind a deserted hotel.

After he was gone, Amdu took hold of the prow of a caïque and dragged it to the water's edge. He did the same with the five other caïques. When he was done he looked up and saw the fisherman standing on the hotel's back porch, leaning against the rail. Amdu waved to him. The fisherman shrugged and turned an empty pocket inside out, and Amdu did the same. The fisherman shouted something in Italian that ended in "Africa." Amdu could tell from his tone that "Africa" was being used as an insult. He wanted to communicate to him what the fisherman had missed, never having traveled to Africa, presumably. He'd missed the feeling of walking barefoot along a trail of burlap bags stuffed with peanuts or riding on a spotted horse across the sun-baked land in Kaolack. He'd missed the experience of being a young boy writing stories about himself with his fingertip in the dust of the street outside his home. He would never hear what Amdu Diop could have told him, including information that might have been useful, such as advice about the shirt he'd chosen to wear, which was blue. Amdu could have warned him that blue is the mosquito's favorite color!

"Buona giornata, signore." Amdu made a motion with his hand as if to tip his cap. The fisherman grunted and waved Amdu away, clearly indicating what he wanted to say: Go on, go back to Africa, black man. And that's where Amdu was heading, though he was taking his time about it, for he had a need to absorb the experience that was about to end, to saturate himself with the island that he was obligated to leave behind.

Instead of sticking to the coast, he turned inland to cross the wooded Punta Pina, following a dirt road in a general southeastern direction and then bending more directly south. He walked through a herd of goats being driven forward by a boy who was no older than seven or eight. When the boy spotted Amdu, he dashed behind a juniper hedge. Amdu could see him creeping behind the bushes and he pretended not to notice when the boy whistled for his goats to catch up with him farther down the road.

Amdu felt as massive and obvious as an elephant among all those bleating, jangling goats. As he moved among them he thought about how the girl named Adriana would have laughed at him. He wondered what she was doing right then back in her stone palace by the sea — probably playing a tired old song on the piano, he imagined. He started to hum a marching tune in her honor.

Across a field, smoke rose in a thin column from a small bonfire. Amdu kept walking, though more slowly, respectfully increasing the distance between himself and the timid goatherd up ahead. He passed an old cart abandoned along the side of the road. He passed a concrete, windowless shed with a collapsed roof. He passed a one-wheeled motorcycle lying on its side in a ditch. In the story he would have liked to tell about himself, he would find the missing wheel in the field and attach it to the motorcycle, and then he'd ride around the island before he returned to his ship, taking advantage of his last hours of freedom to see all the sights. That story, however, would have depended upon a miracle, and he was done with miracles.

The goatherd steered his goats down the drive leading to a

farm in the valley. Amdu stuck to the road, believing from its direction that he could follow it all the way to the marina where his division had come ashore. But the road abruptly ended at a low, crumbling stone wall bordering an uncultivated field. Rather than backtrack and find another road, Amdu set out across the field.

The sun was fiercer on the open land, and when he saw a barrel cactus roasting on top of a hillock, he felt a sudden urge to break open the fleshy tip and suck out the juice. He started to cross over to the cactus but stopped when he felt the sting of nettles on his ankles. He continued along the edge of the field, drawn instead toward the tempting shade of a grove of fruit trees in the distance.

As he climbed over another stone wall he realized that the landscape was familiar. He had passed through the same fields before, on the night he ran away from the war. The grass had been silver in the hazy moonlight, and the windfall fruit had had a bitter smell. He recognized the pattern of the uneven furrows beneath his boots and the gnarled, broken trees. Now, in daylight, neglect made the orchard look peaceful and inviting. It was the same orchard, with the same decrepit trees and the tall weeds and the shed that should have been nearby. But he didn't see the shed where he thought it should be. Perhaps it was on the opposite slope, hidden by the crest. He climbed to the highest point and scanned the land around him. To his surprise, farmhouses dotted the south and west, almost within calling distance. He concluded that he had been mistaken about his whereabouts, that this must have been a different orchard on a different hill.

Continuing across the crest, he found himself standing at the edge of a singed, blackened ring of earth, the ashen crust over the dirt flat and cracked, the trees nearby charred on the side that would have faced the fire. He knew at once that he'd been right about the orchard and this was where the shed had been, where the soldiers had raped the girl and stabbed her in the throat to silence her, where Amdu would have lost his tongue if he'd been caught, the place he'd run from, where he'd been unable to help. He didn't know whether the villagers or the soldiers themselves had burned down the shed. He didn't need to know in order to imagine the walls splitting from the heat and crumbling, the flames stretching in tall, swaggering figures, swelling, wavering, the wood popping, sparks flying, melting into the darkness. He didn't have to witness the fire to feel the throbbing heat on his face. And he didn't have to know whether the woman standing about twenty meters away, in an open space that once must have been the central path cutting through the orchard, was the mother or the aunt or just a neighbor of the girl who had been killed. She wore a bulky dress the color of the ashes at Amdu's feet, with a brown kerchief tied over her head, and she was bent under a bundle of wood she carried on her back. She stood motionless, propped over her walking stick, staring at Amdu. For a long while he stared back. Between them was the invisible, implacable truth of what had been done at this spot, though the actual role that he had played receded behind the current perception. He could guess what she was seeing. He, Amdu Diop, who knew himself to be a good man, was thought to be a murderer of children. His crime was unforgivable, even to a woman who might have been generous with forgiveness. The motionlessness of her stance conveyed both the accusation and bafflement of the only question she had to ask: how could he have let it happen? By staring at him, absorbing him with her gaze, she thought she'd find her answer. Staring back at her, he wished he could convey an adequate response and offer consolation to the woman. But she would spend the rest of her days refusing to be consoled. Whatever her relationship had been to the murdered girl, she was destined to remember and to keep remembering as long as she was alive.

The leaves of the fruit trees crackled when a gust of hot, dry wind blew through the orchard. It was a desert wind — silky with particles of sand too small to see — and it stirred in Amdu a craving to go home. At home he wouldn't be held responsible for what had happened on this island. He would be measured solely by the expectations of heredity, resuming his place as the firstborn son of his grandfather's firstborn son, using his advantages to reinforce the family's distinguished reputation. Even if he had given up hope of proving himself exceptional, at home in Dakar he could still be known as a respectable man.

There he could be what he wanted to be, as long as this did not keep him from becoming what he was expected to be. Here he was what he was. There he would study to be a doctor. Here he was a murderer. There his parents would find him a suitable bride. Here he was alone. There he could enjoy the feeling of belonging and from his privileged position embrace a variety of influences. Here he couldn't make himself understood. There he believed in dhikr, the remembrance of God; he believed in authentic holiness; he believed that anyone could be a saint. Here he was a stranger, a foreigner, an invader, a barbarian, *un negro*, a soldier of the Thirteenth Senegalese Regiment in the Ninth French Colonial Division who, by running away from the place where a girl had been murdered, had forfeited the one meaningful gift he could have offered the people of this island — the gift of testimony. Here he had kept his mouth shut. Here he had persuaded himself that with enough faith and the proper magical incantation conceived as prayer, he could revive everything that had been lost. And here he had come to his senses and understood that some forms of suffering cannot be rectified with a miracle.

Here he stood convicted — rightly so. If instead of running away from the scene on the first night of the invasion he had gone to the French field commander Lieutenant General Henri Martin and told him what he'd witnessed, there would at least have been an investigation. But he had lost any credibility he might have had and denied those who were involved either by their actions or their relationship to the dead girl the chance to experience the effects of justice. Even a halfhearted investigation overseen by a military tribunal would have been better than this: a woman's staring eyes and a memory as unalterable as the hard-baked crust of ash in a neglected orchard. Here, this circle of ash before him, was what he couldn't change.

And here, paradoxically, was where he wanted to return. Here — not just this place where he was responsible for crimes committed during a night of chaos, but this entire island he and his comrades had come to liberate. Although he knew clearly enough that he had to leave, although in his heart he really wanted to leave, he also wanted to come back. To spend the remainder of his humble life here rather than there. To plant himself in the middle of these ashes, to live as though he belonged for long enough so that he finally did come to belong.

Did this make sense? Probably not. Amdu wouldn't have tried to explain himself. But locked in the gaze of a woman who would never forgive him, he could imagine what it would feel like to experience himself completely as himself, without potential. To the peasant woman he was beyond redemption. But he remained alive, and life filled him with a powerful desire to earn the right to be who he was.

Amdu began to feel as if he and the old woman were the only two inhabitants of the island. For a long while they stood as still as the trees around them. But eventually the woman decided that she'd seen enough, or that watching was a futile effort resulting in nothing more than tired eyes. She turned away and carried her bundle down the east side of the hill, leaving Amdu alone.

He would have liked to remain there until nightfall and longer, to be there — here — marking the place. But his feet carried him into the hot, gusting wind. His feet remembered the course they'd already traveled and carried him toward the blue water glittering in the distance, through a meadow buzzing with a thousand bees, and toward the marina where he had jumped with his comrades from a rubber boat. He couldn't help it — his feet continued to take him in the direction he'd set out, toward the ship that would bring him home and the life he had been born to live, a life he would resume, though only temporarily, for already he was planning his return.

It cheered him to think about how after the war, after he'd taken his exams and had been certified as a doctor, he would come back to this island by his own means, under no one's command. Ten years from now he would find the girl named Adriana, who by then would be a woman.

As he walked toward Marina di Campo he composed in his mind the letter he would write as soon as he had settled into his berth. He would write directly to the girl's mother to thank her for all she'd done for him. Then he would go on to express his respectful interest in her daughter and, tactfully, to broach the subject he'd been so reluctant to consider: the possibility of marriage. Confident that he would secure his own parents' permission when he returned home, he would make the proposal himself. He would ask the signora to ask her daughter to wait for him. It might take many years, but he would come back for her. He hoped she would be patient. She had to grow up, and he had to finish his studies. Truthfully, he considered their union natural and inevitable. He would tell the signora everything that needed to be said in order to convince her of the sincerity of his interest, and he'd conclude with a gracious, sincere apology, in case she found him presumptuous.

Although the sea was visible from the top of every slope he climbed, he didn't seem to draw any nearer to it, and his journey lasted through most of the day. He wandered across farmland and through villages he didn't remember from the night he'd crossed the island. He followed dusty roads that curved in wide spirals, heading north when he wanted to go west and east when he wanted to go south.

At last he came to a place where he recognized the silent bungalows on the terrace above the sea and the well that had swallowed his rifle. Somewhere embedded in the dirt were bullets that had been meant to kill him. Look at me, he wanted to shout. I am alive. The streets in this hamlet were as empty as they'd been that first night. It was strange to see the shutters closed against the sun, just as they'd been closed against the war. He paused to examine the produce outside a grocer's — a paltry array of withered lettuce, onions, and hard black plums the size of walnuts. No one was attending the store, as far as Amdu could tell, and no one appeared to receive the money he didn't have after he helped himself to some fruit.

It was wrong to steal the plums, of course, though in the story he was telling himself he would come back to the island and find the grocer and pay him what he owed. Without paper and pen, he couldn't leave a message to explain. He was sorry for this. The grocer, if he was watching from behind the door at the back of the store, as Amdu suspected, would consider him a thief. How easily a man accumulates guilt, he thought. But he wasn't a saint and would never be a saint. He was who he was, just a young Sene-galese rifleman biting into a plum, heading home.

FRENCH OFFICERS SUNBATHED on the beach at Le Ghiaie. Amer-ican officers ate lemon ices. British officers drank the beer the German officers had left behind and traded news of the Battle of Saipan. Over the wire a field correspondent who had accompa-nied the Allies to Elba wrote that eighteen hundred German and Italian prisoners had been taken over the three-day period of fighting. By the nineteenth of June, the remaining machine-gun nests had been dealt with and the white flag of surrender hoisted at Porto Longone. By the twentieth, a Tuesday, the prisoners were on their way aboard a Royal Navy brig to England. On Wednes-day, the journalist set up a typewriter at an outdoor table in Piazza Repubblicà. "There is said to be little doubt that the landing was probably the most difficult ever attempted," he wrote, stopping to mop the sweat from his neck with a cocktail napkin. "The initial stages resembled Gallipoli in the First World War."

On the day that Amdu disappeared from La Chiatta, Mario re-turned to Portoferraio and approached the journalist, intending to ask him if he'd seen or heard of any Africans wandering around the port dressed in civilian clothes. But after Mario introduced himself, the journalist made a preemptive offer to buy him a beer. He was American, though he spoke enough Italian to make a basic exchange of information possible. The conversation that followed was full of talk about the weather, for which the journalist knew a variety of phrases (fa caldo, il cielo è chiaro, il tempo è molto bello!). Their talk turned naturally to the war, and Mario learned that the Allies were within seventy miles of the German front on the mainland. But in response to the Normandy invasion and the American advance across the Cherbourg Peninsula in France, the Germans had sent "dynamite meteors," as the people were calling them — a phrase he said in English — to explode over London. Mario admitted that he didn't understand. A dynamite meteor? What is that? It is a plane without a head, the journalist explained — senza una testa, capisce?

"Sì, sì, ho capito," Mario lied.

The journalist, pleased with his ability to make himself understood in a foreign language, told Mario something about an encounter that he'd witnessed on Capo d'Enfola between French Colonial shock troops and a German battery strongly placed between granite outcrops. When the smoke cleared, the journalist had gone forward to examine the battleground and found the corpse of an Allied soldier, an African man, cut clean in two by machine-gun fire. To demonstrate, he flattened his cocktail napkin into a square and ripped it in half. "Così," he said, though he pronounced it as the English word *cozy*.

Mario had been planning on telling the journalist about the Senegalese soldier who had run away from La Chiatta — a renegade soldier would make a good story for an American paper. But he thought better of it after the journalist ripped the napkin. Instead, Mario promised to introduce him to the captain of the carabinieri and also to the current mayor of Portoferraio. He didn't add that he himself hoped to be mayor someday. The journalist said he'd appreciate the introductions, and he went on to ask if there were any Fascists left on the island. Mario didn't disclose that he had registered as a Fascist in 1922 during the period Il Duce called "la fiumana," the flood, when to save oneself from the violence directed against the Socialists it was necessary either to join the Fasci or leave the country. Mario had even gone through a period of wearing white spats, just like Mussolini, though he was never one of the savage nationalists who drove the country into war. He told the journalist that the few remaining Fascists who hadn't been captured by the Allies had joined the retreating Germans. To lighten the mood, he recited the lyrics to a song the local squadra used to sing about Il Duce. He repeated the song so the man could write down a translation: *He's an electric current, his voltage runs up high; lay hands on Mussolini, and probably you die.*

The journalist asked Mario to explain why Italians hadn't revolted against the Fascists after Matteotti's assassination twenty years earlier. Mario pointed out that it was the king who had appointed Mussolini in the first place, and the king had protected him in those early years. Without the king, Mussolini would never have consolidated power to become a dictator.

What did Italy need with a king? the journalist asked.

"It is difficult for Americans to understand our country," Mario conceded. He let his gaze drift toward a pair of carabinieri standing on the opposite side of the piazza. "I hope we meet again," he said, and he bid the journalist good day.

From Piazza Repubblicà Mario meant to continue toward the quay — he knew he'd find African soldiers there and hoped to find Amdu Diop among them. He surprised himself, though, by taking a diversion along a series of side streets. At first he allowed himself to wander somewhat arbitrarily, partly because he thought a renegade soldier would do the same and partly to assess what might be salvageable in the apartment buildings that had been set on fire by the retreating Germans. Somehow civilian forces, including women and old men, had managed to contain the fires before they spread across the port, but three blocks of buildings had been abandoned. People were still camped out in the Municipio, and some families who had returned from the hills to find their homes destroyed had set up tents right in the street.

It was strange to wander past the charred, empty buildings behind Piazza Repubblicà and from there up into the oldest quarter of the port, where on the narrow streets winding toward Fort Stella the stone houses stood unmarked in any visible way by the invasion. Even the pots of cyclamens had survived intact.

It was obvious that there weren't any Senegalese soldiers in this quarter, but still Mario pressed on. Alone, he could admit to himself that he wouldn't have known what to do with Amdu if he'd found him. Truthfully, he didn't want to find him. He was glad the African had gone away — he never wanted to see or hear of him again.

He ended up on the street where Rosa, his mistress, had lived for eight years, ever since she'd arrived from Pianosa after the death of her husband, a prison official. She originally came from Sardinia and she planned to return to her family there once she'd paid off her husband's debts. Mario had met her at the trattoria where she worked as a waitress, behind the Mercato Vecchio. She was too coarse and plump to be called beautiful, and with her fiery temper she was an unpredictable mistress, though always satisfying. He had visited her regularly for two years. He wasn't sure why his interest had faded — perhaps because of the distractions of the war and the occupation. Now, as he approached her house, his desire ached like a hollow stomach. He had gone too long without making love. The thought of his abstinence made him irritable, and though he knew he was to blame, he was hurt that Rosa hadn't bothered to contact him over the past months.

The midday smells of cooking drifted through open windows. Outside a closed door, three cats ate from a dish piled with cold spaghetti. At number 34, the windows and shutters on the ground floor were closed, but on the upper floor the windows to the bedroom were open and the shutters propped aslant.

Rather than ringing the electric bell, which hadn't functioned for the two years Mario had visited number 34, he called to Rosa. When no one appeared, he called more loudly. The cats eating from the dish next door scattered. A shutter across the narrow street was flung open, and an older woman whom Mario didn't recognize leaned over the sill. She contemplated him for a moment, apparently judged him deserving, and shouted at the top of her voice, "Rosa! Rosa, dove sei?"

"Vengo subito," a voice answered from inside the bedroom. One of the shutters lifted, and Rosa's sleepy face appeared at the window above. She squinted down at Mario. Though her eyesight was poor, she had always been too vain to wear glasses. "Is it you?" she asked him.

"Sì, sì."

She disappeared. The old woman across the street continued to lean on her elbows, watching as Mario waited. His irritation increased as the wait extended over a minute. How long did it take to walk down a single flight of stairs and open a door? He wondered if Rosa meant to leave him standing in the street. Perhaps this was her response to his long absence. She would humiliate him like this, in front of her neighbor. Then he would humiliate her. He would leave and never come back. Good riddance.

But just as he was preparing to give up Rosa forever, the door opened and a hand reached out and pulled him by the wrist. Once he was inside, the door slammed shut behind him.

The entrance hall was narrow, the space illuminated only by the daylight that managed to extend across the bedroom and down the stairs. Mario's resentment began to settle into dull regret. Instead of the fragrances of fresh-cooked food, the stink of damp wool and greasy, stale smoke from fried fish saturated the hall. Why had he ever thought he would find comfort here?

In reply to his unease, Rosa planted her lips on his, her kiss startling him with warmth. Yes, this was the kind of comfort he'd been seeking. He grabbed her by the hips, but she peeled his hands off and began teasing him with questions. Why hadn't he come to visit her? she demanded. Did he love someone else? Had he been sick? Had he been too busy to spare an hour now and then? Was he in trouble? Was he in debt? Didn't he care what happened to her? What if she had been killed in the invasion? She'd heard that the French Colonials had been roaming the island looking for girls and women to assault. What if they had come to number 34? What would Rosa have done? A poor widow with no one to protect her. Why hadn't Mario protected her? Didn't he love her? Didn't he care that she was all alone in the world?

He didn't bother to answer her with words. Rather, he nestled against her with a tenderness she must have found unusual, since in the past he had approached lovemaking in a hurried, businesslike fashion, as if to keep reminding her of the limits of his commitment. He felt no inclination to limit himself, however, now that his regret had evaporated.

He tugged her open-necked dark blouse free of her skirt and slipped his hands inside her bra. He had forgotten how soft she was. Even if he had remembered the fact of her, he hadn't remembered the sensation of touch. It all seemed new to him, and the novelty made him feel youthful and vigorous but also profoundly respectful. He cupped the lower bulge of her breast and pressed his lips into the warm pocket of flesh. He licked the film of her sweat along the flat crevice of the sternum and filled his mouth with her areola. How lovely and soft and salty she was. He imagined that her compliance was more pronounced than ever, her hunger matching his own.

He held her around the waist, half-carrying her up the narrow staircase to her bed, to the matrimonial mattress he'd paid for himself. He was pleased to see the familiar cream-colored woven spread, and he wasn't bothered to notice, in the light slipping beneath the slanted shutter, a few circles of stains on the spread. This was just what he expected of Rosa — stains and dust and a lush, inviting warmth.

He kicked off his shoes and trousers and sat patiently while she unbuttoned his shirt. He shrugged when she exclaimed at the small bandages on his back — he insisted it was nothing, and she asked no questions. He undressed her slowly. In her haste when she'd found him waiting outside her door, she had pulled on stockings without garters, and when he discovered this she let out a silly giggle, which delighted him. He caught sight of their reflection in the mirror above the bureau. They moved together easily. But when she bent to take him in her mouth, as she had often done, he caught her and held her face between his hands and kissed her again, sinking his tongue deep inside her, feeling the uneven surfaces of her back teeth, and at the same time nudging apart her thighs and entering her, pushing with a long, gradual thrust as far as he could go.

His only disappointment was that it ended too quickly. He was confident that he'd fulfilled her, and he enjoyed the warm pride that had replaced his desire, but he couldn't shake off the disappointment. At first it came to him like the initial awareness of reality upon waking from a good dream. But after he'd put on his clothes and gone down to the kitchen to light the single burner so that Rosa could have her tea, he felt the disappointment growing like rain that slowly, almost imperceptibly, turns from a drizzle into a steady downpour.

She was a loyal woman — he knew as much, and he welcomed her dependence on him. After all these months, she had continued to wait for him. He would have heard if other men had started visiting number 34. Surely she could have taken another lover, had she wanted one. Or she could have made herself available to the Germans, who were eager for female company. But Rosa had remained determinedly alone.

As they drank tea together, Rosa recounted her experience of the invasion — which mostly involved sitting right there in the kitchen, holding her hands over her ears to block the noise of the bombs exploding around the port while she wondered if she was going to die. Half listening to her, Mario asked himself if they would be better off married. If they shared a home, they could make love every day. And yet he knew this wouldn't happen. He didn't want to make love every day, and he didn't want to drink tea with Rosa. In fact, he didn't much like her. Maybe this was the source of his disappointment — though he loved the warmth of her and the feeling of moving with her and being inside her, he didn't like listening to her thoughtless chatter afterward. Or maybe he disapproved of her self-absorption. Through two cups of tea, she hadn't asked him what he'd been doing during the invasion. She didn't seem to want to know how he'd been wounded. True, the wounds on his back weren't grave, but they were more than the nothing he'd pretended they were. Rosa should not have believed him when he'd said that. She was a silly woman and would never be more than an occasional pleasure.

She was too concerned with her own needs to notice his disappointment. She asked him to bring a bottle of aleatico next time he visited. Also, she hadn't eaten any meat for weeks. If he had any sausage to spare, she'd appreciate it. Would he come for supper the following Wednesday and spend the night? And could she borrow fifty lire?

His wallet was empty, he lied, but he promised to bring her the money on Wednesday. She remained in the kitchen while he let himself out. He noticed water puddling on the doorstep of the house across the street, and he looked up to see the old woman watering her geraniums. She called buongiorno to him. He answered her with a cold greeting and walked away, down the street and out of the shadow of Fort Stella.

Unsure where to go next, Mario tried to recall what he had been intending when he'd left La Chiatta, after the pandemonium caused by the dog and the soldier and Ulisse's boys. The dog, it turned out, wasn't dead — it wasn't even injured — but the soldier had disappeared. Of course he had disappeared. Permitted to wander unattended around the property, he ran away like a thief without thanking his kind hostess or saying good-bye to Adriana, who had foolishly come to trust him.

Mario was convinced that the soldier had stolen something small and valuable, even if Giulia wouldn't admit that anything was missing. Also, he guessed that the soldier had a more significant secret. Guilt had brought him to La Chiatta in the first place.

Guilt had kept him away from his regiment. It was easy to commit an actual crime during a night of chaos. If the renegade soldier hadn't eaten from the corpse of a German, then he had set a wounded man on fire. If he hadn't set a wounded man on fire, then he had participated in the assault on Sofia Canuti.

Mario was aware as he headed back toward Piazza Repubblicà that the disgust aroused by the thought of the African soldier helped to relieve the disappointment he'd felt after making love to Rosa. It was good to be reminded of unfinished business, even if he couldn't precisely define what that business entailed. He had some imprecise notion that the citizens of Elba needed to be stirred into action. Although the soldier had disappeared, he must still be held accountable. Every one of the French Colonials should be held accountable.

He arrived at the office just as Dino was letting himself out and locking the door. He accepted Dino's invitation to join him for pranzo at the Albatros in via Roma, though Mario would have preferred to eat at Olga's in via dell'Amore — the street of love — if only for the sake of the street's ironic relevance to a man who has just visited his mistress.

He was glad when they met the brothers Sergio and Marcello Pirelli outside the trattoria. "Come eat with us," Mario proposed. He was glad to be in the company of men and glad when Alonso Benassi asked them to join him and his friends at a long table. A big, boisterous group of men — all of them, except Dino, over the age of fifty, all of them native Elbans, all of them vocally sharing their rage at the reports circulating about the random atrocities committed by their self-appointed liberators — in particular, the negri of the Ninth French Colonial Division. Sergio said he hoped Mario and Dino were pressing for investigations. Alonso pointed out that the privacy of the families involved must be respected — what's done is done, he said, arousing loud protests from both Pirelli brothers. Sergio insisted that there could be no peace until the barbarians had been punished. Alonso believed that adequate revenge wasn't possible during a time of war, and all they could hope was that God would enact his own forms of vengeance. Dino expressed some confidence in the Allied forces' military tribunals, but Mario scoffed at that. The Africans were animals, he said. You can't put a pack of monkeys on trial.

He had meant to tell the men about the Senegalese soldier, but instead he fell into a tense silence after his last comment. If he admitted that his sister-in-law had harbored the soldier, the men would ask too many questions. It was frustrating to be trapped into secrecy. He couldn't even admit that earlier in the week he had alerted French officials in Marciana Marina. The lieutenant had gone himself to search, but thanks to Giulia's clever deceptions, he failed to find the soldier at La Chiatta, which made him Mario's responsibility, or so the men would assume if he told them about him now. They'd want to know why Mario hadn't reported the renegade to the carabinieri — or why he hadn't asked his friends for advice. He wouldn't be able to answer them.

The waiter appeared with their first courses of steaming soup. For a few minutes the men concentrated on the pleasures of the meal. But as they finished their last spoonfuls, one man, Filippo, a friend of Alonso's, cleared his throat and said lowly, "In the absence of the law, there are other methods."

Perhaps it was his tone that made the other men sit up and listen — his voice was almost too soft to be heard and yet remained carefully articulate. After a pause to let his audience contemplate the implications of his proposal, he went on to meditate aloud upon the nature of evil. There was no going down from where they had arrived, said Filippo. They had been dragged into the mire of humanity's filth, to the bottom of existence, to hell on earth. And here in hell, one evil act begot another. If they sinned, it was because others had sinned against them. The worst had happened, and the worst would happen again. But this time it was up to them to choose the victims. If they matched one crime with another, if they participated in an action that they knew to be evil, it was out of necessity rather than any sense of moral superiority. They would do what they had to do.

Filippo swished his wine and studied it through the glass, like a scientist examining liquid in a beaker. Mario had only known him from a distance, as Alonso's friend and as a pharmacist who limited his working hours to the evening shift. He was not a homely man, though Mario found him repulsive. The skin above his beard was pale and waxy. The pink tip of his tongue kept appearing to lick away the residue on his lips. His confident attitude was so smooth that it seemed rehearsed. But his voice was mesmerizing, and he presented his plan, whatever it entailed, as a possibility that he was sure would prove irresistible. Maybe he didn't have a plan — it was hard to tell what he was suggesting with his murky allusions. But his manner and voice suggested a ferocious intention, even if he wouldn't come right out and explain himself.

The waiter moved among them, replacing their bowls with plates bearing watery spinach topped with fried eggs — an image that seemed to express the unspoken meaning of Filippo's intricate discourse. The yolks were like keen yellow eyes, like the eyes of feral cats in the darkness. Yellow eyes that saw what only Filippo knew was going to happen — evil to match evil, evil as the inevitable outcome following the events of the last six days. Soupy yolks surrounded by the gelatinous white of nothingness on a bed of overcooked spinach — this was what Filippo had been talking about. This was the only food left for consumption on their damaged island, where whatever would happen next would follow naturally from whatever happened before.

Good and evil and the unquiet faculty of the soul, the seed going forth from itself, frittering its unity away, time breaking from eternity, hatred gathering itself in opposition until all that's left in life is sin and despair. A man does what he has to do, Filippo was saying. In this sense, every man is a soldier on a battlefield where the smoke is so thick he can't see his hands before his face. Groping, stumbling, he does what he has to do to survive.

Somehow Filippo managed to give to his nonsense the force of irrefutable logic. Though the speech confused Mario, he didn't dare ask questions. No one asked questions, and Mario had to presume that he was alone in his confusion. The other men, including Dino, nodded and murmured in agreement throughout the rest of the meal, as Filippo continued to hold forth. Mario could only conclude that the men had participated in previous discussions, and the knowledge they shared gave them the ability to interpret what was essentially a secret code — Filippo's code, simultaneously instructive and obfuscating, like all effective codes used during a time of war.

Mario left the restaurant with the pack of men but separated from them on the street. He didn't know whether to feel resentful for his exclusion or excited by the prospects contained in Filippo's obscure words. He didn't know what those prospects entailed. There seemed to be a general consensus that something momentous would soon occur, and that whatever would happen, set in motion at an earlier point, could now proceed accordingly, thanks to the approval of all who'd been sitting at the table.

Mario imagined that his confusion was similar to that of an illiterate peasant who has just come from voting in an election. He couldn't clearly explain who would be involved or what the final outcome would be, but whatever it was, he knew it would be significant. Dino, Sergio, Marcello, Alonso, and his other friends — they all agreed with Filippo that a man must do what a man must do. And Mario, by not raising his voice in objection — how could he have objected to such vagueness? — had essentially cast his vote, making it unanimous.

SHE IS IN BED, that's where she is, in a hospital, with tubes in her nose and needles in her hands and monitors attached to her chest and fingertips. She doesn't actually remember the period when she was unconscious or much about the activity focused on her for the past hour, but she is aware of the relief saturating her body. Mysteriously, the embolism has partially disintegrated on its own without traveling to some new precarious juncture; her lungs are pumping greedily; her heart is glad to welcome the Coumaden that helps to thin her blood. She has been promptly measured, analyzed, and diagnosed by a pulmonary specialist. Soon she will be subjected to more extensive tests in order to determine further treatment.

It seems as if only a minute earlier she was looking out the window at the graffiti on the warehouses while she listened to the murmur of the other passengers on the train to Penn Station. She remembers in particular the prominent voice of a man sitting behind her. He was talking about the inconvenience of a flight delay, she recalls.

Lying on the stiff hospital bed, stable and blissfully unattended while the nurse is off tracking down her family — her daughter in Queens, her husband in Rahway, her son in Port Jervis, whoever can be reached first with the telephone numbers Mrs. Rundel has been able to provide — she remembers feeling cheated. No one warned her that her life would be over before she could finish saying what deserves to be said.

She remembers that on the train she had put aside her newspaper to rest her eyes. She remembers feeling a tightening sensation throughout her body even before she was aware of any discomfort. And at the same time she felt a strange fatigue, as if she knew beforehand that she wouldn't be able to resist what was about to happen. Communication seemed imperative. She remembers looking for the cell phone in her purse. She was desperate to talk to Robert, if only to tell him that she needed to talk to him.

Without her phone, she couldn't get in touch with her family. She remembers feeling a brief surge of envy when she realized that the man sitting beside her on the train had his cell phone. Now she wonders if he used his phone to call for help. She wishes she had a way to contact him or anyone else on the train so she could find out what happened in the blank space between then and now.

She watches from a distance as a male nurse enters the cubicle and checks the fluid level of the IV. After he is gone, Mrs. Rundel continues to ponder the puzzle of her situation. What can't she remember? She can't remember what she can't remember.

She comforts herself by reviewing the reliable facts of her existence: the presence of her husband and children in the world, wherever they are at the moment, the friends she will see again, the sensation of air touching her skin, the fresh smell of oxygen, the stale, pervasive stink of antiseptic, the steady pattern graphed on the monitor, the anticipation of a full glass of water, and the time of day: only 10:23, if the clock on the wall is correct.

Which corresponds to 10:32 on the watch of the woman who helped save Mrs. Rundel's life. She routinely sets her watch ahead to keep herself from being late for work. She'll be late for work today. But what an excuse she has! She can't wait to tell her boss. He has his own cholesterol and blood-pressure problems, so he'll appreciate the fact that his secretary had the wherewithal to perform CPR and he won't blame her if she's absent for his first appointment. She can take her time getting to the office. Although she already ate breakfast at home, she can stop at a café and enjoy a coffee and croissant. Surprisingly, she is ravenous.

Unlike the financial adviser, who in his office on the seventeenth floor looks out the window at the building across the street and is physically revolted by nothing more than the dark outline of a block of filing cabinets visible behind the tinted plate glass. He can't imagine ever feeling hungry again.

Or the student sitting in the back of his forensics class. Although he purchased a bagel at the train station, he hasn't been able to bring himself to eat it. He keeps thinking about the swampy liquid that spilled from the mouth of the drowned man he tried to revive.

Or the adulterous husband who left his former lover a long message, a message he knew would never be answered. He has no early meeting and is taking his time getting to work. He wanders along Seventh Avenue thinking about love and loss and the enviable release of death.

The software designer, waiting to be interviewed for a job he desperately needs, is too nervous to be thinking about the incident on the train. Nor does his friend the lawyer, in his office five blocks away, give Mrs. Rundel another thought. He has just learned that a trial for which he has spent months preparing has been indefinitely postponed.

Meanwhile, across town, in a committee room at the United Nations, the Polish woman finds that the experience on the train that morning makes any issue concerning basic human sustenance that much more relevant. When it's her turn, she speaks in a low, precise voice, with burning passion.

And inside Bloomingdale's, the thief is trying to decide between a blue suede suit and a black silk jacket. Why not both?

Outside

S HE'S NOT THINKING ABOUT THE WAR. SHE'S NOT REMEM-
bering the night she spent hiding inside the kitchen cabinet.
Rather, she's thinking about how her husband will appear at her
bedside any minute, and he'll plant a kiss on her mouth, pressing
his lips against hers with the force of gratitude and relief and a
tinge of desperation that will extend the contact beyond a routine
greeting, husband and wife, old man and old woman, Robert
Rundel welcoming Adriana — Dree, as he calls her — back to
life, assuring her with a kiss that he will love her forever and at the
same time asking for her impossible assurance that she won't let
death steal her away from him, kissing her to demonstrate that he

depends upon her to be there, in time, alive and responsive, just as she depends upon him.

With Robert's arrival imminent, she's too full of anticipation to be thinking about a Senegalese soldier named Amdu Diop. She's not remembering the last time she ever saw him that morning in the boathouse, when, as if to hide his embarrassment, he pulled the tarp back between the barrels to cover the den full of mewing kittens. She's not remembering how even as she searched for some sign of him in the fields outside her bedroom window, she already knew that he was gone. She's not thinking about missing him, and how later that same day, six days after the launch of Operation Brassard, word spread across the island that the two warships belonging to the Ninth French Colonial Division had been ordered to depart for the mainland.

Wired to monitors in a hospital cubicle, she's not dwelling on something that happened sixty years earlier. She's not puzzling over the information that accumulated in the aftermath. She's not considering how in the days and months that followed the liberation, she was repeatedly surprised by what she hadn't even thought to ask. When she was a young girl, she couldn't adequately appreciate the fact that what she called knowledge was based in large part on assumption. But then, one by one, so many of her assumptions proved wrong. She was wrong about the people involved. She was wrong about methods and backgrounds and motives, along with all sorts of details of varying significance.

And she was probably wrong about what had never been disproved. For instance, she liked to imagine that after the soldier named Amdu left La Chiatta, he had been driven in a jeep to the piazza in Marina di Campo, where members of his regiment were stationed, and when he stepped from the jeep he was greeted with cheers. At some point she assigned names to Amdu's friends —

Moussa, Alioune, and Khalam — as though she were naming the kittens in the boathouse. She even convinced herself that she could have understood what they were saying in their own dialect.

She imagined them cursing Amdu, praising him, ridiculing him, calling him a coward and a hero. She was sure, though, that they listened soberly while he told them that he couldn't remember where he'd been or what he'd had to do to survive, though he knew he was lucky to be alive — see here, he'd say, showing them the scab where the bullet had grazed his shoulder.

Praise the God of Abraham.

Praise Allah.

Praise your own good luck.

But tell your brothers, Amdu: why didn't you hear them calling your name when they sent out a search party for all those who were missing? Were your ears stuffed with manure? Six days you were nowhere. Everyone thought you were dead. But you're not dead. Lieutenant, come see what the tide washed in! Our ugly little mascot boy, dressed like a clown.

Adriana didn't ask herself whether the Senegalese soldiers even had a word for clown. Or whether they were all from Dakar and shared the same dialect. In the scene that she repeatedly imagined through the years, Amdu Diop, wearing her grandfather's clothes, was teased because he looked like a clown.

Don't you know, he's back! Brother Amdu has decided to return from his vacation. Oooeee, crack him on the head. Here's one from your mother!

No one ever told Adriana what really happened when Amdu was reunited with the French Colonials. She could only guess that it was a joyful reunion. She pictured the soldiers lifting Amdu above their heads and carrying him across the piazza while others gathered to hoot, mocking him, she presumed, only because they were too proud to express their relief. The boy they thought was dead had come back to life. Their favorite little brother. How could he not be everyone's favorite?

Although she never learned the exact truth about Amdu's return, she did find out that the troops of the Ninth French Colonial Division were treated to a feast that night — their last night on Elba. Though most Elbans chose to stay at home, those who did attend the celebration later described how some of the Africans used jerry cans as drums, others danced in their bare feet, and a brave musician from Fetovaia, who called himself Pino Solitario, played the accordion. The troops drank beer and whiskey — only the officers filled their glasses with sweet Elban aleatico. There was plenty of bread and spaghetti, and down on the beach the French cooks were frying squid in huge vats of oil over open fires.

Those present later reported that the Africans could leap as high as the top of the Torre. Adriana imagined that Amdu was one of the dancers — the one who jumped the highest and stomped in dizzying circles around Pino Solitario. Sometimes in her dreams she was there, standing at the edge of the crowd, watching Amdu dance and beating time with her hands.

Her husband will arrive within the hour, if the traffic isn't heavy. When he comes he will kiss her and then pull up a chair, and they will talk about her ordeal. With his prompting, she will try to trace the sequence backward from her current situation to her departure from the house that morning. She will try to describe everything she remembers, up to the moment when she fainted on the train. At some point it might occur to her to mention that she'd been thinking about the story she'd told the previous evening — the story of the war.

The story ends on the night of the victory celebration in Marina di Campo, though it took months and even years for Adriana to learn certain facts. She's still not able to verify all of her suspicions. For example, she's not sure where her uncle spent that night — whether he was in Portoferraio or Marina di Campo. And she's not sure if Amdu Diop even participated in the celebration.

What she does know, even if she has no reason to think of it at the moment, is that Luisa's nephew, Paolo, left for Marina di Campo with Lorenzo Ambrogi early in the evening on the twenty-third of June. Instead of returning to his home, he joined a group of men and boys in Piazza Alighieri. Though the celebration hadn't begun, the carabinieri had already been warned to expect a crowd, and a military ambulance was stationed nearby. Although most Elbans didn't plan to join the celebration, they shared the sense that history was about to move elsewhere. History would continue to follow the war, leaving the island of Elba behind.

The two warships anchored offshore were like massive guards waiting to take their captives away. The men loitering under the portico had heard different rumors about where the Ninth French Colonial Division would go next — up to Genova, some said, or to France. They smoked cigarettes and cast sly glances at one another, as though to acknowledge the innuendo hidden in their words.

Filippo, the pharmacist from Portoferraio, wasn't there, but his friend Alonso Benassi was, along with the Pirelli brothers. They had come not to watch the Colonial soldiers celebrate their victory but to watch them leave. This group of Elban men, along with a few attentive boys, would wait all night, if necessary, for the satisfaction of bidding good riddance to the savages.

Later, Paolo would tell Adriana that he smoked a real Cuban cigar that night, which made him thirsty, so he stole a flask from a table in the piazza and drank half a liter of wine by himself, and then, feeling sluggish and bored by the conversations of the men, he found a quiet doorway to sit in and promptly fell asleep. He slept for hours and would have preferred to go on sleeping — his dreams were pleasant, full of drumbeats and the antics of masqueraders — but shortly after midnight he was knocked awake by the booming of an explosion, which at first he took for thunder.

Although Adriana never had the chance to visit Senegal, in the years following the war she searched for the scanty information available about the country. Later, when she was a young woman studying at university, she pored through more-substantial sources, reading privately, without supervision, until she came to consider herself something of an expert on West Africa. She knew the distance between Dakar and Saint-Louis. She knew the annual per capita income, the vicissitudes of the peanut crop, the frequency of drought, and the customs of the Wolof. She even managed to find an outdated copy of *La Condition Humaine*, the newspaper for the Senegalese Democratic Bloc, at a newsstand in Livorno in 1953, and she read for the first time about the country's leader, Léopold Sédar Senghor.

Senghor was a poet, a Roman Catholic, and a Socialist. Adriana liked to imagine that Amdu would have been a member of Senghor's party and supported the Federation of West Africa. With his education, he could have helped draft the new constitution. She was convinced that everywhere he went, he would have been appreciated. Sometimes she even conflated Senghor and Amdu — in her imagination, Amdu became the president of Senegal, and Senghor was the boy who had fled to La Chiatta to escape the war.

Yet no matter how much she learned about the country, the soldier named Amdu continued to elude her. Still, she was a determined girl, resistant to disappointment — spoiled, Amdu would have said — and she couldn't completely resign herself to ignorance. Even though with time she was absorbed by other preoccupations and her memory of Amdu lost clarity, she never stopped hoping that he would become newly visible and available to her at some future point. As long as she couldn't forget him, she couldn't give up the idea that someday her limited knowledge would be supplemented.

She went on waiting for Amdu to return, if not in person then in the stories she would hear about him. And many years later, when she was going through her mother's papers, she was sure she would find the letter Amdu had written to Giulia Nardi from his berth just hours before the Ninth French Colonial Division was scheduled to depart from Elba. That she never did find a letter she attributed to her mother's efforts to protect her — Giulia would have thought that by destroying the letter and keeping its contents secret, she was sparing her daughter. But Adriana was already convinced that a letter existed.

Dear Madame. No, no — he should address her as Singora. Sinora. How do you spell *signora?* He can't send a proposal of marriage that is full of mistakes. But truly, it feels good to hold a pen in his hand once again. And it feels good to be back in his upper bunk, soon to be on his way home. How easy it has been to resume his life as a soldier. He remains in a state of shock, according to the medic, who didn't question Amdu's claim that he has no memory of the time between the launch of Operation Brassard and his return to the marina. He is sorry to have to bend the truth a little,

but it is for everyone's good. Now no one has to waste time on a
court martial, and Amdu can go home on medical leave.

As much as he has come to appreciate this island of dreams and
is eager to return in style someday, he longs to be at home. He
isn't sorry to give up the military life. He has to agree with the
lieutenant general that he is cut from a different cloth and will
never successfully move up through the ranks of the Tirailleurs.

In the story he would like to tell about himself, he is still a no-
bleman — a jambur, in Wolof — but he would also admit once
and for all that he is something of a coward. A few enlisted men
grumbled that they saw him running from the battlefield. If he
was nicked by a sniper's bullet, he deserved it, they said. Probably
the men complaining are the same troops he ran from in the orchard. Surely at least some of them are still alive. He learned from
his friend Khalam that the captain in charge of the battalion was
killed later that first night by mortar fire. They found his body, but
he had no face left, Khalam said. Or perhaps it was Moussa who
told him this. Moussa, whose holy ancestor had preached that all
faithful followers were assured a place in heaven despite their sins.
Anything is endurable as long as there's heaven at the end, Moussa
insists, following his ancestor's belief, and Amdu agrees. They are
good friends, Moussa and Amdu. Amdu could be the good friend
of anyone — African or European, Christian or Muslim or Jew.
Even the men who disapprove of him would come to like him if
they spent time with him.

It must be acknowledged, however, that he neglected his duty
while he lived like a prince in a stone palace by the sea. He has no
excuse. With chagrin, he'd have to say that he enjoyed himself.
He listened to a young girl play the piano. He fed pine nuts to the
birds. He brought a dog back to life. He lived at La Chiatta like a
member of the family, like a brother to the girl and a beloved son

of the signora. And though he can't see into the future, he can deduce the logical progression of the sequence that began with the first night of the liberation. Follow the sequence through time, into the bright, clean rooms of La Chiatta, away and back again, to what is most easily understood as destiny but that Amdu recognizes as the inevitable point when everything falls into place and the pattern, no matter how complicated, becomes clear.

Dear Madame-Signora, your daughter is a child. God willing, someday she will be a woman in need of a husband. No — he'd better not suggest that the girl would need anything. She would want a husband? Or she would receive many proposals from many men, and she would have to choose. That is better. Amdu Diop will distinguish himself as the most farsighted suitor, offering himself and his respected name ten years in advance of their actual engagement.

It is possible that during the interim, rumors about Amdu will reach Madame-Signora and her daughter. As much as he has been praised for his good heart, he is considered by some to be less than reasonable. True, he used to exaggerate his potential — he even, pardon his blasphemy, believed himself to be something of a saint. But he is done with all that. In the years to come he will work to the best of his abilities, no more and no less. In his conversations with God he will no longer trade his future talents for current miracles.

To all the good people of the island of Elba he wants to say that he is sorry for whatever went wrong with an invasion that was planned and initiated on their behalf. No one should ever suffer needlessly. But don't believe that the loved ones you have lost will never be recovered. The ashes will give up the dead. The sea will give up the dead. Death will give up the dead, all sins will be forgiven, and heaven will welcome anyone who wants to live.

There's happiness ever after for you. Everything's forgivable, amen.

Amdu, who is used to believing whatever he wants to believe, believes that he has found his future place in life at La Chiatta. Now he must convince the residents of La Chiatta that he is worthy. In his long absence, they might forget his charms and remember him only as a representative of the Allied division that brought both freedom and atrocity to their island. Experience is full of contrary influences, and proximity tends to strengthen persuasion. While he is off in Africa studying to be a doctor, another man might arrive at the palace by the sea and try to persuade the madame-signora and her daughter that he is superior to Amdu.

He can only hope that they will be patient and wait for him.

To the famiglia Nardi, he wants to say: vi ringrazio — merci beaucoup. He wants to say that as unlikely as it might seem, the twisting, turning chain of events leads invariably to his return. He wants to assure them that he isn't foolish or insincere or easily distracted. He is Amdu Diop, the grandson of a general. He wants to sign the letter *with love*.

Alone in her bedroom on the last night the Ninth French Colonial Division spent on Elba, Adriana Nardi found herself imagining Amdu as a child — first as a pudgy infant holding his toes, the disk of his thick, coarse hair looking like a plate balanced on the top of his head, then as a toddler running bowlegged across a courtyard, then as a young boy climbing up onto the rim of a well while his mother screamed at him to get down, then as an older boy who demonstrated for all the weary adults around him what it really meant to be alive. A boy with strong, knobby legs and thin arms that could bend backward like a bow around the double joints of his elbows. A boy who liked to jump like a rabbit across the room.

Though he was a soldier, Amdu hadn't finished growing. Adriana imagined what he'd look like as a man — a head taller than her uncle Mario, with a black cap of a beard on his chin, a narrow chest, long limbs, and feet as wide as palm leaves. Then she imagined him as an old man, with a gray mist of hair, his shoulders stooped. She pictured him with spectacles for reading, looking up as she entered the room, looking over the rims of his glasses so for a moment he seemed to have four eyes.

She'd left her shutters open to let in the cool night air. Later, she would remember hearing the noise of the soldiers celebrating across the island in Marina di Campo, though she must have made this up, since the sounds couldn't possibly have traveled that far. But when she thought back to that night, her memory distorted time and distance. She heard the soldiers celebrating and she quietly hummed along to the music of Pino Solitario's accordion.

Though it would seem strange to someone else that a soldier she had hardly known should have filled her thoughts so completely, it didn't seem strange to her at all. Just the fact that he was so different from anyone she'd ever met would have been enough to keep her interested. And yet there was more — the effect of him, her confidence that she was absolutely right to be impressed, the sense of belonging in the world that he inhabited, the plain admiration she felt, even if she didn't know him well enough to know what, in particular, she admired.

She had given up the notion that Amdu Diop had some sort of miraculous or magical power. But she didn't soon forget the pleasure of his company, and as the hours passed that night — June 23, 1944 — and she drifted toward sleep, she found it comforting just to think about him and to let her memories get mixed up with her ideas about the past and the future. Over and over, she reviewed every minute of the short time she'd spent with him. She pictured him in his own home with his family — his mother and father and sisters. She imagined him studying in a library. She imagined coaxing him to jump off the highest rock at Viticcio.

Although she would have been suspicious of an interest in her that went beyond what she considered appropriate, she felt entitled to claim him as her own. Even if she didn't adequately know him, she knew what she felt.

During the course of her long life, Mrs. Rundel spoke about the liberation of Elba on several occasions, sometimes in response to related stories she'd read or heard and sometimes in reply to questions put to her in conversations. But she spoke to her husband at length about Amdu just a few separate times, and only once when her children were present — the previous night, when they had all gathered at a restaurant for her seventieth birthday.

She knew her family loved to hear her stories about Elba. Since she had ordered an appetizer of calamari, she told them about the giant squid she'd once seen stretched out on the quay in Portoferraio. She went on to describe the dangerous rocks at Viticcio. Her children had visited the island when they were young, but she hadn't taken them to Viticcio. They would be shocked to see the rocks where she had learned to dive, she said.

Her daughter reminded her that she'd said the same thing before.

"It's amazing I survived," she added.

Her son said, "You always say that."

"Or even that I learned anything at all in those provincial

schools," she continued. She laughed when she thought about how she had believed the rumors that there were diamonds on the volcano called Volterraio. She'd spent hours digging on the slopes and never found anything better than pyrite and quartz. "Diamonds, no." The German soldiers had started the rumors.

Her son wanted to hear about the German soldiers and the occupation. her daughter wanted to hear about the liberation. Adriana recounted the history as simple summary, but she included the story of spending the night hiding in a cabinet — a story she knew she'd told them before. Then Robert urged her to tell the children about the Senegalese soldier.

"What Senegalese soldier?" Max, her son, asked.

Anna said she'd recently seen a film about Senegalese soldiers who were bombed by the French military in their own camp after returning to West Africa after World War II. It was based on a true story, Anna said. And was it really true that the Senegalese went to Elba? Certo — of course — Adriana found herself surprised that this wasn't common knowledge. Of course the Senegalese went to Elba. And one of them came to stay at La Chiatta.

Over a dish of sea bass and potatoes, she told her children the story of Amdu Diop. Robert filled in, gently adding details that his wife managed to leave out. But he didn't remind her to tell the children what Amdu had written in his letter. He couldn't have reminded her, since, after all these years, she still had never mentioned it to him. How could she tell him about the contents of a letter that she had never read?

Say your body has been in the world for seventeen years, four months, three days, and five hundred and twelve minutes. Say you've already sealed the letter you just wrote and addressed the envelope and placed it for safekeeping in the empty leather box that once held a pair of field glasses. You buckled the lid closed to keep the letter safe from the prying eyes of your comrades and you asked one of the boat pilots ferrying soldiers from shore to deliver it to whatever trustworthy Italian he could find.

Say you've already had a good long piss and even briefly admired the invention of the urinal. Lying on a thin mattress in the berth of a warship, staring at the ceiling, you admire the pattern of bolts holding the steel plates in place. You pretend that the ceiling is the sky, the impressions in the bolt heads are stars, and the rust streaks are the tails of comets. You pretend that there's a fresh night breeze blowing through the cabin and that the coughs and sighs of your exhausted comrades in their bunks are the sounds of the nocturnal life along the Saloum River — wild dogs, monkeys, fruit bats, tree frogs.

The surface of your skin is the place between what you are and what you're not. You feel the air with your fingertips, then you entwine your fingers and feel the fact of your hands. You try to identify the varying sensations that come with being yourself, from your head to your bare toes. On your scalp you feel a slight itchiness and wish that you had borrowed a bar of the honey-colored soap you washed with at La Chiatta. On your face you feel chalky dust settling — just to think about it makes you sneeze, and the one sneeze feels so satisfying that you do it again. Achoo! You feel the thump of the foot that the irritated soldier beneath you has kicked against the bottom of your bunk in response to your loud sneezes. He is telling you to shut up!

You feel your biceps bulging when you press the palms of your hands together. You feel the hollow of your deep-set navel. Between the ridges of your hips you feel a tightening sensation that reminds you of a tortoise withdrawing into its shell, as though your self-awareness were a shadow crossing the path, giving your body reason to hide. Yet the same shadow rouses your penis into action — you feel it stiffening and, along with your awareness of pleasure, you feel a new eagerness to finish whatever it is you've started. You don't want the pleasure to end, but you can't wait until you've reached the culmination. Never and until. Wanting and wanting. Life is never less than interesting. You can't think of a time you've ever been bored. Doesn't it feel fine just to be in the midst of something that deserves to be completed?

He, Amdu Diop, knows himself to be the proud inhabitant of a strong, healthy seventeen-year-old body. Above all, he feels safe inside himself, as though his skin were as thick as the ship's armor plating. If he were running a race, he'd be running his fastest — not to win, but to reach the finish line in the shortest time possible.

Audible through the walls is a distant groaning, recognizable as the sound of the thick spindles of the bower capstans turning, drawing up the dripping cables. The ship is weighing anchor. Half of the Ninth French Colonial Division is leaving Elba. The second ship with the rest of the troops will soon follow.

In his bunk, surrounded by thick bodies just like his own — bodies sweating and murmuring in sleep, bodies turning, bodies resting, bodies recovering from the night's celebration — Amdu is feeling pleased with himself. He is pleased that he wrote the letter he intended to write. He is pleased that his ship has ample ammunition, though he'd prefer that it wouldn't need to be used. He is pleased that Operation Brassard is officially over. He is pleased to be the grandson of General Diop. He is pleased to be a citizen of Senegal and a resident of Dakar. He is pleased to be so amiable. He is pleased to imagine that the steel bolts are Andromeda and Pegasus, and the rust streaks are comets flying close enough for him to reach out and touch. He is pleased to be where he is. He is pleased to know that he doesn't necessarily have to repeat his mistakes. He is pleased by the depth and diversity of the colors of the spectrum. He is pleased to have to struggle to keep himself from laughing aloud, and at the same time he is pleased with his capacity for solemn wisdom. He is pleased to be a Roman Catholic. He is pleased to be a brother to his sisters and a son to his parents. He is pleased to be a young man with advantages. He is pleased to think about the children he will father. He is pleased to hum a marching tune — softly, so as not to disturb his comrades.

He is too absorbed in his pleasure to bother devising a reasonable hypothesis to explain why the rumbling of the anchor chains has turned into a distant booming that quickly is growing louder. He doesn't trace the sound from the initial explosion that pierces the armor casing of the midship bilge keel and ignites the ammunition in a handling room, which then collapses the center girder and blows open the floor of the lower deck, sending pieces of steel plates into the combustion chamber, where the boiler explodes. Amdu, along with every other infantryman in the cabin, feels the vibration of the booming simultaneously against him and inside him. He is shaking and shaken, his muscles are useless, solidity dissolves, the boundary he has just been appreciating no longer exists, there is no edge to himself, no surface, no difference between Amdu Diop and the world. Before he can begin to understand what is happening, everything turns to liquid.

At the dinner in honor of her seventieth birthday, Mrs. Rundel paused and coughed briefly into her napkin. Her family remained silent while a waiter refilled their water glasses. When the waiter was gone, Anna asked if the soldier's body had ever been identified. After hearing from her mother that as far as she knew, his body hadn't been recovered, Anna asked if she could really be sure that the soldier had been on the ship that was blown up in the Golfo di Campo. Couldn't he have been on the second ship? Maybe he went home to Senegal and was absorbed back into his life there and that's why she never heard from him again.

Another waiter arrived at their table and distributed dessert menus. When he received no reply, he offered to return in a few minutes. Mrs. Rundel sipped her water and watched over the lip of the glass as he walked away.

"I did not need to be told what happened that night. I just knew. It is strange, I admit it is strange, but I knew."

"How did you know?" Anna asked.

"Era impossibile, lo so, ma sapevo tutto."

"Oh, come on, Ma . . ." protested Max. He understood Italian but didn't have the patience to listen to his mother speak it when the subject of discussion was important.

"Okay. I'd been lying awake in bed for hours. I couldn't fall asleep that night, so I was humming to myself, just, you understand, mmmm hmmm. Luisa used to call it my habit of humming. It was the way she kept track of me, she liked to say. Even if she could not see me, she could hear me. I think she exaggerated. And she was wrong to insist that I stopped humming the night I spent hiding in the cabinet. She mixed up the dates. I stopped humming the night the Fasci blew up the Allied ship. I heard the explosions from across the island. It was like the sound of fireworks, but I knew it couldn't have been fireworks. And then there was a silence like the silence inside the cabinet — my room became so still and quiet, and I could do nothing but wait. I didn't have to wait long.

In a moment I heard our neighbor's dog howling in the field. The night was perfectly silent, and then Pippa began to howl and didn't stop. Poor Pippa. I remember thinking of a bow sliding back and forth across a single string of a violin. But no one was playing a violin. It was Pippa howling. That's how I knew what had happened. Because of the dog."

The waiter was back, standing behind Anna's chair. He hovered with a pinched smile until Mrs. Rundel stopped talking, and then he asked if they were ready to order dessert.

"Sì, sì, sì, siamo pronti, we are ready, now or never," Mrs. Rundel said, picking up the menu and shrugging a couple of times to indicate that she had finished with her story.

From the portico in Marina di Campo, the explosions inside the Allied ship were less than spectacular. For an hour or more, the men had been watching the boats transporting the Africans from shore, but when they heard the first detonation followed by the series of booms, they weren't even sure which ship was involved.

Paolo woke in the doorway with a parched mouth and an aching head. He drew his arms inside the short sleeves of his shirt to protect himself against the rain. Then he discovered that there was no rain. He pushed himself to his feet and walked groggily to the portico, where he found the group of men standing in a row, as though watching football from the edge of a field. It seemed to him that the French officers and the few dozen Africans who hadn't yet boarded the boats were the players of competing teams, shouting and running frantically back and forth along the sand. But there was no ball to kick and there were no goals marked. Watching them, Paolo felt stupid, as if he'd forgotten the rules of a familiar game.

"What happened?" he finally asked.

At first, none of the men bothered to answer, though Sergio was kind enough to offer Paolo what was left of his cigarette.

"What happened?" Paolo repeated after awkwardly tapping off the long ash.

"Justice," said Sergio.

It was then that Paolo noticed the thick cord of smoke pouring from one section of the ship and the orange flames flashing inside a gaping hole in the hull. Smaller explosions were still following in quick succession, almost like the rattle of machine-gun fire. From this distance, he couldn't tell whether the forms falling into the sea were men or pieces of the ship.

"What is justice?" he asked.

Two of the men — Sergio and his brother — let out a grumbling laugh. Paolo knew what they were saying with their laughter. They were saying, Go ask your mamma. They were saying, Grow up.

In her hospital room, Mrs. Rundel recognizes the quiet urgency of her husband's voice as he identifies himself to a nurse out in the corridor. When he appears at the door, she smiles weakly to reassure him. His exclamation upon seeing her comes out as a puff of an "Oh!" She hears his Manchester childhood in that simple syllable, his education, the long-ago past, as well as the love that prevented him from ever adequately preparing for her death. This man who has shared her bed for almost fifty years. Neither one of them would survive long without the other.

He steps toward her and leans over. Just as she expected, he kisses her, pressing his lips to hers beneath the oxygen tube. It is a long, desperate, loving kiss, a kiss containing fifty years of kisses, from the first kiss in the Place des Vosges in 1956 to the kiss in their first shared bed in that filthy hotel room to the kiss on their wedding day to all the routine kisses — hello, good-bye — kisses of congratulations, kisses of clever seduction, reviving kisses at the end of a long day, kisses of apology, kisses of gratitude, kisses of celebration, quick pecks in passing, kisses enlivened by the action of their tongues, kisses filled with foreboding, kisses of relief, kisses to make up after an argument, easy kisses, tender kisses, grinding kisses, kisses before intercourse, during, after, wet kisses, dry kisses, kisses to comfort, kisses to persuade, kisses to punctuate a joke, kisses interrupting stories that would prove impossible to finish.

She reaches out for him, misses his hand, and instead grabs his wrist.

"I'm fine," she says.

"You're fine," he echoes.

The sergeant who carried the case containing Amdu's letter had just finished loading his landing boat with his final group of drunken infantrymen when the explosives were detonated. When other explosions followed, the sergeant thought that the Germans had returned. The soldiers in his boat must have thought the same, for they were already jumping out into the shallow water and running off in search of cover. The sergeant followed them, leaving the case in the boat and the boat to drift back out to sea.

The next morning the landing boat was found by a fisherman floating offshore of Capo Stella. The fisherman towed the boat back with him to the beach at Lito, where he pulled it ashore to examine it. He found a pistol, two left boots, and the field glass case. He unbuckled the case, saw that there was an envelope inside, and was about to open the letter and read it when a group of young boys came running across the sand to see the boat. The fisherman set the case on the sand and let the boys climb inside the boat. He tried firing the pistol to entertain them, but the trigger was jammed.

The next day the boat was returned to the French Colonials in Marina di Campo, but the black case sat unnoticed on the empty beach at Lito. The case remained there just above the waterline for three nights and four days, until it was found by a girl who had come with her brother to the beach without their mother's permission. They were intending to go for a swim, but when the girl found the case, she decided she wasn't interested in swimming anymore, to her brother's disappointment.

The girl brought the case home, and the next day she gave it to her cousin in exchange for a comic book. She kept the letter. After she discovered that it was written in French, she put the sheet of paper back in the envelope and hid it beneath her mattress because she didn't want to have to tell her mother where she had found it. Months passed before her mother discovered the letter when she was turning the mattress. By then, her mother didn't care that the girl and her brother had gone without permission to the beach at Lito. She did care, however, that the girl had opened an envelope that wasn't addressed to her. For this crime, the girl's punishment was to deliver the letter herself, by hand, to Signora Nardi of La Chiatta.

She sat on the handlebars of her brother's bicycle all the way across the island. The journey took more than three hours. Once they arrived at the villa, the girl was too frightened to face Signora Nardi, so instead she set the letter on the sill outside the kitchen. She called hello through the open window and turned and ran as fast as she could after her brother, who was already wheeling his bicycle down the drive.

On a bright fall day in the year 1944, in the quiet of the midday rest, a woman's hand reached from the dark interior of La Chiatta and caught the tip of the envelope between her forefinger and thumb.

Joanna Scott is the author of seven previous books, including *The Manikin*, which was a finalist for the Pulitzer Prize; *Various Antidotes* and *Arrogance*, which were both finalists for the PEN/Faulkner Award; and the critically acclaimed *Make Believe* and *Tourmaline*. The recipient of a MacArthur Fellowship and a Lannan Award, she lives with her family in upstate New York.